FIRE, FOG AND WATER

FIRE, FOG AND WATER

MIKE MARTIN

OTTAWA
PRESS AND
PUBLISHING

ottawapressandpublishing.com

ISBN (pbk.) 978-1-988437-28-6
ISBN (EPUB) 978-1-988437-30-9
ISBN (MOBI) 978-1-988437-29-3

Printed and bound in Canada

Design and composition: Magdalene Carson at New Leaf Publication Design

To Joan, my muse and constant support.
Thank you for continuing the adventure with me.

FIRE, FOG AND WATER

1

Sergeant Winston Windflower was not happy. That was unusual. Anybody who knew Windflower would say he was almost always happy. Today though, anyone who saw him could tell he was certainly not happy. The funny thing is, if someone dared to ask him why he was so unhappy, he wouldn't have been able to say because even he didn't know.

Everybody from his wife, Sheila, to his friends at work, to Molly the cat—if she could talk that is—would tell you that he was not a happy man. The only ones who were exempt from his blistering wrath were Lady, his collie, and the joy of his life, little Amelia Louise.

He started the day off fighting with Sheila, and that was unusual. He never fought with Sheila. She would say later that he picked the fight. He would say that it was already there; he just jumped in. None of that mattered. They fought, and some harsh words had been exchanged. Windflower left in a huff, something he had never done before.

He was still in that huff when he got to work at the RCMP detachment in Grand Bank. The rain, drizzle and fog didn't help his mood either. It had been raining or drizzling or foggy every day that it hadn't snowed, which was every second day. He didn't know what made him madder, rain or snow, but he knew for sure that he was sun-starved. And he knew he was angry.

Things didn't improve at work. His second-in-command Corporal Eddie Tizzard got an earful for eating crackers in the lunchroom. He looked shocked, and more than a little hurt, when Windflower yelled at him. He was always eating in the lunchroom and anywhere else he could get a snack. So what was the problem in doing that today?

Constable Yvette Jones was next in line to feel Windflower's fury when she arrived at his office to ask for some leave so she could visit her boyfriend in Manitoba.

"Didn't you just have leave?" asked Windflower.

"I did at Christmas, and it's only a few days over Easter," said Jones.

"It's always a few days, then a few days more," Windflower snapped back. "Doesn't anyone care about anybody else around here any more?"

Jones felt like she was going to cry — and she never cried — when she was shooed out of Windflower's office. She passed Constable Rick Smithson who was off duty but had a requisition form in his hands and was headed towards Windflower's office.

"Not today," Jones suggested.

"It's only to upgrade our printer," said Smithson, the resident tech expert.

Jones shook her head. "I wouldn't."

Smithson thought he knew better and walked into Windflower's office with his requisition.

"What do you want?" demanded Windflower. "Don't be asking me to approve more funding for your toys. That guy in Marystown is already screaming at me. Are you deliberately trying to get me into trouble?"

Smithson started to mumble a response but gave up under the stony glare of his superior officer. "I'll come back tomorrow," he finally said.

Windflower just scowled as the younger officer slunk out of his office.

Jones was standing at the counter in the lunchroom when an ashen-looking Smithson came by.

"Told you," she said.

"I'm going home," was all Smithson said in response.

"Me too," said Tizzard. "I was just having a snack at the end of my shift when he started yelling at me. He's got a real bee in his bonnet."

"More like a hornet's nest," said Jones. "I've never seen the boss like this."

"Me either," said Tizzard. "But he's got a kettle full of steam, and unless he figures out how to let go of it, he's going to blow."

They were still commiserating when Betsy Molloy, the office administrative assistant, came into the room.

"Lord alive! He's a cranky-bones this morning," said Betsy. "I said good morning, and he just snarled."

Minutes later they heard Windflower stomp out of the Grand Bank RCMP Detachment, and as they peered out the window, they saw his Jeep peeling away from the parking lot.

Windflower arrived home, hoping to make some sort of peace with Sheila. But she and the baby had left. There was no note or indication about where they'd gone or how long they'd be. Only Molly and Lady were left behind to greet him. He brushed off Molly, grabbed Lady and threw the dog's leash into the back seat of his Jeep. Molly was highly miffed, but Lady was thrilled that she and her master were apparently going on an adventure.

It wasn't an adventure for Windflower, though. All he knew was that he needed to get away from other people and from his life, at least for a little while. The day was dark, gray and foggy with rain clouds threatening to drop more miserably cold moisture on him and everyone else. At least it wasn't snowing, he thought, which was a definite possibility in the netherworld of March weather in Newfoundland. In fact, the last snow dump had melted away, leaving mini-snowbanks of a crusty brown nature, and pools of water that would linger around all day and turn into skating rinks during the night.

Windflower knew he needed to get out, breathe and think. As a resident of Grand Bank, he could get close to nature pretty quickly when he needed to. That was a real blessing for him. His head was so muddled as he drove to the trail past the Grand Bank Clinic that all he could think about were problems with no solutions. There was trouble at home, trouble at work, even trouble at the beautiful old B & B where springtime had revealed a massive leak in the roof. Luckily, they'd found it before it completely destroyed the lower levels of the building, and they'd managed to patch the roof. But that was a temporary measure. The whole roof would have to be repaired, and that was going to cost at least $10,000, which was a lot of money he and Sheila didn't have right now.

Windflower parked the Jeep and let Lady out of the back. She was so happy, she ran around the car three times before heading off to explore the area around them. Windflower smiled, despite his mood. Maybe that's why he still got along with Lady. She was happy to be with him and to just be alive. The dog ran back to get him and to tell him what a wonderful day it was. At least that's what Windflower heard.

"Okay girl. Let's go," he said, once he got his insulated runners from the trunk. He ran up the trail, followed close behind by Lady. He sprinted through the woods to the top of the hill and stopped at the lookout. He was out of breath but finally feeling wonderful with a runner's high that came from lack of oxygen and a rapidly increased heart rate.

He paused for a moment to take in the view of the town, partially obscured by a massive fogbank beginning its intrusion into Grand Bank. It was like it was eating the town alive, street by street and block by block. He was sure that by the time he got to the bottom, the town would be completely consumed, just like his dark mood, now returning, was taking over his day. He gazed at Lady and then took off down the hill. It was a bit greasier on the descent because less snow had melted in this area of the trail. He slowed a little, but as he neared the bottom, it wasn't enough.

He reached a precarious turn and felt one foot slide off into the distance in front of him. When he tried to correct, the other foot followed its partner and his head and torso soon fell into step. Seconds later he was sliding underneath the branches of the trees by the side of the trail and deeper into the wooded area. He stopped abruptly next to a large boulder buried under the snow.

At least he thought it was a rock. He noticed it might be something different when Lady started sniffing and poking at it.

"What is it, Lady?" he asked. "Did you find something?" He thought the dog may have uncovered a dead animal like a rabbit or vole. But Lady's frantic digging told him it might be something bigger. He pulled himself up on his hands and knees and moved Lady aside. He started digging around the area where the dog had made an opening. At first, he found a carpet, an old-style large rug that had been rolled up. As he managed to pull back more snow, he could see that there appeared to be something inside it.

He pushed back some of the carpet. At first, he felt it. Then he gazed down at the human head, its hair frozen and matted with blood.

Sergeant Windflower reached for his cellphone.

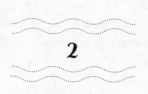

2

Windflower managed to crawl out of the bush and pull Lady out with him. He didn't want her to interfere anymore with what certainly looked like a crime scene. There was almost no way that a person could wrap themselves in an old carpet and slide in here alone. It sure looked like foul play. But that wasn't up to him to determine, at least not yet. He asked Betsy to alert the town coroner and Windflower's friend, Doctor Vijay Sanjay, to help determine that.

But Doc Sanjay wasn't the first to arrive; Tizzard and Jones got there first.

Windflower showed them the body and barked at them to secure the scene. He walked down to his car to put Lady inside and to warm himself up. Then came the paramedics, and he briefed them about the location of the body and was told that Sanjay was en route. A few minutes later the diminutive coroner arrived. Not knowing Windflower's dank disposition, he greeted the RCMP officer in his usual friendly fashion.

"How ya getting on b'y?" asked Sanjay. "Da fog's some tick b'y."

For the second time that morning, Windflower couldn't help himself from smiling. His old buddy's habit of trying out the local slang always broke him up.

"It's good, Doc. Nice to see you, even if it is under less than favourable conditions," replied Windflower.

"Dead body, I hear," said the doctor.

"Wrapped in an old rug just off the trail up there. I stumbled on it accidentally."

"Know who it is?"

"I didn't turn the body over. Figured we've already interfered enough."

"Is everything okay? You seem a little off. No Newfie response and not even any Shakespeare."

Windflower thought for a moment before responding. "I'm okay," he finally said. "Some extra stress these days."

Sanjay looked at his friend closely. "You can talk to me anytime you know. I've got a beautiful bottle of Scotch, and Repa would love to make you some fresh samosas. It's an Oban 14-year-old Highland single malt. It's described as smoky with a hint of salt air, and it's said to taste like a really good kiss from someone who has a little whisky on their breath."

Windflower laughed again, despite himself. "That would be nice. I'll give you a call," he said. "Let me know what you find out. I'm especially interested in what you might think about time of death."

Sanjay waved goodbye as he lugged his black bag up the trail. He shouted back to Windflower. "Remember, 'You can't cross the sea merely by standing and staring at the water.'"

Tagore, thought Windflower. He was Sanjay's favourite poet. Besides being a famous poet, Rabindranath Tagore was also an artist and musician who had reshaped Bengali music and literature. Sanjay revered him as the Bard of the Bengalis, and Windflower had grown to love his beautiful poetry as well. But today he was in no mood to feel better. He wrapped himself in his scowl and drove back to his office.

He stopped along the way to drop Lady off at the house. There was no sign of Sheila or little Amelia Louise, but Windflower reminded himself that wasn't particularly unusual. Sheila often had errands to run, messages she called them, and she was still the mayor of Grand Bank for a few more months until she returned to school part-time, a decision she had made just a couple of months ago. She wanted to eventually do a Master of Business Administration but had to clear up her scholastic records and complete the course load for an old degree program she had started several years earlier but had never finished.

Windflower supported her. Yes, he was sure of that. But he had a nagging feeling in his gut about being left behind or out of place or maybe just plain angry. Molly got the brunt of his discomfort next. She approached in her gentle, pleading feline way for some attention and stroking from her master. But she was met with a snarl and definite "no" from Windflower. The cat slunk away to sulk and show the world how badly she had been treated. But since her world right now consisted only of Windflower and Lady, who was already curled up on her bed in the corner, it was fruitless. If cats could sigh, she sighed her loudest plaintiff meow and went to her own corner of the kitchen.

Lost in his dark mood, Windflower was oblivious to the cat's pain. He thought about writing Sheila a funny, yet remorseful, note but couldn't think of anything except how he was still hurt from their morning fight somehow. He was in bad shape emotionally. Pitifully so. Uncle Frank would call it sitting on his pity pot. Maybe he should call Frank. But that thought and the one to write Sheila a note vanished when his cellphone rang. It was his boss from Marystown, Acting Inspector Richard Raymond. He paused for a moment to collect himself before answering.

"Windflower."

"What's going on over there, Sergeant? Another dead body on your watch," said Raymond.

Windflower wondered how he could know that. Did he have spies in Grand Bank watching him? Before he could test out that theory, Raymond continued.

"Your admin told me you are investigating a death near the clinic," he said.

"Yes, Sir," said Windflower. "I was out for a run this morning and happened to find a body in the brush near the trail. Doctor Sanjay is there now, and I hope to have his preliminary report soon."

"Age, height, any strange markings?"

"I don't know, Sir. I didn't want to disturb the scene. There might be more evidence nearby."

The acting inspector decided Windflower needed a policing 101 lesson. "Getting the basic info doesn't disturb anything," said Raymond. "We learn that at the academy, Sergeant. Time wasted in an investigation cannot be found again."

Windflower thought about saying something smart in return but decided to hold his tongue instead. That just left an opening for another salvo by his superior.

"Where does one get the time for a run in the middle of the day anyway? Maybe you have too much time on your hands over there in Grand Bank. I was thinking that maybe we could transfer one of your crew to HQ. We have lots of work to keep us busy," said Raymond.

Now Windflower was in serious trouble. He could actually feel his blood boil and the colour in his face increase in intensity. He wanted so badly to tell the acting inspector exactly what he thought of him. But somehow his inner angel saved him. "Sorry, Sir. I have to go. I have another call. Maybe it's Doctor Sanjay. I'll send you a report tonight."

Windflower closed the phone and looked around for something safe and soft to hit. His pets stayed in their corners and pretended he wasn't there. He paused, counted to 10, then counted another 10. By the time he got to 50, his breathing was almost back to normal. He even felt better enough to absent-mindedly rub Molly when she came back towards him. He took one long breath and left.

He was on his way to the office when his Jeep seemed to take a turn of its own toward the Mug-Up café. The small restaurant was hot and full, but Windflower managed to get one last seat in the far end away from the bustle of the morning. He ordered a coffee and muffin from Marie, the long-time waitress, and surveyed the scene in front of him. People were chatting and greeting each other like they hadn't seen one another in years. Yet Windflower knew that they likely had the same visit yesterday and the day before that. He nodded his thanks to Marie when she brought him his coffee and a warm blueberry muffin with butter.

"Morning, Sergeant," came the friendly and familiar voice of Herb Stoodley as Windflower was digging into his muffin.

"Good morning, Herb," said Windflower, greeting his friend and, most recently, his tutor in the magic and mystery of classical music. "How is Moira doing?"

"She's coming along fine," said Stoodley. "But it's made running this place a challenge 'til she gets back on her feet."

"That was a nasty fall. She's lucky she only broke her ankle."

"Don't tell her that," warned Stoodley. "She's getting angry that she can't get up and go like she's used to. Can't say as I blame her. I guess that fate is awaiting all of us, but we have to maintain a good attitude. 'With mirth and laughter let old wrinkles come.'"

Windflower almost smiled at that last quote. It was his cue to reply with a rich Shakespearian ditty of his own. But instead he gathered up the last crumbs of his muffin and drained his coffee mug. "I have to get back," was all he said.

"Winston, are you okay?" asked Herb.

"I will be," said Windflower as he stood to leave.

"I'm here if you want to talk," said the other man.

Windflower nodded and went to the cash to pay his bill. He waved goodbye to his friend who was still standing in the area near his table. "That's two people who've offered help this morning," he mused out loud. "I guess I'm not hiding what's going on with me very well. Maybe I should talk to somebody."

That thought lasted until he opened the front door to the RCMP detachment and heard the screaming.

3

W hat the heck is going on in here?" Windflower asked nobody in particular.

There was a man lying on the floor with Smithson on top of him and a frantic woman nearby yelling at the police officer to let the man go. Betsy was hiding out in her workstation and peeked over the cubicle wall when she heard Windflower.

"Constable Smithson brought that man in," she said, pointing at the two on the floor. "And then she shows up," she added, waving her hand up towards the woman.

Windflower quietly took the woman's arm and guided her to his office. His calmness seemed to work as the woman meekly went along and the man beneath Smithson stopped struggling. This allowed Smithson to get the man up and propel him down the hall and into a cell. Windflower heard the cell door slam shut and Smithson's steps coming back up the hall.

"Would you like a cup of tea?" asked Windflower of the woman. She nodded that she would.

"Betsy, would you get this woman a cup of tea?" he called out, before telling the woman he would be right back. He then motioned for Smithson to join him in the back room.

"What's going on?" asked Windflower.

"I was on my way home when I spotted Vince Murray going the other way," said Smithson. "We've got a warrant for his arrest for breach of conditions. So I pulled him over. He got a bit snippy, but I managed to get him back here. Then she showed up, and the place went crazy."

"His girlfriend?"

"Daphne Burry. I've seen her at the lounge a few times, sometimes with Murray and sometimes with her friends. She's been barred from there now for causing fights, and the bartender accused her of trying to steal a bottle from behind the bar."

"Nice," said Windflower, his tone making it obvious he didn't think her behaviour was nice at all. "Vince Murray's the car thief, isn't he?"

Smithson went through his notebook. "Was part of a gang in St. John's sending cars to the mainland in shipping containers. Then from there, from Halifax to be precise, they were being resold all over the world, mostly to Russia and then back into Europe. Apparently a very lucrative operation. Some say it's still going strong."

"Okay," said Windflower. "Do the paperwork and send him to Marystown. They can do the transfer once they get him in front of a judge. You don't want to press any more charges from the ruckus this morning, do you?"

"And have more paperwork? No, thanks. I'll write Murray up and take him over to Marystown this afternoon. So what's going on with the body you found?"

"Too early to say." With that, Windflower abruptly turned away from Smithson and walked back to his office. Betsy was standing in the doorway, and the other woman was sitting by his desk holding a cup of tea.

"Miss Burry, we haven't met. I'm Sergeant Windflower."

The woman scowled at Windflower and continued to sip her tea. "I don't have to tell you nuttin'," she said.

"Listen. We can do this the hard way or the easy way. We can charge you with obstructing justice and probably a lot more, or you can be nice, say goodbye to your boyfriend and go home. You pick," said Windflower.

The woman started to bite back, and then realized that this cop wasn't playing games. She laid her cup on his desk and stood up. "Let's go," she said.

Windflower called Smithson who took the Burry woman back to see Vince Murray. He handed Betsy the woman's cup, and finally alone in his office, he closed the door. A few minutes of peace and quiet, he thought. But only a few it turned out, because his cell-phone rang.

"Good morning, Sergeant." It was Ron Quigley, Windflower's

old boss who had been seconded to RCMP HQ in Ottawa for a year to serve on a task force looking at the opioid crisis and developing a new police response.

"Good morning, Ron," said Windflower.

"Do you miss me?" asked Quigley playfully.

"More than you could imagine. Raymond is driving me nuts."

"I know," said Quigley. "I'm sorry they imposed him on you. I think they wanted to get him out of Nova Scotia. He wasn't my first choice, that's for sure."

"How's Ottawa?"

"Ottawa is great. You know I love Newfoundland, but Ottawa actually gets something that looks like spring. How are you doing?"

"I'm okay. But between Raymond and a leaky roof at the B & B, I've got my hands full."

"How's that baby girl of yours?" asked Quigley, hoping mention of his daughter would take his mind off his problems for a few minutes.

It worked. Windflower smiled as he thought of Amelia Louise. "She's wonderful," he told Quigley. "But not so little. And now that she's mobile, she's a handful, too."

"That will keep you in shape," said Quigley. "Call me if you need anything, okay?"

"Okay, Ron."

After Windflower hung up, he wondered why so many people were offering to help him. He had already had two offers that morning, and Quigley made three. And he hadn't even asked for help. He didn't have any more time to think about that, though, as his cellphone rang again.

"Good morning, my little rabbit," said the quiet voice on the other end of the line in Alberta.

"Good morning, Auntie Marie, how nice to hear your voice," said Windflower. "How are you feeling these days?"

"I'm okay," said his aunt. "Slower, but okay. I hear you need help."

"How did you know I needed help?" he asked. "I didn't tell anybody I wanted help."

"Your spirit did. Your allies came to me in a dream and woke me up. That's why I'm calling you this early from Pink Lake. That's why your allies are here. To help you when your spirit is low."

"What do I have to do?" Windflower was bewildered, but he was always open to Auntie Marie's suggestions, even if he didn't always understand them.

"You have to accept the help that's offered to you," said Auntie Marie. "We are never truly alone in this world. There are always allies here with us and on the other side. But if you scorn or rebuff them, they will go away. So welcome them in and offer them your most special gift, your time."

"Thank you, Auntie. I just don't know what's wrong with me these days."

"That's why you have to have good practices, like ceremony, in your life," said his Auntie. "When you do those things, all is right in this world, and you have many more gifts to bring to your family and your community. What are you not doing today? That is your first question."

"I guess I haven't been smudging, praying or asking for help and guidance," Windflower admitted.

"How that's working for you?" asked his aunt, laughing.

"It's not funny, Auntie!" Windflower was feeling exasperated. Even his beloved Auntie had no sympathy for him.

"It sure is funny," said Auntie Marie. "Let's say you were cold and had a pile of dry wood and kindling and you refused to start a fire. I think that'd be pretty funny. Do what you know works, and it will work for you. Now, how's my baby?"

"She's perfect. We will try and come visit this summer. How is Uncle Frank?"

"Frank is well. He has an apprentice dream weaver, and they are out on the land on a vision quest. He will do another one with you if you come. It is time for you to move into another role in your life."

"What is that role?"

"You already know the answer to that question. That's why you are so uncomfortable. You don't want to accept it yet. But you will. Goodbye, my little rabbit. Be well."

Once the phone went dead, Windflower opened his door and walked to the front to see Betsy. She was waiting for him.

4

Corporal Tizzard is on his way back," Betsy told Windflower. "Constable Jones is staying there to protect the scene. He said he's asked the town manager to put up a sign and a barricade, closing the trail 'til further notice. I've called forensics and advised that we have an incident. Anything else I should do right now?" Betsy was all business.

"No, that's fine. Later today, when we get more information, I'll get you to work with media relations to put together a statement. But for now, we say nothing," said Windflower.

"Some people already know something's up. I certainly won't tell them anything."

"Tell anybody what?" asked Eddie Tizzard, who walked in on their conversation.

"Is Sanjay still over there?" asked Windflower.

"He was leaving with the body to go back to the clinic. Jones is still there. I was thinking that we could stay there for the day and then get Smithson to rig us up a light and a camera so that we can monitor the trail from over here," suggested Tizzard.

"Are you trying to do my job now?" asked Windflower. "You don't have any authority here. I make the decisions."

Tizzard looked at his boss with his mouth open and checked with Betsy. She looked as dumbfounded as he did.

"Okay. I mean, yes, Sir," Tizzard stammered. "My shift is over. Is it all right if I go home?"

"Go," said Windflower. "Let me know if Doctor Sanjay calls," he said to Betsy and walked back to his office. He shut the door, and if he could've, he would've screamed. He knew he had just screwed up, with Tizzard of all people. They truly had been through the wars together. What was going on with him?

A few minutes later there was a timid knock on his door. It was Smithson.

"I can take Murray over to Marystown now if that's okay with you," he said.

"Fine," said Windflower. "But before you go can you see Jones at the crime scene? Tizzard thought we might be able to set up a spotlight and camera, so we don't have to stay there overnight."

"Sure, I can do that," said Smithson, happy to put his technical skills to good use. "I've got a spare camera at home that I can use, and there's a big spotlight in the back."

Windflower thought about saying something like "whatever," but for the first time that morning, he wisely restrained himself. "Good," he said instead, and while Smithson was hoping for more, he settled for a wave of dismissal from his sergeant.

Windflower's cellphone rang again. When he looked down, he could see it was from Sheila.

"Hi, Sheila."

"Hi, Winston," said Sheila, a little cooler than usual, at least in Windflower's perception. "We're coming back from the town office. I hear there's some trouble up at the trail behind the clinic."

"We found a body this morning," said Windflower, omitting the fact that he had been the one to find it.

"Do we know who it is?"

"Not yet. Doc Sanjay is working on that. Listen, Sheila, about this morning . . ."

Sheila cut him off. "Let's not talk on the phone," she said.

"Okay," said Windflower, more than a little tentatively.

"We need to sort out what's going on, and we need to do that in person. Can we make time to do that when you come home tonight?" she asked.

"Sure. I'll try to come home early."

Sheila had assessed the situation. "You've got a dead body. Come when you can. I'll make supper, and if you're a little late, I can heat it up for you."

"Thanks, Sheila, that would be great."

"Okay, bye," she said abruptly.

"I love you, Sheila." But she was gone.

Now Windflower knew he was in trouble, big trouble. If Sheila was giving up on him, his life was over. He needed to come up with a plan pretty quickly to deal with the raging fire on his home front. But time was not on his side.

"Doctor Sanjay on line two," came Betsy's voice over the intercom.

"Paul Sparkes," said Doctor Sanjay.

"What?" asked Windflower.

"Your dead man is Paul Sparkes," said the doctor.

"That's the guy who was reported missing just before Christmas."

"That's the one. I checked the photo on file and it matches along with his general description. That should at least give us an outside window on time of death. I'm kind of surprised though. He's still frozen solid inside that carpet. No real signs of decay or animal intervention that you'd expect to see."

"Yeah, it's been mild enough for the snow to melt a few times since the New Year. What do you think it means?"

"I think our man has been kept frozen somewhere," said Sanjay. "Somewhere north of here or . . ."

"Or in a cooler," said Windflower, finishing the sentence.

"I'm not the police officer, but you would need a large deep-freeze."

"Like a commercial or walk-in freezer."

"Exactly. I have to continue my work. Do you want to get someone to make the identification?"

"Thank you, Doc. I'll get Betsy on it."

Windflower punched the intercom and called Betsy into his office.

"Can you pull up the file on Paul Sparkes?" asked Windflower. "See if there's a next of kin or contact."

"Is that the dead man?" asked Betsy.

"It looks like it," said Windflower. Then he decided to change the subject to a more delicate matter. "Betsy, have you been talking to anybody over in Marystown?"

"What do you mean?" she wondered.

"The acting inspector knew about the dead body when he called me this morning."

"I didn't tell him," said Betsy, her face turning red and her voice rising a little. "I would never betray the confidences of this office. I'll get the file." With that, she turned and marched out.

"Betsy . . . ," Windflower started to say, but his administrative assistant was gone. Great, he thought. Now Betsy hates me, too.

He tried to turn his mind to a stack of unread paperwork but didn't have the head or heart for it. He was still shuffling papers around when Betsy returned, laid the file on his desk and marched out again.

He thought about following her but decided against it. Let her cool off first, he thought. He opened the file marked Missing Person: Paul Andrew Sparkes. The picture paper-clipped to the folder was a mug shot of the missing man. Not missing anymore, Windflower thought wryly. Sparkes was in his mid-thirties and had stringy, brown-black hair and faded blue eyes that looked like they were a long way from the jail or detention centre where the photo was taken. He was described as 5'11", Caucasian male, with one finger missing from his left hand and multiple tattoos, including one on his torso of a python. His nicknames and aliases included Sparky, Robert Winter and Snake.

There was a long list of arrests and charges dating back to when Sparkes was eighteen. And there's probably more stuff before that but not recorded on his adult file, thought Windflower. Born in Rencontre West. That was around Ramea, where Tizzard was from. He'd have to talk to Tizzard about that. The latest charge, the one where he was out on conditions while awaiting trial, was possession for the purpose of trafficking in a controlled substance. Most likely opiates of some sort. That had become the drug of choice in rural Newfoundland and was wreaking havoc in every small community throughout the province, including Grand Bank.

Windflower also noted that Sparkes had been diagnosed with FASD when he first entered the prison system. Windflower knew a little about Fetal Alcohol Spectrum Disorder. It had been a big deal back in Pink Lake when he was growing up and in the many remote communities he had been in contact with during his stint working in British Columbia. What he knew about it was that not all people with this disorder got into trouble. In fact, many of them were nice, kind, maybe a little slow, but not bad people at all. Others were the mean, violent kind. Some experts said that only a fraction of people affected by this condition, caused when their pregnant mothers drank alcohol, ended up in prison. But that didn't jibe with another number that Windflower had seen. Ten to maybe 30 percent of all those in Canadian prisons had some degree of FASD.

It looked like Sparkes may have missed the kindness gene.

5

Windflower tried to recall Sparkes, but at some point all the bad guys melded into one. He thought he might have seen him around the Marystown RCMP, but not in Grand Bank. None of that was important right now, not to Sparkes, that was for sure. He scanned the file for the name and number of next of kin. He had a brother in Terrenceville, William Sparkes, also known as Billy Sparkes or sometimes Big Billy Sparkes. Windflower called the number.

"Ello," a woman answered.

"Can I speak to William Sparkes please?" asked Windflower.

"Billy? Yeah, just a sec," said the woman. "Billy, someone's on da phone fer youse."

"Yah," came a man's voice.

"This is Sergeant Winston Windflower from the RCMP in Grand Bank. I have some bad news about your brother Paul. I'm afraid he's dead," said Windflower.

"Ded, whaddya mean ded?" asked Billy Sparkes.

"His body was found on a trail in town here. It was just discovered this morning. We will need somebody to make a positive identification, but we are pretty sure it's your brother. I am sorry for your loss."

"I bet youse are." Billy Sparkes' tone was definitely sarcastic.

"If you can come by the detachment, we will escort you to see his remains," said Windflower.

"Can we take 'is body?"

"Once the coroner finishes his autopsy, he will release the body."

"We'll be over tomorrow mornin'," said Sparkes.

Windflower started to say something else but realized that the phone had gone dead. He walked to Betsy's area at the front. She took off her headphones and took out her pad.

"I spoke to Billy Sparkes, the brother of the deceased. He will be by tomorrow morning. Can you get whoever is here to go with him to the clinic and let Doctor Sanjay know he's coming?" He handed the file back to Betsy. "Thank you, Betsy," he said. "I have to go out for a few minutes." Betsy took the file and nodded but didn't say a word. Man, she is really mad, thought Windflower.

The rest of the afternoon was a bit of a blur. Forensics called back and said they were coming in the next morning. Raymond called three times for updates, but at least he was handling the media from over in Marystown.

Around four o'clock, Windflower said goodnight to Betsy, who still wasn't talking to him. She nodded dismissively as he was leaving. But he knew Betsy wasn't his biggest problem. That was waiting for him at home. He needed advice and he needed it fast. Herb Stoodley might be just the man for that. Windflower drove back to the café to find Herb. He was in the kitchen cleaning up.

"Did you want a sandwich?" asked Stoodley when he saw his friend come in.

"I need some advice," said Windflower.

"Turn that open sign around on the front door and lock it. I'll make us some fresh tea. Are you in a big rush?"

"Not particularly. I'm kind of dreading going home to be honest."

Stoodley nodded sympathetically. "Ah, woman problems," he said. "Well, it's good that you came to Uncle Herb. It's not that I have all the answers. But I have made most of the mistakes. Didn't you tell me that part of wisdom is learning from our mistakes?"

"That's one of the Grandfather Teachings."

"Then I am a very wise man. But before I share my wisdom, some music to soothe our savage souls." Stoodley reached up and found a case with a disc and put it into the player.

The violin and cello started slowly, and the music soon filled the room around the two men as they sipped their tea. The rest of the orchestra joined in, and Windflower felt himself relax for the first time that day, maybe even for the first time in a long time. He let the music wash over him. It felt like the waves of the ocean.

"What was that?" he asked as the music slowed and faded away.

"It's Pachelbel's Canon in D. It's wonderful, isn't it? This music comes from the 1600s, but it was lost and forgotten until 1919. When I hear it, I think of the quote by Tagore. 'Music fills the infinite between two souls.'"

"That's amazing. I guess you must be seeing a little of Doc Sanjay."

"Just here in the café. He's worried about you." Stoodley took a deep breath. "And so am I."

Windflower felt like bolting but forced himself to stay. "I am in big trouble at home," he finally blurted out.

"That's the first step," said Stoodley. "Admitting you have a problem."

"It's like I've lost my voice. I don't even know who I am anymore. I've turned into a husband and a father and a Mountie. But who am I, really? I feel overworked and under-appreciated."

"Wow," said his friend. "How long have you been carrying that around? That's an awful lot of weight for one person."

"I know my life is wonderful. But somehow, I just can't feel it," said Windflower, looking into his cup of tea while fidgeting his fingers. "Maybe I'm just depressed from the weather around here."

"None of us likes the weather. But you've been here, what, seven or eight years now? It's the same weather every spring. RDF—rain, drizzle and fog—with snow always not far off."

"That's true," said Windflower, now sipping his tea. "Maybe it's cumulative. All that fog and drizzle building up in my system."

"If that were the case, I would've turned completely into fog by now and drifted off to sea. My experience, for what it's worth, is that my happiness is not dependent on the weather or anything else outside of me, not even the people as close to me as my family. It's about what's going on up here or in here," Stoodley said, pointing to his head and then to his heart. "What's happening at home?"

Windflower sighed. "I really love Sheila, and Amelia Louise is my world. But, something's just not right with us these days. I suspect that most of it is me, but I need some stuff from Sheila. I don't know how to ask for it."

"What are you afraid of?"

Windflower stayed silent for over a minute, then rose to leave. "Thanks for the tea and the chat," he said.

"'Those who own much, have much to fear,'" said Stoodley as Windflower unlocked the café door. Windflower nodded and went out into the late afternoon.

Windflower knew that he had a lot going for him, that was for sure. Maybe he was just ungrateful. There was one sure remedy for that. He opened the trunk of his Jeep and took out his mobile smudge kit that was under the spare tire. He placed the basket on the front seat and drove over to the beach.

He parked the Jeep and walked down the slippery rocks carefully until he came to a small sheltered place just out of sight of the road behind him. People would see his vehicle, but he was safe from any prying eyes. He took out the earthen bowl and unfurled his medicine kit. Inside were his sacred medicines. There was a little each of sage, tobacco, cedar and sweetgrass, and he put them into the bowl. Windflower also added a little reindeer moss, which he gathered every year from the barrens outside of town, because it sparked easily when he used a wooden match to light the medicines. When the smoke had started, he took his large feather and circulated the smoke over his head and all over his body. He paused at his heart to pray for wisdom and kindness. He finished the smudge by directing the smoke under his feet to give him strength to stay on a good path in this world.

After he had smudged, he stayed completely still for about a minute to allow the sacred medicines to fully inhabit his body and his mind. Then he turned his thoughts to what he was grateful for. Sheila and Amelia Louise were the first ones to come to mind, and he spent another minute thinking about what exactly he was grateful for when it came to these two, special people. Then he allowed his thoughts to go to Auntie and Uncle, a few of his last remaining relatives, and then to his friends at work and in the community. By the time he had finished giving thanks, he felt refreshed and energized. I am a very rich man, he thought.

With the sun now setting over the ocean and the sky filling with light and all the colours of the universe, he got in his Jeep and drove home, grateful for his life and grateful to be alive.

6

When Windflower walked through his back door and into the kitchen, he was immediately hit with aromas that were at once delightful and totally surprising. His eyes watered as if he were going to cry, and his stomach grumbled to remind him that he had nothing to eat since that muffin at the Mug-Up in the morning.

"What is that smell?" he almost gasped as he walked into the living room.

"Fish stew," said Sheila, handing him Amelia Louise before the little girl jumped out of her arms. Molly and Lady circled his feet as he danced with his baby daughter and sang her a nonsense song that she loved. The baby squealed, the dog barked, and the cat made herself as large as possible to make sure she wouldn't be left out of the fun.

Windflower brought the baby into the kitchen and strapped her into her high chair. He got both animals a treat and went to the sink to wash his hands. Sheila gave Amelia Louise a small bowl of rice with some pieces of vegetables that had cooled and been cut into small pieces, and some pieces of bread. The baby thought the bread was great fun and stuffed some in her mouth, hurling the rest over the side, where Lady and Molly fought over each piece, finally retreating to their corners with their new, prized possessions.

Windflower sat at the table and buttered his own chunk of bread as Sheila laid a bowl of rice and stew in front of him. He paused for a moment to inhale the flavours. "Coriander," he said.

"That's easy," said Sheila. "You can see that. What else?"

Windflower sniffed deeply. "I'd say a touch of chili powder, and I can see the bay leaves. I'm guessing cumin, but there's something a little strange in there too. Whatever it is, it smells wonderful."

"Some turmeric and panch phoron. I got it and the recipe from Repa. She said the dish is called muri ghonto, and she used to make it back home in India. She gets a large fish head and cleans it and then adds all these spices. I guess it's a traditional Bengali recipe. The panch phoron is actually a combination of spices that are dry roasted. She gets it sent over once a year," said Sheila.

Windflower tasted the broth. "Oh, my goodness. That is fantastic," he said. "We should make this at the B & B this summer."

Sheila did not respond to the last remark, but Windflower may not have heard her anyway. He was long gone into fish stew heaven. Sheila cleaned up Amelia Louise and her food, which was much of it, that had fallen to the floor and had not yet been picked up by the scavengers.

"Help yourself if you want more," she said. "We'll be out in the living room."

Windflower cleaned his bowl of stew and then added a refill. When he was done, he put the dishes in the dishwasher and the kettle on to boil. He went to the living room and became a human version of Twister with two animals and a very happy baby crawling all over him. Sheila went upstairs to start Amelia Louise's bath while Windflower finished the clearing up and made tea. When the tea was ready, he brought two cups upstairs and sat in the bathroom to play with the baby for the last few minutes of bath time.

He took her out of the bath and brought her into her bedroom where he put a diaper and pajamas on her. She squealed and squirmed the whole time. Then he handed her over to Mommy for her last feeding. When that was done, Windflower read her a story. Tonight's story, an illustrated version of The Velveteen Rabbit, was about a toy rabbit that longed to be real. Amelia Louise loved the story but not enough to overcome her drowsiness. Before long, her eyes closed and she was fast asleep.

Windflower laid her gently in her crib and turned on the monitor. Sheila had already gone downstairs, and Windflower found her sitting in front of the fireplace.

"Thank you for dinner. That was wonderful," he started.

"No worries," said Sheila. "It was fun to make something

different. Repa is such a good cook. I was so pleased when she offered me this recipe and the spices to make it."

"I know that I have not been very pleasant to live with these days. I'm not even sure I can explain it. But I do not want to be anything but kind, gentle and loving towards you. I love you, Sheila."

"I love you, too, Winston."

"I know that, Sheila, and thank you. I have some work to do. But I want to do it here, with you by my side."

"Why don't you talk to me, Winston? Or your friends. Every one of them has called me to ask how they can help."

"That's how you got the recipe from Repa. Did Herb talk to you, too?"

Sheila nodded. "And Ron Quigley," she added.

"Auntie Marie called me this morning as well. She said I needed to seek out my allies for help. I will do that starting first thing tomorrow. Right now, I have a date with a near-frantic collie."

Windflower looked intently at Sheila, who was now smiling. That made him smile in turn. When Lady almost pulled Windflower out of his chair, Sheila's smile broke out into a laugh, and she watched Lady run to the kitchen and grab her leash in her mouth.

"Saved by a dog," she said good-naturedly. "Come back quickly. I've missed you."

Windflower and Lady had a brisk walk around town, which was much too short for her liking, and he was back home in 15 minutes. He made sure to fill the pets' bowls with food and water and then headed upstairs. Sheila was waiting for him.

Windflower went to bed feeling happy, the first time he had done that in a long time. To love and be loved were great gifts, he thought, as he snuggled into Sheila for the night and drifted off to sleep. Soon after though, he woke up. But it was in a dream. He knew he was dreaming because he was outside, and he wasn't cold, despite the fact that he was wearing his pajamas. He looked for his hands. That was one trick to vivid dreaming that he had learned from Uncle Frank, along with his Auntie Marie, a master dream weaver as well. Knowing he was dreaming, he patiently waited for something to happen, because something always happened in these types of dreams.

He took notice of his surroundings, another key to understanding the dream world. It was early spring back home in Alberta by the looks of it. There was still a little snow underneath some of the trees, but there was a smell of fresh earth and life in the air. It was growing dark as he entered a clearing in the forest of tall trees, and he could see a fire in one corner. He thought he saw people around the fire, but when he got closer, he could see they were animals.

There was a moose, a young deer and a rabbit. All of them seemed to look back at him as he neared. When he came almost close enough to touch them, the rabbit started to shake and shiver and then ran off. "He'll be back," said the moose in a surprisingly loud voice that startled Windflower. "We've been waiting for you," said the moose. "What took you so long?"

Windflower opened his mouth to speak, but nothing came out. When he finally did manage to squeak out something, he heard a voice. It sounded like Sheila. "Winston, are you okay?"

Windflower rubbed his eyes and said, "I'm fine, just a dream." He cuddled in closer to Sheila, and after a while, she fell back to sleep. Windflower spent a few more minutes trying to figure out what had happened, and then, despite himself, he was pulled under again. When he finally woke for good, it was to hear Amelia Louise on the monitor. Sheila was still sleeping, so he crept quietly out of their bedroom and into their child's room where he turned off the baby monitor. Then he took Amelia Louise and held her high above his head. She squealed, and he laughed. It was his favourite time of day. Maybe it was hers, too.

7

Windflower made a promise to himself to start over anew that morning. He thought about his day as he walked Lady around town. There were few people stirring this early in the morning, and he took a glimpse of the sun between the clouds as an omen of better things ahead. He had a quick breakfast with Sheila and Amelia Louise and then went to work early, actively trying to have a good day. He started by making a fresh cup of coffee. Once at his desk he reached inside a drawer for a notebook marked 'Gratitude.' He had used it over the years to write down all the things he was grateful for. When he thought of something else, he added it to the ever-growing list. This morning he added his dreams and his allies. Both may have been there already, but it wouldn't hurt to add them again, even if it was just as a reminder to himself.

Such reminders were important because he had learned, especially as he got older, that whatever he was grateful for, he got to keep. That was true of things and possessions but equally true for people and relationships. He got another reminder when Eddie Tizzard showed up at his office door with a box of muffins.

"Partridgeberry muffin?" asked Tizzard.

"That's a good one," said Windflower, and he wrote partridgeberry muffins in his gratitude notebook, alongside Eddie Tizzard.

Tizzard took a bite of muffin. "They are good," he said. "Fresh, too."

Windflower laughed and followed him back to the lunchroom. They were still sitting there and laughing when Betsy came in.

"Somebody's in a good mood today," she said.

"I'm planning on having a good day," said Windflower. "Have a muffin, Betsy."

Betsy got a cup of coffee and sat at the table with the two men.

"My dad always said the sun was still up there, even if we can't always see it right away in the morning," said Tizzard. "Hope is believing that it will still shine."

"Let's hope so," said Windflower. "These dark gray days are getting me down."

"But the days are getting longer," said Betsy.

"Maybe you've just got sad," said Tizzard.

Windflower and Betsy stared at Tizzard. "I don't mean feeling sad. I mean Seasonal Affective Disorder. Your body might need more light. My dad got one of those special lights. He says it mimics the sun."

"Did it work for him?" asked Betsy.

"Yes, but he said he missed getting up mad about the weather like everyone else, so he turned it off," the corporal dead-panned. Both Windflower and Betsy laughed.

They were all enjoying their coffee and snacks when the two RCMP officers' phones beeped. "It's Smithson," said Tizzard, beating Windflower to the draw.

"There's been an accident," said Windflower, after answering Smithson's call and listening briefly. "On the road to Fortune, near the new subdivision. One person seriously hurt."

"I'll head over there," said Tizzard.

"Give me a call when you get there," said Windflower. "I'll text Smithson back to get him to close the road."

"I'll call highways," said Betsy. "They'll divert people down below Fortune and send them back the other way."

Windflower nodded. Betsy had been through this many times. It would take time for all the evidence to be collected and debris cleared. "Is forensics coming in this morning for the Sparkes case or did they arrive last night?" he asked Betsy.

"They were only coming this morning," the administrative assistant responded. "Corporal Brown said they should be here by ten or so."

"Great," said Windflower. "We can get them to take a look at the accident scene, too, when they're here. Let me know when they arrive. I'm going to the clinic to check in with Doc Sanjay."

"That would be good," said Betsy. "The media are calling for an update."

"Okay. I'll let you know. If he has anything, we might be able to schedule a press conference."

"Thank you so much. You know what they're like."

Windflower nodded again and left to go to the clinic. He thought about going past the accident scene, but the two other officers could deal with that. He was coming around the turn near the brook when he heard the siren and then saw the flashing lights of the ambulance. He pulled over to let it pass and then followed it to the clinic. He parked near the emergency entrance and watched as the paramedics went to work.

The driver jumped out of the ambulance and ran to the back to open the door. Assisted by the paramedic inside, he pulled the gurney and their patient out and then through the emergency door where they were met by two nurses and an on-call doctor. Together, the team rolled the patient down the hall towards what Windflower knew was the clinic's intensive care area.

Windflower decided he would check on the accident patient later. For now, he had to see the coroner. Doctor Sanjay's small office and examination area was down the corridor from the reception area. As he passed through, Windflower said hello to the on-duty nurse and smiled at the two people in the waiting area. Once he got to Doctor Sanjay's office, he could hear activity behind the door marked Dr. V. Sanjay, Coroner. He knocked and was called to enter.

The doctor was on the phone. "I'll send the sample by taxi this afternoon. Can you check for the normal range of drugs? Narcotics, opioids, painkillers, you know the drill. Thanks."

"I'm ordering some tests," said Sanjay. "If I can get the samples in by tonight, my associate in the lab will run the base set of tests. It won't find traces, but it will show if our late friend wrapped in a rug was intoxicated when he passed away. Rather suddenly by the looks of it. I am still thawing him out, so I don't have a sense of how he died yet, or when, but at first glance I would suggest he was hit with some blunt object. But I could have called you with that news. It's nice to see you, but why are you really here this morning?"

Windflower blushed a little. "I need some help to get back on track," he said.

"Well, I guess we should see if there's anything physically wrong with you first. Although, I have to tell you that the longer I practice medicine, or maybe it's because I'm getting older, I'm not sure most of what's wrong with us isn't up here." The doctor tapped his forehead.

"What do you mean?" asked Windflower.

"I am thinking that there is more of a connection between our emotional health and our physical well-being than we once believed."

"It's not all in our heads," Windflower protested. "You can't think your way into cancer or diabetes."

"No, but people who have good emotional and mental health tend to be healthier overall. Studies show that they have better and faster recoveries than people who are depressed or anxious. But let's start by checking your blood pressure and heart rate. Then we'll do some blood tests. Might as well send them into the lab tonight, too."

Windflower went through a basic physical under the careful watch of Doctor Sanjay. He was about to leave when the doctor stopped him and wrote him a prescription.

"What's this?" asked Windflower.

"Read it," demanded the doctor.

Windflower had to squint to make out the handwriting on the prescription, but when he did, he burst out laughing. "You are invited for Scotch and samosas this Friday night. Under order of Dr. V. Sanjay."

"I'll be there," said Windflower, reaching to shake hands with his friend. "I have to go see what's going on with the patient from the accident."

"So that's what all the commotion was about," said Sanjay. "I've got to get my package ready to go to St. John's. See you Friday. Repa will be so pleased you are coming."

"Tell her thank you for the fish stew recipe. Sheila made it last night. It was so delicious."

"She will be more than pleased. I will be sure to pass your good wishes along."

As he was leaving the office, relieved his doctor's appointment was over, Windflower remembered he had another piece of business to take care of with Sanjay. "The brother of the deceased will be over sometime today to make the identification," he said.

"He should be a bit more thawed by then," said the doctor. "Although he will be just as dead."

8

Windflower walked back down the corridor of the clinic and stopped at reception to get an update.

"She's still in intensive care," said the nurse.

"Do we know who it is?" asked Windflower.

The nurse pulled up the form on her computer. "Daphne Burry," she said.

Windflower thought for a second and then remembered. Daphne Burry was the frantic woman who was in the detachment. "Can you get the doctor to call me when she's free?" asked Windflower.

"I will, Sergeant."

Windflower was driving back down the highway towards the accident scene when his cellphone rang. He pulled over to the shoulder to take the call.

"Windflower," he answered.

"Good morning, Sergeant," said Corporal Ted Brown, head of the RCMP Forensics Unit. "You've been busy around here. I thought Grand Bank was the RCMP retirement home."

"Yeah," said Windflower. "Nothing ever happens in Grand Bank, and then everything happens all at once. I'm glad you're here. Can you come take a look at this accident? It just happened this morning."

"Down towards Fortune, right?"

"Correct. I'm on my way there right now."

"See you soon."

When Windflower arrived, he saw Smithson and Tizzard at the barricade across the highway. He parked next to them and walked over.

"Forensics is on the way here," he said.

"Betsy told us," said Tizzard. "We haven't done anything but secure the scene."

"No vehicles?" asked Windflower.

"Looks like hit and run on a pedestrian, Sir," said Smithson.

"Witnesses?" asked Windflower.

"Only the person who saw the woman on the side of the road," said Smithson, pulling out his notebook. "Bobby Pike. He was driving to work at the plant when he saw her. According to him there was nobody else around. She wasn't moving so he called 911. The paras took the call and then called me. They said she was alive but unconscious. They took her to the clinic."

"It's Daphne Burry," said Windflower. "I was at the clinic to see Sanjay."

"What?" asked Smithson. "That woman who was at the detachment yesterday with Vince Murray? I didn't see her face before the paramedics had her on the stretcher."

"Same one," said Windflower. "Here comes forensics," he added as the white van pulled up to the barricade. "I'll stay here with them. Why don't you two do a foot canvass of the neighbourhood, see if you can find any witnesses? Somebody may have seen something."

The two other officers went off to their task while Windflower walked towards the white van to greet the crew from forensics.

"Hi, Ted, how's it going?" asked Windflower.

"Morning, again," said Brown. "So what do we have?"

"Looks like a hit and run," said Windflower. "We're just doing the neighbourhood now. One person hurt, in serious condition at the clinic."

"Okay. We'll get to work," said Brown. He started directing his crew to take pictures and measurements from the scene. Windflower watched until his phone rang.

"What's the latest on the Paul Sparkes' death?" asked Acting Inspector Raymond. "Anything on cause? Or do I have to come and lead this investigation myself?"

"We're working on it, Sir," said Windflower. "But we also have a hit and run this morning. The woman is in hospital in serious condition."

"Didn't you learn to multitask yet?" asked Raymond. "I expect a full report on my desk by the end of the day. And deal with the media yourself. I'm tired of holding your hand."

Windflower wasn't going to let that go. But luckily for him, and probably for the acting inspector too, Raymond was gone before he could respond. That left him muttering to himself when Brown came back to talk to him.

"My guys are all set up. Why don't you show me the other scene, the one on the trail? Might as well take a quick look at that before it starts raining," said Brown.

Windflower looked up. Sure enough, dark clouds hovered. He thought he felt a drop hit his cheek. Whatever sunlight they had, it looked like that was over for the day. It's probably Raymond's fault, he thought to himself, but somehow he actually said it out loud.

"He's a real prince, isn't he?" said Brown. "He had one of my crew up on charges. Accused him of stealing equipment. He took a camera home with him for his daughter's birthday party, with my permission. I just about freaked out."

"He's been a challenge, that's for sure. I'll give you a ride over to take a look around," said Windflower.

When they arrived, the entrance to the trail had been marked off in bright yellow police tape. Brown went over the light and camera that Smithson had set up so the scene could be monitored back at the detachment. "Nice job," he said.

"Smithson," said Windflower. "He's our resident techie."

"Nice to have an expert like that. Froude is gone now, back to headquarters. You remember her? She was a crackerjack, but with all the illegal cyber stuff going on, they needed her over in commercial crime."

Brown gazed up the trail. "Okay, let's go have a look," he said.

As the two walked, the rain started to peck. By the time they reached the place where Windflower had found Paul Sparkes' body, there was a steady downpour. The canopy of trees kept them somewhat sheltered, but they both turned up their collars against the rain.

"This rain might actually help a little," said Brown as he peered into the bushes. "Footprints will be long gone, but I'll get my guys to come up and do some soil samples. If we're extremely lucky, there might be some blood or other evidence. A long shot, though."

"We take what we get," said Windflower. "We're having trouble with time of death, too, because it looks like our deceased may have been killed and frozen before he was dropped off here."

"In that case, it's unlikely that we'll find anything. But you never know. Criminals are never as smart as they think they are. They always make mistakes. That's why we do a thorough investigation."

"Exactly, and to keep the bosses off our backs," said Windflower. "Let's go. I'm getting soaked."

9

When Brown and Windflower got back to the accident scene, Brown's guys were packing up.

"Finished already?" asked Windflower.

"There wasn't much to see," said Peters, one of the forensic technicians. "We've got pictures of the scene to send you. There's no sign of braking, and we've taken shots of the marks by the shoulder over there. Sure looks like a hit and run to me."

"That's not up to us to determine," Brown reminded the technician. "We just report what we see."

"I guess we'll have to talk to witnesses," said Windflower.

"I didn't realize you had any," said Brown.

"We have the pedestrian lying in the clinic, for one, and I hope to find more in the neighbourhood," said Windflower. "Someone always sees something. We just have to find them."

"Okay," said Brown. "My team will go to the trail now and start going over it with a fine-tooth comb. We're staying at Granny's tonight. Want to join us later for dinner?"

"I think I'll have to pass on dinner, but I'll try and come over for breakfast in the morning, if that's okay."

"Perfect. We'll have breakfast before we head out. I can give you a verbal update then. If Tizzard is around, tell him to come along, too. He's the funniest guy ever."

"Will do," said Windflower, nodding to Brown and Peters. He drove back to the detachment where Betsy was waiting for him. "The media are calling about the dead man," said Betsy. "And people are asking about the accident. You also have visitors, Big Billy Sparkes and his wife."

"Can you see if we have a file on Daphne Burry?" asked Windflower. "She's the woman in the accident."

Betsy nodded, but said nothing, which meant to Windflower
that she already knew.

"How did you know about Daphne Burry?" he asked.

Betsy started to stammer. "I got a call from Ethel at the clinic,"
she finally said, fully expecting to get an earful from her boss.

Windflower surprised her. "That's great, Betsy," he said. "I'm
glad that we've such a good information-gathering system in our
detachment. Keep up the good work. We'll talk about the media
after I see our visitors."

"Yes, Sir," said Betsy, beaming as Windflower turned to head
down the hall towards his office. He was feeling pretty good about
that interaction, too. That didn't last long.

"Why da 'ell can't I bring my brudder 'ome?" said the man.

Windflower turned around to check out what was going on.
"Good day. I'm Sergeant Winston Windflower. I'm sorry for
your loss. What did Doctor Sanjay say?" Windflower asked as he
motioned Billy Sparkes and a woman accompanying him into his
office.

"Dat little brown injun said we'd 'ave to wait whilst my brudder
tawed out," said Sparkes. He was now standing and yelling close to
Windflower's face.

"Sit down, and we'll see what we can find out, okay?" said Windflower. He sized up Sparkes, who was a large man with an even
larger beer gut and had long, stringy hair hanging out from underneath a dirty baseball cap. Windflower tried to exude confidence, but
he wasn't all that sure how the clearly enraged man might respond.

"Sit down, Billy," demanded the woman. "No point gettin'
arrested over dis, is der?"

Big Billy glared at the woman, who if anything was a bit larger
and more dangerous looking than the Mountie. He didn't want to
tangle with her today, he decided. That could actually be worse than
getting arrested.

"Thank you, Ma'am," said Windflower, and as he picked up the
phone in his office, his two guests sat down. When Doctor Sanjay
answered, Windflower put the call on speaker. "Good day, Doctor.
It's Windflower. I'm with the family of the late Paul Sparkes. Can
you please advise us when you will be able to release the body?"

"Well, Sergeant, as I mentioned to them, I still have to do some tests when the body is completely unfrozen. I will likely not be in a position to release the body until tomorrow."

"Thank you, Doctor. Would you be able to facilitate transport of the remains to Terrenceville after you have completed your work?" asked Windflower.

Sanjay sensed that this was a group conversation. "Absolutely, Sergeant. I could do that. I simply want to make sure that we leave no stone unturned to collect any evidence that will assist the authorities in finding out who did this horrible deed."

"Thank you, Doctor," said Windflower. After he hung up, Windflower turned to Sparkes and said, "We will arrange transport of your late brother's body to your hometown, if that is acceptable."

The woman looked particularly pleased, but her husband was not convinced. "All dis talk about carin' about my brudder and 'elpin' us is all baloney," he said. "Youse guys never did anytin but 'urt me and my brudder ever since we wuz kids. I don't expect anytin from youse."

"Send 'im to Green's Funeral Home," said the woman. "We'll look after 'im from der."

"Thank you," said Windflower. "Before you go, do you have any idea about who might have wanted to hurt your brother?"

"My first guess would be youse," said Sparkes. "Youse always 'ad it in fer Paul. And if it wasn't youse, youse know who."

"What do you mean?" asked Windflower.

Sparkes stood up and laughed in Windflower's face. "My brudder wuz a small fish. 'E may 'ave stole a few tings along da way, but 'e never really 'urt anybody but hisself. Look around. People dat 'as money calls da shots. Dat's who killed Paul. C'mon, Missus, let's go."

With that, the pair left, and Windflower watched out the window as they drove away. He was left with a sense that there was a ring of truth in what Billy Sparkes had just said. But that didn't help much. He was still left with many more questions than answers.

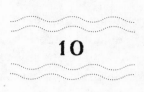
Windflower's questions about his cases would simply have to wait. There were just too many of them about the accident that put Daphne Burry on the side of the road and an equal number about the poorly hidden body of Paul Sparkes on the trail. They would have to wait, too, because Betsy Molloy had questions of her own and made it clear she needed answers.

Windflower spent a few minutes with Betsy going through all the information they had, which wasn't a whole lot. He helped her draft up a brief media release on the accident.

"A woman in her twenties is in serious condition after being struck by a vehicle on Highway 210 east of Grand Bank in the early hours this morning. The driver left the scene. RCMP are investigating and would appreciate anyone who witnessed this accident to call the RCMP Grand Bank Detachment."

"That's perfect," said Windflower after Betsy had read it back to him. "You can let that go and send a copy to Marystown to the attention of Acting Inspector Raymond."

"Will do," said Betsy, clearly still happy from their previous interaction that day. "What about the other case?"

"Let's schedule a media briefing for tomorrow morning, 10 o'clock. Hopefully Doc Sanjay will have more to give us on Paul Sparkes' early demise by then."

Betsy nodded she understood and left to do her media work. Windflower was about to go to the back to get a snack when his intercom buzzed. "Doctor White on line one," said Betsy.

"Good morning, Doctor," said Windflower. Danette White was the newest doctor on board at the clinic, fresh out of medical school and eager to get to work. This was her first placement after her internship, but according to all reports she was both confident and capable.

"Good morning, Sergeant. I'm calling you about Daphne Burry. She's got substantial injuries but, surprisingly, is in fairly stable condition now. Broke both her legs and at least one arm, but we don't know the full extent of any internal injuries," said Doctor White.

"Is she conscious?" asked Windflower. "Did she say anything?"

"She's in a lot of pain, so we've had her heavily sedated. We'll keep her sedated for now until the swelling goes down. We will wake her up tomorrow morning if all goes well, but I'm not sure how coherent she'll be."

"Okay. Will you let me know of any changes in her condition? We're going to put out a statement saying that a woman has sustained serious injuries after being struck by a motor vehicle."

"Thanks for the heads-up," said Doctor White. "I think serious is a good way to describe her condition. Even if the internal damage is minimal, she has a long road to recovery. The rumour is that it's a hit and run. Is that true?"

"It may be," said Windflower. "But we're still investigating, I'll let you know if we have more information on that front. Thanks for your help."

"No problem," said the doctor as she hung up.

Windflower checked his watch, but his stomach told him that he hadn't eaten since breakfast. Having no other pressing responsibilities and before his phone rang again, he snuck into the lunchroom. He got himself a few Purity Cream Crackers, buttered them, added thick slices of cheddar cheese and topped them off with sliced apple.

"Lunch?" asked Tizzard as he waltzed into the room shortly after Windflower had shut down.

"You must smell food from a distance, do you?" asked Windflower while Tizzard helped himself to a couple of crackers and loaded them with cheese.

"My dad would say that I have impeccable timing when it comes to food," said Tizzard.

"Speaking of food, you're invited to breakfast with the forensics crew tomorrow morning."

"Too bad, but I can't. Carrie is coming over tonight. I won't see her 'til I get off in the morning."

"I understand. Young love. Moving on, did you have any luck with the canvass of the neighbourhood?"

"That's what I came back to tell you. We found someone who said they heard a woman scream, and when they looked out of their house, they saw a black or dark-coloured pickup speed away. Smithson is talking to the witness now."

"I guess no licence plate or ID?"

"Nope. Should we re-open the road? It looks like forensics is done."

"Yes, tell Smithson, and I'll get Betsy to let highways know. Are you going home to get a break?"

"On my way now," said Tizzard. "Just wanted to give you the info—and get a little snack."

Windflower plugged away at the office for another couple of hours but realized that the cheese and Purity crackers were not nearly enough. He phoned Sheila to make inquiries about supper.

"I've got good news and bad news. The good news is that I found the last of Beulah's salmon pies in the freezer," said Sheila, referring to her friend who helped out at the B & B. "I'll make a little salad and put on some peas and carrots."

"That is good news," said Windflower. "So what's the bad news?"

"Our roofing contractor came by. There's more damage than he first thought. About three-quarters of the slate tiles are gone or going, and there's some rot and mould underneath them. He is suggesting a full replacement. That way they could replace all of the wood and put a tin roof on for 20 to 25 thousand."

Windflower whistled softly. He stayed silent.

"I told you it was bad news," said Sheila. "But I guess we knew there might be more trouble than we could see."

"Or than we could afford," sighed Windflower. "Oh well, let's talk about it tonight."

"Okay. Come when you can. Levi Parsons came by and walked the dog. That's one less thing for you to do."

"It's great that we have Levi around. I hope he'll stay in town again this summer to help us with the B & B. I'll be home in a little while."

"Okay, bye."

Windflower thought about the B & B. That was certainly not good news about the roof. Was this really the future he wanted or just a money pit to sink him and his financial future? He tried to be optimistic, but it was difficult rising above this latest setback. He was about to pack it in for the day when he remembered that he had to write a report to Raymond. Or I could face his wrath in the morning, he thought as he weighed his options.

He stared at his computer for a few minutes and finally wrote everything he knew about the body found on the trail. He named the dead man and noted his record. He described finding the corpse and what Doctor Sanjay had reported so far. He noted that the coroner was waiting for the body to thaw, which was imminent, and for the tox reports. Then he told what he knew about the hit and run and quickly hit send. Just as quickly, he left his office and headed for home.

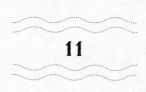

11

The usual family chaos awaited Windflower as he opened the door to his house, along with a surprise. Carrie Evanchuk, Tizzard's fiancée, was there with Amelia Louise in her arms.

"Carrie, what are you doing here?" asked Windflower.

"I thought you'd be glad to see her," said Sheila, coming to give him a hug and a peck on the cheek.

"I am," said Windflower. "How are things in Marystown?"

Evanchuk almost grimaced but quickly recovered and said with a smile, "They're good. Busy. Not as much fun as Grand Bank."

Windflower wanted to ask about Raymond but didn't want to disrupt the happy familial scene. Plus, he was hungry and could smell dinner in the oven.

"Are you staying for dinner?" he asked.

"Carrie has agreed to grace us with her presence," said Sheila. "But I have to give our little darling here a feeding first. She will eat a little solid food, but she's still looking for Momma."

"It must be about the bonding," said Evanchuk.

"Do you want to have kids?" asked Windflower, petting both Lady and Molly at the same time.

"I think Eddie and I would like a couple," she said. "Not right away, though."

"Why don't you help me set the table?" asked Windflower.

In the kitchen they were putting plates and cutlery on the table when Evanchuk spoke. "Can I talk to you about work for a minute?"

"Sure," said Windflower.

"I think I'm being bullied, and I'm having trouble figuring out how to deal with it," she said.

"If you feel you're being harassed, then you likely are. I know you and your work, and you are not a complainer."

"Ever since Acting Inspector Raymond took over, it has been very difficult. I took the position under Inspector Quigley, and we had a great relationship. Now I don't even think I'm doing a good job. I might have to leave."

Windflower raised his eyebrows. "I find Raymond difficult, too," he said. "But I don't have to work with him every day. It must be awful."

Evanchuk looked like she was going to cry. That's when Sheila came back with the baby, ready to put her in her high chair, but Amelia Louise called out for her dada.

"We'll talk later," said Windflower reassuringly, and he took his daughter in his arms and waltzed her around the kitchen.

"Talk about what?" asked Sheila.

"Just work stuff," said Windflower. "But you better feed us Mounties soon. We're starving."

Both Sheila and Evanchuk laughed at Windflower, and little Amelia Louise thought it was pretty funny, too.

Windflower put her back in her chair and Sheila gave her a small bowl of food. Both Lady and Molly perched below her in great expectation. They were rewarded for their vigilance. That kept everybody amused as Sheila dished up salmon pie and vegetables for the adults.

"This is sooooo good," said Windflower as he let the flavours of the pie enter all of his pores. He took one bite and pronounced it perfect.

"What is that flavouring?" asked Evanchuk. "And the crust is absolutely delicious."

"I think it's dill. I would give my right arm to be able to make pie crust like Beulah," said Sheila.

"Thank God for Beulah," said Windflower, already holding up his plate for more. "And you, too, Sheila," he quickly added.

Windflower was halfway through his second helping when they heard someone at the door.

"Unca, unca, unca," screamed Amelia Louise.

Tizzard came in the kitchen and immediately went to the little girl. She wrapped her arms around his neck and wouldn't let go even when he sat at the table. Tizzard didn't seem to mind. "I hope I'm not too late."

"You mean I have to give up my leftovers for this guy?" asked Windflower, feigning a little outrage.

"Here you go, Eddie," said Sheila. "You have to fatten him up, Carrie. He's still a growing boy."

Tizzard beamed as he was handed a plate with the last of the salmon pie. Evanchuk rolled her eyes. "Veggies?" asked Sheila.

Tizzard recoiled in mock horror. "Don't ruin a great meal," he said. He made fast work of the pie as Amelia Louise struggled to get down. Once finished, he carried the baby out to the living room where they and the two animals squealed and had a noisy good time.

Windflower and Evanchuk cleaned up, and Sheila sliced up the remainder of a pound cake and put strawberries and whipped cream on top. After dessert was done, Sheila and Evanchuk went upstairs to get Amelia Louise ready for bed.

"Did she talk to you?" asked Tizzard.

"Your suggestion?" asked Windflower. "I seem to always be in hot water with that guy. So I'm not sure I'm the right one to talk to about Raymond."

"You're the only one. If she doesn't sort this out, I think she'll quit the Force."

"I'll talk to her again after the baby's been put down. Still not convinced I can help."

"Do your best. That's what you taught me."

12

Amelia Louise reached first for her daddy and then for Uncle Eddie. Windflower let Tizzard read her a bedtime story, and when she started to close her eyes, he took her up to her room and laid her in her crib. He kissed her gently on the cheek and turned on the mobile above her head. By the time it had completed its rotations, she would be under.

Downstairs, Tizzard was saying his goodbyes.

"Somebody has to work around here," he grumbled.

"See you tonight," said Evanchuk.

"See you, Eddie," said Sheila and Windflower in unison.

"I guess I should be going, too," said Evanchuk. "Thanks for a wonderful dinner."

"You're welcome, Carrie," said Sheila, coming closer to give her a hug.

"Why don't you walk around the block with me," suggested Windflower. "Lady would like the company."

Sheila looked at him quizzically, but she seldom questioned his motives around his work or police colleagues. "See you soon," she told them. "I've got a date with a book and my slippers."

Lady was very excited to have not only her master but a special guest on the night's stroll around Grand Bank. It was both clear and still, rarities for the time of year. Dry, too, thought Windflower. His next thought was that it wouldn't last long.

Evanchuk and Windflower were silent as they walked along. Finally, he broke the ice. "I know it's tough, but you have to speak up for yourself. There are just too many guys in this outfit that will push you around if you don't. It's changing, but that's the culture we inherited."

"I'm not afraid," said Evanchuk.

"I know that," said Windflower. "You are a strong and confident woman and a good RCMP officer. Don't let him take that away from you. You will have my full support. I can phone Ron Quigley if you want."

"Thanks for your support, but let's leave Inspector Quigley out of it for now. I need to fix this myself."

"Okay, but you need to tell Raymond which behaviours are upsetting to you, and you need to ask him to stop. If he does, that would be great. If not, you'll have to file a complaint. That's how to deal with a bully."

"I know. It's just not easy."

Windflower nodded in agreement. "But 'you can't cross the sea merely by standing and staring at the water.'"

"That sounds like Eddie's dad."

"Tagore."

After walking a bit more, Windflower suggested they return to the house. He had been right about the weather. As they made the turn up the street to home, he felt the cold wind on his face and saw the eternal fog starting to shadow the streetlights. He said good-night to Evanchuk and watched the young constable walk slowly back to her cruiser with her head down. She seemed lost in her thoughts. Windflower told himself to add her to his prayers.

When Windflower and Lady went back inside, all the lights were turned out downstairs.

"Come up to bed," he heard Sheila say.

"I'll be right there," he said.

It was sometime in the middle of the night that Windflower thought he heard a noise. Then he realized he was dreaming again.

The noise seemed to be coming from downstairs, so in his dream Windflower felt himself walk downstairs towards the sound and a dim light. When he arrived, he was back in the clearing, but this time there was only the moose sitting around a much smaller fire.

"Where are the others?" asked Windflower.

"I'm the only one stubborn enough to stay," said the moose.

"Why is the fire so low?" asked Windflower, suddenly realizing that he was cold and shivering, even in his dream.

"That's your job," said the moose, and he started to walk away slowly. As the moose was disappearing into the forest, Windflower saw a small boy standing near the edge of the clearing. He stared directly at Windflower and then followed the moose.

Windflower stood watching, and there was suddenly a swoosh above his head. He ducked, reactively covering his head. A bird, a red-tailed hawk, had flown by, missing him by inches. He stayed as still as possible and tried to calm his breathing.

The hawk perched on a rock near the middle of the clearing, and Windflower cautiously approached.

"I can see the future," said the hawk.

"Tell me," said Windflower.

"I can only see the future on this side of the world," said the hawk. "But if you are not careful, that fire will go out. That is your spirit fire. It nourishes all parts of you."

"What do I do?"

"Ask for help."

Windflower returned to a deep, calm sleep, and it was nearly light out when he stirred. He heard Amelia Louise gurgling on the monitor and felt Sheila rise and go to her. He stayed for a few moments longer, recalling the vivid dream.

Sheila was feeding the baby, so he went downstairs, said hello to Molly and Lady and put on a pot of coffee. He and Lady had a brisk walk around the block, trying to avoid the gathering pools of water from the steady rain. At least, he was. Lady seemed quite content to not just step, but almost dive, into the really big puddles.

Seeing that Lady was wet already when they returned home, Windflower let both her and Molly out in the back with him while he did his morning routine. After he smudged, he said his prayers, noting Carrie Evanchuk for special attention. He also prayed for courage and patience, the courage he needed so he could say or do what was needed, and the patience to keep his mouth shut when things didn't go his way.

13

Windflower brought two cups of coffee upstairs with him and took a wiggling Amelia Louise out of Sheila's arms. He laid the baby on the floor and watched as she crawled away from him and then stood and ran back, teetering all the way, but having so much fun that both parents had tears of laughter running down their faces.

"She is so much fun right now," said Windflower.

"And so much more work," said Sheila. "She is on full speed all the time when she's awake. Luckily, she still takes naps. Otherwise I'd never get anything done."

"It must be hard," said Windflower. "I'd love a few days of napping myself."

"Why don't you do that, then?" asked Sheila.

Windflower shrugged. "Not easy," he said, "especially with Raymond running shotgun on me."

"He's not very nice, is he?"

"No. But it's only temporary. I'm more worried about Evan-chuk."

"That's what you were talking about last night?"

"Yeah, I guess he's been pretty rough on her."

"You'll help her."

"I'll do my best," said Windflower as Amelia Louise climbed over him and started sticking her fingers in his eyes, his ears and anywhere else she could reach.

"What should we do about the roof at the B & B?"

"You know the roof problem feels a bit like my life," said Wind-flower. "It is wonderful and beautiful on the outside, but it's getting a little old and creaky and leaky on the inside. I love it. I just can't seem to manage it all."

"We can sell the B & B if you want."

Windflower shook his head. "We'd just lose all the money we've poured into it. Plus, I think it's part of our future, her future." He pointed to Amelia Louise.

"We can build any future we want. But it seems to me it's decision time when it comes to the B & B."

"I don't know. Let's take a couple of days to think about it. Now, I've got to go see the forensics guys. I love you, Sheila."

"I love you, too, Winston."

"Dada, dada," said Amelia Louise.

"Someone else loves you, too," said Sheila.

"I know. I'm blessed. Thank you, Sheila."

Windflower drove past the darkened B & B on the way to his breakfast with Corporal Brown and Tizzard at the motel where most government personnel were housed when they had business in Grand Bank. It was raining so hard that all he could see clearly was the outline of Grand Bank's grand old lady, the Thorndyke Inn. Despite the rain, it was a beautiful sight with its Queen Anne Revival style of architecture and three full storeys. Along the full length of the front of the house was a sun porch with large panes of glass. Magnificent was his first thought. Expensive to maintain was his second.

Be that as it may, his grumbling stomach wouldn't let him linger any longer, and he drove to the motel. Tizzard's vehicle was out in front alongside the forensics van. He parked and ran through the parking lot to the restaurant entrance.

"Morning," he said to Tizzard, Brown and the rest of Brown's crew, all sitting at two tables pushed together near the back wall. The waitress brought him coffee, and he ordered the breakfast special with eggs over medium, crisp bacon and whole wheat toast.

"Quiet night last night?" he asked Brown.

"Yeah, in bed by ten," said Brown. "Pretty hard to get in trouble around here. We didn't get much from the site search at the trail. But we did manage to get a few partial footprints."

"We'll have to check them against yours though," said Peters. All of the men including Windflower and Tizzard laughed.

"I sent you the report on the hit and run," said Brown as Wind-flower's breakfast arrived. "Nothing new. Did you find witnesses?"

"One man who said he saw a black or dark pickup drive away," said Tizzard. "I'll check with Smithson today to see if he found anybody else."

"That's tough, a dark pickup isn't much to go on," said Brown.

"We go with what we have," said Windflower, scooping up his eggs with his toast. "You guys heading back soon?"

"We're going to Clarenville," said Brown. "Domestic case. I'll spare you the details. But it's not good. That and kids in accidents are the hardest ones to do. We've put a debriefing process into every big case now."

"That's a good idea," said Windflower as he gathered up the last morsels of his food and put them into his mouth. "I remember having nightmares when I first started on highway patrol out west."

"Okay, we're off," announced Brown. "Breakfast is on us. You can buy us dinner the next time we end up here."

"You're on, and thank you," said Windflower.

"Yeah, thanks," added Tizzard.

Windflower and Tizzard got a refill on their coffee and stayed for a moment after Brown and company had left.

"Thanks for helping Carrie last night," said Tizzard. "She's going to talk to Raymond this morning. He's coming over for the media conference."

"We better make sure that everything is all set up then," said Windflower. "Let's go."

They didn't have to worry. Betsy had the room arranged and a draft of the media statement on Windflower's desk. He scanned it and made a few changes, including a note at the bottom asking the public to help by coming forward if they had witnessed the acci-dent on the road to Fortune or had seen a black or dark-coloured pickup driving away from the vicinity. Since there were two major incidents being investigated, he also asked for the public's help in reporting anything suspicious that they may have seen around the trail in the last few months.

"Somebody always sees something," said Tizzard as he read over Windflower's shoulder.

"That's my theory," said Windflower. "Aren't you going home?"

"I'm going to catch up with Carrie. She may want to talk about her meeting with Raymond."

Tizzard went to the back to get a coffee, while Windflower tried to move some of the paperwork in his basket along. But he didn't have much time as the media started arriving. He noticed they were setting up when Windflower caught sight of a very agitated Carrie Evanchuk rush by his office. He didn't have time to catch her before Acting Inspector Richard Raymond was standing in the doorway of his office.

"Ready to go?" he asked with half a smirk.

"I'm ready," said Windflower. He walked into the boardroom where the TV cameras turned on him and the press reporters snapped his picture. He took the handout from Betsy and walked to the podium. He was surprised when he felt Raymond's presence behind him and even more surprised when his superior officer came and stood beside him.

Betsy looked at him with an expression that said she wasn't just surprised but was a little horrified, too. This was not the way they did media conferences. Inspector Quigley often came to the media shows, but unless he was invited, he did not speak or participate. Windflower felt uncomfortable but managed to smile at Betsy and went straight to his media statement.

14

After reading the statement, Windflower asked the reporters if they had any questions. The first was from the beat reporter with the Southern Gazette who asked if the suspicious death on the trail was a murder. Windflower replied that the coroner was still investigating, and they would have more to say about the matter in the days ahead. He also said that at this point they were ruling nothing out and asked again for the public's help in reporting anything they might have seen or heard regarding the case.

The next question was if the public should be worried that there was a murderer on the loose in Grand Bank. It was from the NTV reporter who often tried to sensationalize cases in order to get a bit more profile for herself. Windflower started to respond, hoping to dampen her enthusiasm, when he felt Raymond nudge him aside.

"I am Inspector Richard Raymond from Marystown RCMP HQ. Let me deal with this question. I want to assure the public that we are monitoring the situation in Grand Bank very closely and that we will not hesitate to put additional resources into this community to ensure that everyone can be safe in their homes and on the roads."

Windflower stood there dumbfounded and watched as Raymond took over the media conference from that point on. That had never happened to him before, and he really didn't know how to handle it. Finally, he woke out of his daydream and stepped in front of Raymond.

"I want to thank Acting Inspector Raymond for coming this morning. If you have any further questions or requests, please contact the Grand Bank RCMP Detachment. Thank you and good day." With that, Windflower left the room and walked quickly past the still-stunned Betsy. He didn't realize it right away, but Raymond

stayed behind and schmoozed with the reporters. Windflower went
into his office and closed the door.

He tried to stay as still as possible and let the anger run through
his body. Uncle Frank had taught him this technique, and it had
saved him many times before. He imagined his anger to be fire
flowing through him like molten lava. He could let the fire move
from the top of his head all the way down his body and then flow
out through the soles of his feet. It worked best when the earth was
directly below him, but today the carpet and underlay on the office
floor would have to do.

He could feel his temperature start to subside when he heard a
knock on the door. "It's us," said Tizzard. "Me and Carrie, can we
come in?"

Windflower didn't want to see anybody, but he couldn't say no
to Tizzard. "Come in," he said.

"Betsy told us what happened. That was awful," said Tizzard.

"He is not a nice man," said Evanchuk. "I've decided to take a
leave of absence. I can get a doctor's note."

"That's probably a good idea," said Windflower.

"I'm going to run over to see Sheila and the baby before I head
back," said Evanchuk. "Thank you for your help."

Windflower nodded as Evanchuk left. He was about to go, too,
when Raymond appeared in his doorway again, this time looking
particularly pleased with himself. That was too much for Windflower. He thought about counting to 10 but didn't get past two.

"You can't treat people this way," he said.

"Excuse me?" said Raymond.

"Being nasty, bullying people, demeaning them. None of us
signed up for that." Windflower's voice was getting louder despite
his best efforts.

"I'm in charge," said Raymond. "What I say goes around here."
The acting inspector's face was now a bright red, and his voice was
getting loud, too. Betsy came in from the front to see what was
going on, and the last media guy, the reporter from the Southern
Gazette, stopped on his way out to see what was happening, too.

Windflower could feel the fire starting up again in him. "You
don't do any of the work, and you want all of the credit. The way
you treat Evanchuk is horrible. You should be ashamed of yourself."

"Evanchuk is nothing . . . ," started Raymond, and the next thing Windflower knew, the acting inspector was on the floor and somehow Tizzard was on top of him. Windflower managed to pull Tizzard off, and Tizzard and Raymond were screaming at each other.

"You're suspended," screamed Raymond, waggling a finger at Tizzard. "He assaulted me. In public. In front of you and all these witnesses."

"It was an accident," said Windflower.

"This was no accident," said Raymond. "You're suspended 'til further notice. And lucky you're not being charged with assault. And you, Windflower, zip it. I've heard enough from you today, unless you'd like to be suspended, too."

Windflower wasn't afraid of Raymond and he wasn't afraid to speak. But he had no idea what to say. So, he took Tizzard by the arm, and they walked out of the building. Whatever just happened wasn't good and hanging around could only make it worse.

"Go home," he said to Tizzard. "I'll call Sheila and get her to tell Carrie to go see you."

Tizzard didn't say a word but turned and walked to his vehicle. Windflower watched as Tizzard drove slowly away. Tizzard never drove slowly. He called Sheila and gave her an update. She said she would get Beulah to look after Amelia Louise so she could leave and be with Carrie and Eddie. That was good, thought Windflower. What was not good was the look on Raymond's face as he stormed out of the building.

"He assaulted me. You saw it, and so did other witnesses. One from the media. Your friend is done, Windflower. And if you're not careful, you'll be next. I want you to write Tizzard up and send me the report. He is suspended indefinitely until I make my recommendation."

Windflower listened but didn't respond. He still had no idea what to say. Raymond stared at him for a very long minute and then started to walk away. "I want that report, Windflower, or I will have your badge," he shouted.

Betsy came out as Raymond was driving away.

"What will happen to Corporal Tizzard?" she asked.

"I don't know, Betsy. I really don't know," said Windflower.

15

Windflower needed time to think, again. More than anything, he wanted to see Tizzard and Carrie, but Sheila had that front covered for now. And he knew he needed to sort out reality from his emotions, first. The best way to do that was to visit the ocean. Luckily, in Grand Bank, that was never more than moments away. He got in his Jeep and drove out to the L'Anse au Loup T.

The T was a narrow strip of land that jutted out from the shoreline just outside Grand Bank. It had been narrowed and shaped by the ocean for hundreds of years, and pieces of it were submerged at various times by the tide. This made it a bit of an ecological wonder where plants and sea birds of many varieties found a way to thrive. This would continue to be a magical place if the ATVs and their shotgun-toting riders didn't ruin it.

The L'Anse au Loup T had always been a magical and wonderful place for Windflower. When he first came to Grand Bank, he loved to stroll along the beach with Sheila, and now he loved to do the same with Lady, whenever she could persuade him to. He didn't need much persuasion. There was a constant sea breeze in the air, and he would often see a group of seals frolicking in the water or basking on the rocks. Sometimes he would pick a bouquet of fresh wildflowers and carry them home to Sheila. He always felt a little better after he had been to the T.

He hoped that magic would work again today, but he had a lot on his mind. All his problems had just been magnified by what had happened at the detachment. One way or another Tizzard would certainly be suspended, and it sounded like Evanchuk could be gone as well. Would both of them leave the RCMP permanently? That was an awful thought for Windflower. Plus, he was on pretty shaky ground, too, when it came to his own RCMP career.

What did Uncle Frank say? When you're in deep trouble, stop digging. It will only make things worse. He also said to pause and, in the quiet, ask for help because that would always work. Windflower hoped so as he took in a long breath and held it, then released it and started praying. But instead of praying for something specific, he simply gave thanks. He had learned that when you give thanks for what you have, you always receive more. So he ran through his many blessings. And at the end he laid down a little tobacco on the beach rocks for his friend Eddie Tizzard. He was the one who needed the most help.

Once he had finished his prayers, he felt calm, peaceful and clear-headed. He knew exactly what he had to do. But before he could act on that, he had to answer his cellphone.

"Sergeant, it's Danette White. I thought you'd want to know. Daphne Burry woke and she started screaming about somebody trying to kill her."

"Is she still awake?" asked Windflower.

"I had to sedate her again to calm her down, but she will likely be conscious in an hour or so."

"I'll be over soon," he said.

First, he had to see Eddie and Carrie. He drove over to Tizzard's little house which was on the other side of the brook in Grand Bank. It was near where Doctor Sanjay and his wife Repa lived. But Windflower didn't have time for a social visit today.

He saw Sheila's car out front, and Tizzard's Jeep and Evanchuk's cruiser were in the driveway. The three of them were sitting in the living room. None of them looked happy. When she saw Windflower at the door, Sheila rose and came to give him a hug. He needed that.

"I guess I really screwed up," said Tizzard as Windflower came into the house.

Windflower thought for a moment and then replied, "Yes, but I probably would've done the same thing."

"What happens next?" asked Evanchuk.

"I'm supposed to write a report for Raymond," said Windflower.

Tizzard hung his head, and Evanchuk simply stared straight ahead.

"But I've made a decision," said Windflower. "I'm going to write a full report, one that includes what I've observed and how I've been treated. And if you agree, Carrie, I want to talk about what you told me."

Carrie looked at Tizzard and he nodded. "Absolutely," she said.

"Great," said Sheila. "I'll make some tea, and let's get everybody fired." All the RCMP officers laughed, which was much welcomed after the tensions of the morning.

"You are suspended, though, Eddie," said Windflower. "But Carrie, I'm going to suggest you amend your request for leave to one for a transfer over here to Grand Bank. I'll call Ron Quigley before I complete my report so that he'll understand what's going on."

"That sounds great," said Evanchuk. "You'll need the help, since Eddie will be just lying around."

"I can do the cooking and cleaning," said Tizzard.

"More like eating and making a mess," said Evanchuk.

"You know Tizzard well," said Windflower as he went to the kitchen to see Sheila. "Are you sure you're okay with all of this? I really might get fired."

"If that happens, we'll live with it," said Sheila. "I have watched how miserable you've been in the last little while. So has everyone. Something has to change. 'Something terrific will come no matter how dark the present.'"

"Where did you get that?" asked Windflower. "It's perfect."

"Repa loaned me one of her Tagore books. Now help me bring in the tea tray."

Windflower shared a cup of tea and a ginger snap with Sheila and their friends and then took his leave. "I've got to go to the clinic," he said. "Our accident victim is waking up."

"Good luck," Tizzard shouted as Windflower drove off, waving goodbye.

He stopped in the clinic parking lot and phoned Ron Quigley. The call went to voice mail, so Windflower left a short message. "Hi, Ron. There's been a bit of trouble in Grand Bank. Tizzard's going to be suspended. Evanchuk is worried about her job in Marystown, and I'm even a little concerned for her personal safety. I want to have her here for now. Call me."

16

Windflower put his phone on mute, walked into the clinic and asked the nurse at reception to page Doctor White. He sat in the waiting room with an older couple who were waiting to see the doctor. They looked pleased when Doctor White came out of the emergency area and then crestfallen when she walked to Windflower and not to them.

"Sorry," said Windflower. "I'll only keep her a minute."

He and the doctor walked over to the reception desk to talk.

"She is starting to wake up now," said Doctor White. "But she is in so much discomfort that I'll have to sedate her again fairly quickly. I'm guessing you are going to try to speak with her."

"I need to know if she saw anything, maybe the driver of the vehicle. You said she was screaming about somebody trying to kill her. What did she say?"

"She was pretty agitated, not really making much sense. But I thought I heard her say that somebody was trying to kill her or out to get her."

"Can I see her now?"

"You can, but if she gets too upset, I will put her under. She needs to go to Burin, or maybe the Health Sciences in St. John's, but she's still too unstable. All I can do for her is pain management."

"Okay," said Windflower. "I'll go see her."

"Great," said the doctor. "I'll get the emergency nurse to go with you. If she needs me, she can call. I'm going to look after the couple over there." She spoke to the on-duty nurse who called her emergency colleague. A minute later the other nurse was leading Windflower in through the emergency section to the intensive care area.

Daphne Burry was the only person in the unit but seemed to have every machine and monitor hooked up to her. There were tubes everywhere and lots of noise. Windflower was always surprised by how noisy ICUs were given that the people in them were so sick. But maybe because they were so seriously sick, they didn't really care. Over all that noise, Windflower could still hear Daphne Burry moaning from across the hall.

"She will be dopey," said the nurse. "But this is almost as cogent as she will get. Once she completely wakes up, I'm to call the doctor."

"Thanks," said Windflower as he moved closer to the woman in the hospital bed. "Daphne, Daphne," he started saying slowly and then louder. Finally, the woman opened her eyes.

"Did someone try to hurt you?" asked Windflower.

The woman tried to glance around, looking terrified.

"Did you see who tried to run you down?" he asked, trying to get to the point as quickly as possible.

Daphne Burry looked at him, puzzled as to who he was. Maybe she couldn't even see him clearly, Windflower thought. "It's Sergeant Windflower, from the RCMP," he said.

The woman moaned. "Oh my God, give me something for this pain."

That was the nurse's cue to run out to emergency to get Doctor White.

Windflower was on the clock now. "Daphne. I can help you, protect you. Tell me who's trying to hurt you."

Burry's face was turning red with strain and the muscles in her neck were starting to bulge. She looked at Windflower again. "They want to kill me and Vince," she said. "He tried to run me over." Her voice trailed off and then she started to scream.

Doctor White rushed into the room and pressed the button that would release the morphine into her blood stream. "It'll be okay in a sec," she said.

"Who was it?" asked Windflower.

"It was . . . ," and then the pain medication kicked in, and Daphne Burry almost smiled in relief. Moments later she was comatose.

"Sorry," said Doctor White.

"That's okay," said Windflower. "I know enough now to see that it wasn't an accident and also that she might need protection. Do you have security?"

"We haven't had security since last year's budget cuts."

"I can't spare an officer, but I do have someone I can call. I'm going to post someone outside here until she's ready to be shipped out. She might still be in danger."

"No might about it," said Dr. White, pointing to the medical monitors and equipment. "She's already in serious danger."

"Yes, of course. But we still have to make sure that nobody hurts or threatens her while she's under our care and protection."

"Gotcha. I'll let them know to expect a security guard."

"Well, not exactly a security guard. I was going to ask Richard Tizzard if he would do it."

"I love Richard. It'll be great to have him around."

"Everybody loves Richard," said Windflower. "Thanks for your help."

Windflower checked his phone for messages when he got to his Jeep. There were two from Raymond that could wait and one from Betsy that sounded frantic. He called Betsy.

"Thank you for calling, Sergeant. I've got a man here who says he saw a truck driving fast out of town this morning. He's waiting to talk to you. And Acting Inspector Raymond is looking for you, but you probably knew that already."

"Thank you, Betsy. I'm on my way back over there. Can you call Richard Tizzard and ask him to come by to see me?"

When he arrived at the detachment, there was an older gentleman sitting on a chair next to Betsy. He was still wearing his hat and coat, as if to show anyone who might see him that he was only visiting, and not a guest of, the police station. He stood up when Windflower entered.

"Good afternoon. I'm Sergeant Winston Windflower."

"Yes, Sir. I'm George Follett. I lives down by the beach."

"Why don't you come into my office? Betsy told me you might have seen something that you wanted to tell us about. Betsy, would you mind getting us a cup of tea? Thank you."

Windflower guided the other man into his office and pulled up a chair next to him. He tried to put him at ease. "I think I know your house," he said. "Is it the one with the three dogs?"

"Yes b'y," said Follett. "They're always yapping at something. I sees you down around sometimes with that collie."

"Lady is always a bit surprised by the reception she gets," said Windflower as Betsy handed them both a cup of tea.

"Milk or sugar?" asked Betsy.

"No thanks," said Follett. "I likes me tea strong and black."

"Me too," said Windflower. "So tell me what you saw."

"Well b'y, I was out for a stroll and coming up near the high road when I seen this truck barrellin' down the road. He was going sum speed, I tells ya."

"What kind of vehicle was it?" asked Windflower, sipping his tea.

"It was a pickup. Blackish, but it might have been blue. A Ford. Newfoundland licence plates. I didn't think to check the numbers."

"No worries. Did you see who was driving the truck?"

"Not really b'y. He wuz goin' so fast dat I didn't get a close look. It looked like two of dem in the truck. One guy had a cap on. Might be a Leafs cap."

"Anything else you remember?"

"No b'y, dat's it. Is dat the guy who run over dat young girl?"

"Can't say for sure yet," said Windflower. "But you've been a big help. Thank you so much for coming by today, Mr. Follett."

"You're welcome," said Follett. "I'm happy to help find the person dat done dis."

Windflower shook his hand and led him back out to the front. He stood with Betsy as George Follett got into his car and drove off. His cellphone started to vibrate in his pocket. He checked the number.

17

"Hi, Ron. I'm glad you called," said Windflower as he walked back to his office.

"What the heck is going on over there?" asked Quigley.

Windflower gave Quigley a summary of what had happened, including the incident with Raymond and the information about Evanchuk. "I'm going to write a report, but I'm also going to lay a complaint myself," he said.

"This is going to be messy," said Quigley. "I'm not sure what I can do from here, but I'll call Superintendent Majesky in Halifax. He owes me a favour. I'll get him to allow Evanchuk to stay in Grand Bank until the investigation is complete."

"That would be great," said Windflower. "What about Tizzard?"

"I'm not sure anybody can help with that. Sounds pretty close to assaulting a superior officer. I've never seen a case where there wasn't a dismissal."

"That's what I figured. But I'm going to do everything I can so I'm not helping provide the bullets for his execution."

"Be careful, Winston. Raymond is a dangerous man, and he has his own connections. A guy like that knows where all the bodies are buried. I'll let you know what Majesky has to say. He's no friend of Raymond's. I know that for a fact."

"What's the deal with that?" wondered Windflower.

"I don't know," said Quigley, "except that it goes way back. Majesky would like to get rid of him but can't. He told me that."

"Interesting," said Windflower. "Okay, thanks Ron. Let me know what Majesky has to say."

He was about to walk out of his office when he was met by Richard Tizzard, Eddie's father, on his way in.

"Good afternoon, Richard," said Windflower. "You're looking

pretty spry."

"It's almost April, and as the Bard says, it puts 'a spirit of youth in everything,'" said Richard Tizzard. "Besides, being seventy isn't the end of the world. I heard somebody say that it's the new fifty."

"That's a good attitude," said Windflower. "I guess you heard about Eddie."

"Yes, but you're going to help him."

"I'm not sure how much I can help this time."

"Do your best. That will be enough."

"Thank you for your confidence. I'll do what I can. But I didn't ask you over to talk about Eddie. I have a small job for you, if you're interested."

"Interested?" said the older man. "My life's as tedious as a twice-told tale."

"I'm glad you're interested," said Windflower. "But the job isn't that exciting. I need someone to be security and watch over a patient at the clinic."

"The girl from the accident?" asked Richard Tizzard. "It's Grand Bank," he added, when Windflower gave him a quizzical look.

"Yes, it's Daphne Burry," said Windflower. "Tell them that Doctor White has okayed it, and just set up shop somewhere over there where you can see everybody who comes and goes. Keep a record of all visitors and call me right away if you see anything suspicious. Don't intervene yourself."

"Am I like undercover? Is she really in danger? Is it the boyfriend?"

"Slow down," said Windflower, trying not to chuckle at Richard Tizzard's enthusiasm. "Her boyfriend, Vince Murray, is in jail in Marystown. But she thinks she might be in danger. The job shouldn't be for long. She's likely getting transferred to Burin soon. We just don't want anything happening to her here in Grand Bank. You are my eyes and ears at the clinic. Can you do it?"

"Absolutely. You can count on me. I'm going to go home and pack a lunch, and then I'll be on duty."

"Thank you, Richard," said Windflower. "If anything happens, and I'm pretty sure nothing will, don't get involved. Okay?"

"Okay," said the older man.

Windflower wasn't so sure that everything would be okay at the clinic, but he had to trust that Richard Tizzard would follow his lead. He didn't have a lot of choices. The other thing he had little choice in was writing up his report. He closed his office door, and over the intercom asked Betsy not to disturb him. Then he started to write.

It was slow and tedious, and several times he circled back until he was comfortable that he had told the truth in a way that protected Evanchuk and was the least damaging to Tizzard as possible. As for his own part in this continuing story, he tried to be as honest and factual as possible, noting times and events. He also tried to express his feelings. That part was really hard. Finally, he was ready to send his report, but first he would run it by Ron Quigley. He sent it off by e-mail and sat at his desk for just a quiet moment of reflection.

Next, he did the second hardest thing he had to that day. He phoned Raymond.

"Where's my report, Windflower?" asked Raymond when he answered the call.

"It will be on your desk in the morning."

"Have you got Tizzard's badge and gun?" barked the acting inspector.

"I've informed Corporal Tizzard that he is suspended, and I will follow the procedures," said Windflower. "I am also request-ing that Constable Evanchuk remain in Grand Bank for the time being."

"No . . . send . . . get her back here at once."

"I can't do that. The regulations state that in the event of a complaint, the complainant can request a separation from the person she is filing a complaint against."

"I am ordering you to send Evanchuk back to Marystown. Are you refusing my direct order?" asked Raymond, his voice rising a few more decibels.

Windflower remained calm. "I am simply following protocol. I suggest you consult with your superiors if you require confirmation of the procedures. I will send you the report overnight."

Raymond was still talking, yelling now, when Windflower hung up the phone. Well, that should set a whole lot more in motion, he thought. None of it was within his command.

18

Windflower was surprisingly relaxed when he left his office and turned out the lights. He wasn't completely happy, but at least relieved. The storm was coming, but he had done his best to prepare and was now willing to live with the outcome of his actions, whatever that would be.

Then he remembered he had one more difficult thing to do. He drove over to Tizzard's house again. The lights were all on, and Evanchuk and Tizzard were sitting in the living room.

While they had the TV on, Evanchuk and Tizzard weren't really watching it. At first, they were happy to see Windflower, but then he told them why he was there. Tizzard handed over his badge and went to his bedroom safe to get his service pistol. He gave it to Windflower without saying a word.

"I'm sorry, Eddie, but those are the rules," said Windflower.

"I know," said Tizzard. "But I guess it just hit me. I may not be a Mountie after this."

It was hard to know how to respond to that. Windflower said, "I spoke to Raymond and told him I was sending my report. I also told him that Carrie would be staying here. I tried to smooth the waters with Ron Quigley, so I think we'll be okay on that front."

"What happens next?" asked Evanchuk.

"I guess there will be an investigation, maybe more than one. If I can get some help, we may be able to ask the powers that be to make it broad in scope, looking at Raymond's behaviour overall. But that may not happen," said Windflower. "As we stand today, Eddie is suspended until further notice, and you are on the rotation in Grand Bank. Talk to Jones, and she'll help slot you into the schedule."

"Okay," said Evanchuk.

"I gave your dad a little gig," said Windflower to Tizzard.

Tizzard's eyes gleamed for the first time that day. "He's pretty pumped," Tizzard said. "Told us he was on a secret mission for the RCMP."

Windflower smiled. "I'll see you guys tomorrow. Call me if you need anything."

They were standing in the doorway and waved to Windflower as he drove away.

Sheila, Amelia Louise and Lady were coming up the driveway when he got home. She let Lady off her leash, and the dog ran a few happy circles around him. Windflower reached into the pram and scooped up a squealing baby into his arms. Once everyone was inside, Molly, not to be left out of the fun, nestled up to his legs.

"I thought we could barbeque," said Sheila. "I have a couple of those hot sausages that you like, and I can take a bag of shrimp out of the freezer and thaw them."

"Perfect," said Windflower as he took off the baby's coat and extracted himself from the clutch of his animals. "Let me get changed and I'll fire up the grill."

Sheila put a pot of rice on to boil and gave Amelia Louise a snack to keep her going. Windflower and the pets went out to the back to start the barbeque. When he got back in the house, he noticed Sheila had thawed the shrimp, and they were lying on a board on the counter, next to two fat Italian sausages.

Windflower made a quick marinade for the shrimp with a little olive oil, lemon juice, garlic and cayenne pepper. He didn't have time for anything more elaborate. He placed the shrimp in the bowl and covered it with plastic wrap. Then he took the sausages out to the back and put them on the grill, slicing them about every inch to let some of the fat and juices drain off. He closed the grill to help them along and went back inside.

He took the shrimp one by one and threaded them onto metal skewers. "They're nice and large," he said to Sheila. "Perfect for the barbeque."

Amelia Louise appeared to agree and started saying, "Ba, ba, ba."

"I think she wants barbeque too," said Sheila.

Windflower left the shrimp on the counter and went to check on his sausages. They were cooking nicely as he turned them over and cut them a touch on the other side. They were doing well. "Ready for the shrimps," he said to Lady who was standing sentry at his feet, although if he had asked her, she would have preferred to be wrapping her jaws around one of those delicious-smelling sausages.

He grabbed the plate with the shrimp and went outside. He moved the sausages to the side and left them on a low heat. He turned the grill up to blast and put the shrimp on. They sizzled and steamed for a minute, and then he turned the skewers. A couple of flips and a few more minutes passed, and the shrimps looked ready to go. He loaded up the sausages and skewers and headed back in.

Sheila had made a salad and put a portion on their plates. She scooped up rice, and Windflower laid a sausage and a pile of shrimp on top. He poured a touch of the remaining marinade over them for flavour and sat at the table. "One more thing," he said and went to the fridge. He pulled out a bottle of Thai hot sauce and poured some into a bowl for each of them.

Sheila had given Amelia Louise a little rice with mixed vegetables. Clearly, it was for entertainment purposes since she played with her food much more than she put any near her mouth. But it bought the parents a few minutes of peace to eat their dinner.

Windflower started with a few small slices of sausage first. "Ooh, that's spicy," he said. "Got a bit of an after bite, too."

Sheila cut a shrimp in half, dipped it into the sauce and popped it in her mouth. "Wow, these shrimp are to die for," she said.

"Umm," was all Windflower said and all Sheila heard from him for the next few minutes.

After dinner Sheila cleared up and Windflower took Amelia Louise, Lady and Molly to the living room for playtime. Preparing their tea tray, Sheila heard shrieks of joy and Windflower laughing out loud. She brought the tray out from the kitchen and sat on the couch to watch the fun.

19

The rest of the evening passed quietly until Windflower took Lady out for her evening walk and Sheila gave the baby her bath. He and Lady were enjoying the amazingly dry and mild air on their walk when the sirens sounded. Fire sirens, thought Windflower. They weren't as shrill as ambulance or police sirens. He waited to see if the pitch would increase or decrease. If it increased, that meant the fire truck would be moving towards him. And that's exactly what it was doing. It meant that the fire was somewhere between the brook where the volunteer fire station was located and his house. He thought he smelled smoke, but lots of people still had a fire on these spring evenings.

He ran back with Lady and shouted to Sheila that he had to go out. As he got to his vehicle, his phone was beeping, and when he checked, he saw that Jones was on her way to Coronation Street near the highway. He turned on his lights and raced over. He was hoping it was a false alarm, but those hopes were dashed when he saw the flames coming out of the small bungalow near the end of the road.

Jones had blocked off traffic and was moving people back to what she felt was a safe distance. The fire crew was busy pumping water onto the burning house with one hose and with another was dampening the two houses on either side. Fortunately, they were unoccupied. They were up for sale, a common sight in Grand Bank. The town wasn't dying like so many other communities in the province, but it wasn't growing either. There just wasn't enough to keep young people or young families for the long term, and hence, there were unoccupied houses for sale on nearly every street.

Fire Chief Martin Hodder saw Windflower and came over to see him. "This place is gone. We're trying to save the other two and keep this from spreading."

Windflower nodded and went to help Jones. The spectators moved back a few feet when they saw him coming. "Thank you, Sir," said Jones.

"Whose house is it?" asked Windflower.

"It's Vince Murray's mother's house," said Jones. "Apparently, she's in the Blue Crest Home, and he's been living here when he comes to visit."

"Okay," said Windflower. "Maybe another crime scene."

Smithson came around the corner and met Windflower and Jones. "We've got everybody out of the nearby houses," he said. "The Salvation Army is coming over soon with a school bus and some soup and sandwiches."

"Aren't you supposed to be off?" Windflower asked Smithson. The younger cop shrugged.

"Okay, let's see what the fire department can do."

The Grand Bank Volunteer Fire Department didn't get a lot of calls. Windflower saw somewhere that they averaged only about 15 calls a year. But the 25 members who served as volunteers were well trained and had recently proven their pluck fighting a fire on a fishing vessel in the harbour, preventing the spread of fuel until the Coast Guard arrived. Windflower walked over to where the fire chief was stationed.

"We're lucky," said Chief Hodder. "There's almost no wind, and there's rain in the forecast. First time this year we'll be happy to have rain."

"Anything we can do?" asked Windflower.

"Your guys have done a good job alerting the neighbourhood and keeping people back. That's good for now. We'll need you to secure the site once we're done, if everything goes okay."

"What do you think?" asked Windflower.

"Too early to say, but I'd guess vandalism or arson. I don't think the house was occupied, and empty houses don't often burst into flames."

"We'll check with the neighbours to see if anybody saw anything," said Windflower. As he turned and walked away, he thought he felt a drop of rain, then another. He looked back at

Chief Hodder who gave him a grin and a thumbs up.

"We need to check with the neighbours," Windflower said to Jones and Smithson. "Let's see if anybody saw anything."

"There was one lady in the crowd who says she saw someone jump into a black pickup and take off. Right after that she said she heard a bang and then saw the flames. She's the one who called 911," said Jones.

"Is she still here?" asked Windflower. Jones looked around and saw a thin woman in a red bandana near the front.

"There she is," said Jones, and she went to bring the woman back. "This is Sergeant Windflower. Sergeant, this is Mary Grandy. She's the lady who said she saw something."

"I did," said Mary Grandy. "I just lives across the street there. I was checking to see if the rain had started yet. That's when I saw someone come out of the house. He was running and jumped into the truck and took off. He was going some speed b'y."

"What kind of truck was it?" asked Windflower. "Did you recognize the person?"

"I don't know the names of the trucks b'y. It was a black pickup. And no, I don't think they're from around here. I never seen 'im before. All I really saw was that he had a baseball hat on. I couldn't really get a good look at 'im."

"Was there only one person?" asked Windflower.

"That's all I saw, b'y. It all happened so fast."

"Thank you, Ma'am," said Windflower. "We appreciate your help. If you think of anything else, please let us know."

Mary Grandy went back to the people standing nearby to tell her story of how she was helping the Mounties. But she was rather disappointed that the crowd had thinned because of the rain, which was now steady and hard. So she hurried home to phone all her friends and family and tell them about her adventure.

Windflower turned to his officers again. By now, Smithson and Jones had their yellow slickers on, ready for a long, damp night.

"Smithson, I still need you to check the neighbours once more," said Windflower. And Jones, you'll have to stay until the fire chief gives the all clear. I'm going home. But call if you need me," he said.

Both officers nodded and wished good night to their boss.

20

Everyone was in bed when Windflower got home, even the pets. He filled their bowls and went to the living room to try to unwind. He checked his phone, which he realized had been left on mute. He listened to the first nine messages and saved them for the next day. The tenth was from Ron Quigley.

"'When sorrows come, they come not single spies, but in battalions,'" said Quigley. "You've got your hands full."

"And a house fire tonight in Grand Bank," said Windflower. "Did you see my note?"

"I did," said Quigley. "I know you want to protect Tizzard, and I understand he's your friend. But you do know that this could blow up spectacularly on you?"

"I understand the risks. But either the brass wants to deal with harassment and bullying or I don't want to be part of the Force."

"Well, that's pretty clear. In that case, I think your report will succeed in getting people's attention. I've got a call into Majesky. Waiting to hear back."

"You probably heard from Raymond as well."

"Several times." Quigley let out a deep breath. "He was screaming about you taking Evanchuk away. I told him there was little I could do from Ottawa. I expect he's already on the blower to Halifax."

"Thanks Ron. I'll send my report tonight. I finally figured out how to get e-mail on my phone, thanks to Smithson, though I'm not so sure it's a great idea."

"'Let every man be master of his time,'" said Quigley. "Except when it comes to managing your inbox. Good luck and keep me posted."

"Good night, Ron."

Windflower opened the e-mail app on his phone and ignored the bulging inbox so he could go straight to his drafts. He thought once more about the report he was submitting and then tapped on 'send.' Surprisingly, he felt better almost right away. He went upstairs and had the most wonderful sleep without waking even once. In the morning he heard Amelia Louise playing in her crib. He snuck out of bed and had a few grand moments of father-daughter time before Sheila woke and Amelia Louise got her early breakfast.

Windflower checked his phone as he made a pot of coffee. There were updates from Jones that the fire crew had gone home and that the scene was marked off. She would go back in the morning to check with the fire chief. Smithson had also gone home and would be back in at noon. Evanchuk, who had completed the night watch, was in the office awaiting direction.

He brought a cup of coffee up to Sheila and sat on the bed next to her. Amelia Louise rolled towards him. He played with the baby as he told Sheila about the fire the night before.

"Fire terrifies me," said Sheila. "I can't imagine losing everything you own, just like that."

"Well, luckily no one was living there at the time," said Windflower. "I'm going to head off to work right after I take Lady for a spin around the block."

"Want some breakfast?" Sheila asked. "Or maybe stay home with me and Amelia Louise?"

"Both sound amazing, but I'll grab something at work. And I'll see you later, alligator," he said to the baby who gurgled back at him.

As promised, he took Lady for a walk, but it was brisk, partly because he didn't have much time but also because yesterday's rain had continued through to the morning. They walked down near the brook and then swung up around where the fire had happened. He stopped when they got close to see the blackened mess that was left behind. The rain had taken care of the fire, and the yellow police tape would probably keep gawkers away. But there was something about all the destruction that a fire could cause. And that was something that terrified him, too.

21

After dropping off a soggy Lady back at the house and calling out his goodbyes to Sheila, Windflower drove to the detachment. Carrie Evanchuk's cruiser was parked in front.

"Good morning," he said to Evanchuk, who was sitting in the lunchroom drinking a coffee and staring off into space.

"Oh, good morning, Sir," she said. "I was drifting off a bit there. I'm not really used to the night shift anymore, I guess."

"Maybe you might have a few things on your mind," suggested Windflower, pouring himself a cup of coffee. "Hmm, blueberry muffins." He took one out of the package.

"From Eddie," said Evanchuk. "He knows he's not supposed to be around here, but he said he had to come by to drop off his Jeep. He parked it out back."

"I know it's tough, but we just have to see how this all plays out. I sent in my report last night, so we'll see what reaction that gets."

"Yeah, I know. And I am okay. Plus, I get to spend my time in Grand Bank near Eddie and you."

"Go home and get some rest. You're going to be busy."

"There's some talk that the fire last night was arson."

"Maybe," said Windflower. "I haven't seen too many houses spontaneously combust lately. Plus, we do have a witness that says she saw someone over near there before the fire."

"I guess we should be grateful that there wasn't more damage and nobody got hurt. And that it was raining."

"Whoever thought we'd be grateful for rain around here? I wonder if it will ever stop."

Evanchuk finished her coffee and left for home. Windflower ate the last bite of muffin, filled his cup and went back to his office.

He turned on his computer, but then remembered he hadn't prayed yet this morning. He closed his eyes and offered his thanks for all of nature, even the rain, and for all the friends and allies that were on his path. He smiled when he thought of Sheila and little Amelia Louise and the four-legged members of his family, too. He made sure to offer his prayers as well for Eddie Tizzard and Carrie Evanchuk, that they be given guidance and strength on their journey.

But it was Richard Tizzard who came into his thoughts next. In fact, when he opened his eyes, the elder Tizzard was standing in front of him.

"I was hoping you'd be here," said Richard Tizzard. "She had a visitor last night. Two of them in fact."

"What do you mean?" asked Windflower.

"Last night about nine o'clock, there were two men in a pickup truck who came to the reception desk and asked to see Daphne Burry. I was sitting there and asked them if they were relatives. They looked at each other and just took off. I didn't get their licence plate, but they were driving a black Ford F-150. I'd say 2018 by the look of it."

"You saw them, though?"

"From across the room. One of them had a big bushy beard, and the other had a Leafs hat on. Young guys, in their twenties, average height, wearing jeans, and one of them had a leather jacket. The other was wearing one of those red lumberjack jackets. I didn't see them long 'cause they didn't hang around. If I had a badge, I could've arrested them or something. Anyway, the other reason I'm here is that they are transferring Daphne Burry to Burin this morning. Do you want me to go with the paramedics?"

Windflower, mouth wide open, stared at the older man. "Good job," was all he could think of to say. It seemed completely inadequate, though. And he thought about all the trouble they could've been in had the two visitors decided to challenge Richard Tizzard's flimsy authority. Then thinking about it a little more, he asked Richard another question. "Does Eddie still do his drawing?"

"Yes, I believe so," said Richard.

"I want you to go over to his house and describe the two men. Get Eddie to see if he can draw them. It doesn't have to be exact, but maybe we can match them up."

"Like CSI?"

"Yes," said Windflower with a smile. "That's it."

"But what about protecting the woman?"

"Your mission there is done, and you are discharged from your duty. I'll look after that part. You see if you can get us some pictures to work with."

"I'm on it. It will give Eddie something to do as well."

"Exactly," said Windflower. "I'm glad the RCMP has citizens like you to help out."

Richard Tizzard puffed out his chest and left to go see his son. Windflower was still smiling when Betsy came in his office.

"He's pretty happy," said Betsy. "And you look happy, too."

"Well Betsy, Abraham Lincoln once said that people are usually as happy as they make up their minds to be. I've decided to be happy. And Richard Tizzard was already happy," said Windflower.

"That's a good one. I was reading Dr. Seuss to my granddaughter the other day and decided to start looking up quotes by Dr. Seuss. I found this one: 'Don't cry because it's over; smile because it happened.'"

"That's a great quote."

"And then I found out Dr. Seuss never really said that, but I like it anyway."

"So do I," said Windflower. "Now, who's looking for me today?"

"You've got several messages from Acting Inspector Raymond, one from Doctor White at the clinic advising that the patient is being moved to the Burin hospital, and more from the media looking for some updates on the outstanding cases."

"Tell them we're still investigating. And I know about the clinic. That's part of the reason Richard Tizzard was here. Who's on this morning?"

"Constable Smithson is scheduled for this morning. Constable Jones is supposed to be off, and Constable Evanchuk is on the overnight again."

"Can you see if Jones can do a patient transfer to Burin? I'm going to ask our acting inspector if they can pick up the protection from there."

Betsy went off to complete her assignments. Windflower drew a deep breath and phoned Marystown.

22

Acting Inspector Richard Raymond kept Windflower waiting but finally picked up the call. "I want to let you know that they are transferring an accident victim to the Burin hospital today," said Windflower. "She needs security. There have been threats. We can handle the transfer, but then it's your jurisdiction."

Raymond snorted. "So now you need my help," he said.

Windflower thought about a very nasty retort but held back his anger. "No, just routine police business. I thought you would like to know."

"Yeah, yeah, cover your ass, I get it," said Raymond. "You are still under my authority, Sergeant, and I expect you to carry out my orders. I saw your report, if you want to call it that. You should know that I've submitted my own report. I guarantee you won't like what I have to say about your incompetence and insubordination."

"What are your orders for today?" asked Windflower as calmly as possible. "Although I would remind you that I have a possible murder, a serious hit and run and now a suspicious fire to deal with."

"I want Evanchuk shipped back to Marystown right now," said Raymond.

"Are you ordering me to override complaint procedures?" asked Windflower. "Sorry, I'll have to hear that from HQ."

Raymond was still yelling when Windflower hung up the phone.

"Chief Hodder on line one," Betsy said over the intercom.

"Good morning, Chief," said Windflower.

"Morning. Thought I'd give you a quick update," said Hodder. "I've had a look around this morning. It looks like the fire started in the kitchen but not from the stove. Judging by the burn marks,

I'd say that there was probably an accelerant used. That's usually a telltale sign of arson. But we'll need to do a chemical analysis to be sure."

"You can tell all that from one look around?" asked Windflower.

"I've been doing this for 12 years. Took a course a few years ago, too. Once you see the burn pattern and identify where the fire started, it's just a matter of finding the method that was used. And finding out who did it. But that's your job. I can have a report to you by next week, but I can tell you right now that I believe it was arson."

"Got it," said Windflower. "I guess the only other question I have is whether we should be worried about other vacant homes."

"I'm going to put out a note to the media later today, if it's okay," said the fire chief. "I want to ask people to watch out for suspicious activity around empty properties. That's our best defence."

"Sounds good. I'll set up our file on this one. We do have the report from the neighbour about the vehicle near the scene, and maybe someone saw something else. Thanks."

Betsy came in when she saw that Windflower was off the phone.

"We got a report of a black pickup at an old trailer in Grand Beach," she said. "It's on the back road and on the end. The guy said you can't miss it. It's the one with the wrecks in the front yard."

"Who called it in?" asked Windflower.

"Bill Wilson," said Betsy, checking her notes. "But he's gone to a meeting in St. John's."

"Was the pickup still there?"

"Didn't say."

"Okay, I'll take a run up and check it out. Can you call Smithson and get him to meet me there?"

Betsy went to make her call, and Windflower drove his Jeep out onto the highway and the 20 or so kilometres to the Grand Beach turnoff. He took the turn as directed and followed the road to the end. Bill Wilson was right. The place was easy to spot. There were three rusting hulks out in front with car parts strewn in front and trailing into the back as well by the looks of it. But there wasn't a pickup in sight.

Windflower parked just outside the property, careful not to

disturb the gravel driveway because it looked like it might have recent tire tracks. They were muddy and filled with water but maybe of some value. He pulled out his phone and called Smithson.

"Morning, Boss. I'm on my way," said Smithson.

"Bring an evidence package with you," said Windflower. "There's no vehicle. But we may be able to get prints. Have you got your camera?"

"In the back. I've also got a print kit and lots of baggies."

"Good. See you soon."

Windflower walked to the door of the trailer and peered inside through the grimy window. There was nobody home, but there had been people there not long ago, based on what he could see on the kitchen table. He put on his gloves and pushed the door open, bracing himself for anything that might be on the other side.

He glanced over the dirty dishes and takeout food containers and tried not to notice the stink of garbage and lingering smell of unwashed humans. There was dust, dirt and debris that evidently had been accumulating over a long period of neglect. He was moving around the trailer, carefully poking around in the bedrooms when he heard Smithson arrive.

"What's that smell?" asked Smithson.

"I guess you mean the chemical toilet without the chemicals," said Windflower, closing the door to the small bathroom. "Hold your nose and dust the place and see what you come up with. Make sure you get some from the table and take lots of pictures."

"Got it, although I think I'll try my new scented mask. Cuts odours in half, they say."

"Good luck. I'm going back."

"Strawberry," said Smithson as he sniffed at his mask.

Windflower chuckled. "Sounds delicious," he said.

He started back down the highway to Grand Bank when his cellphone rang. "Good morning, Doc. How ya gettin' on?"

"Best kind b'y," said Sanjay. "Thought you'd want to know. I've got a cause of death on Paul Sparkes."

"Death by shovel in the back of the head?" asked Windflower.

"No, although he was certainly beaten. But that's not what he died from," said the coroner. "Cause of death is insulin poisoning."

"Was he a diabetic?" asked Windflower.

"Nope," said Sanjay, "not according to my testing or the lab results or his medical history, which I got from the Correctional Service of Canada."

"Good work, Doc. How did you get into the CSC files?"

"Well, I have to admit that my friend in St. John's found the extra glucose and alerted me to it. I also have a friend in CSC who was helpful, and it's much easier to get medical info once somebody is dead."

"I heard about a nurse in Ontario who killed her patients by injecting them with insulin," said Windflower.

"It's more common than you think, especially in suicides," said Sanjay. "I'll write it up and send it over. Unless you think that Paul Sparkes beat himself up, injected the insulin and then rolled himself up in a carpet, I think you've got an official murder investigation."

"Thanks Doc. Oh yeah, are we still on for Friday night?"

"I am awaiting it tremendously, my friend. I miss the joy of your company. 'The singer alone does not make a song, there has to be someone who hears.'"

"I'm looking forward to it," said Windflower. "See you then."

On his way back to the office, the rain started to thin out. As Windflower got out of his car, he noticed a rainbow on the horizon. That's a sure sign of hope in any tradition, he thought.

23

When Windflower got back to his office, Richard and Eddie Tizzard were waiting for him.

"I know I'm not supposed to be here, but I'm helping my dad," said Eddie, as a way of explaining his presence.

"That's right," said Richard Tizzard. "He's my assistant."

Windflower laughed. "So why are you here?"

Eddie Tizzard pulled an envelope out of a briefcase at his feet and handed it to Windflower. "It may not be perfect, but it should help," he said.

Windflower looked at the two pencil drawings, one of a man with a beard and the other of a man with a Leafs hat.

"I think they're pretty close," said the older Tizzard. "Now, do I have to go through the books with the mug shots in them?"

Windflower laughed again. "We don't do that anymore. I'll get Betsy to scan these pictures into the system and see if any matches come up. I think I'll get her to ship them out to the media, too, along with a request for help in finding the pickup."

Both Tizzards looked pleased as they left the office, and Windflower watched the pair of them walk down the street. They're probably going for coffee at the Mug-Up, he thought, and at that his stomach grumbled. But his stomach would have to wait because Betsy was standing at the doorway with her pad in her hand.

"How did you know I wanted to see you?" he asked.

"I haven't heard from you all day," said Betsy. "I'm just being proactive."

"Good," said Windflower. He handed her the two pictures that Eddie Tizzard had done. "Scan them into the system and see if we get any matches. Can you also get them out to the media and tell them the men are wanted in connection with the hit and run?"

"Along with the Ford pickup," said Betsy.

"Correct. Is Smithson back yet?"

"Not yet, but Jones is coming from Burin. She dropped off the Burry woman, and she asked that you call her." Windflower reached for the telephone as Betsy took the sketches and left.

"Jones, what's up?" asked Windflower

"Hi Sarge. I escorted the ambulance and saw Daphne Burry admitted to the hospital. Lucas from Marystown was there waiting. He told me that Vince Murray is on the loose. He escaped. Someone cut a hole in the fence and he's gone."

"That's interesting. Did they get it on CCTV?"

"That's what I asked. But somehow the cameras in that area got cut off."

"That sounds professional and like a lot of effort to spring a low-level criminal."

"My thinking exactly," said Jones. "He's obviously a bigger fish than we first thought. Or maybe he knows somebody important."

"Thanks for the update," said Windflower.

Betsy popped her head in again. "Would you like a bowl of soup, Sergeant? I brought in some from last night. Pea soup and dumplings."

"You are a godsend," said Windflower. "Yes, I would love a bowl of soup."

Betsy smiled her best motherly smile and went to heat up his soup. She soon returned with a brimming bowl of thick pea soup with blobs of dumplings floating near the surface. Windflower sipped on the broth and pronounced it wonderful. He continued eating while Betsy walked away contentedly. He dipped his spoon into the soup and carved out a piece of soft and chewy dumpling. With his next spoonful he snagged some carrots and turnip and a large piece of salt meat.

When Betsy returned a few minutes later, he was slurping up the last few morsels. "That was absolutely wonderful," he said. "It hit the spot. Thank you."

"You're welcome. I can get you another bowl if you'd like."

"No thanks, Betsy, I'm great. Stuffed."

She took away his bowl and spoon, and he could hear her singing as she went down the hall.

Smithson wasn't singing, but he was pretty excited when he came into the office. "I got some great prints, especially in the kitchen area, and tons of pictures," he said. "I'm no expert in this, but I'd say there's at least four or maybe five different people's fingerprints in that trailer. By the size of the one of the prints, I'd say there was a woman in there at some point, maybe more than one. I'm going to load them into the national database and see if anyone pops up."

"Do we know who owns that property?" asked Windflower.

"According to one of the neighbours who came to see me when I came out of the trailer, it belongs to Cec Howse."

"Is that Cec Howse from Howse Construction? He's got a million-dollar company going. They're running that project to replace all the culverts on the highway. What's he doing with a rundown piece of property like that?"

"That's him," said Smithson. "The neighbour said that Howse hadn't been around for a while, not that he was aware of, anyway. So we have no idea about who was using the property or for what purpose. I did discover a few shreds of evidence." Smithson held up a couple of baggies.

Windflower took a closer look. There were some seeds and stalks and marijuana roaches, a little white powder residue that he guessed might be cocaine, and a small amount of purple material that looked like chewing gum. "What's that?" he asked. "Chewing gum?"

'I saw a report on TV a little while ago, and then I saw a circular from HQ about something called purple fentanyl," said Smithson. "This might be chewing gum, but I don't think whoever used it were Double Bubble guys. If it is purple fentanyl, it is a mixture of fentanyl and heroin and maybe even carfentanil. Killed a number of people in Ontario last year."

"Shoot," said Windflower. "I hope it's not around here. We've had enough problems with opioids. Give it to Doctor Sanjay and ask him to send it to the lab in St. John's. Good work."

"Thanks, Boss," said Smithson. "I'm going to get these prints in right away."

A rainbow and maybe purple fentanyl, thought Windflower. Mixed omens. One a sign of new beginnings and one of pure death. Lots to think about.

24

Windflower didn't spend a lot of time thinking about his cases or anything else that evening. He packed up and drove home, had a quiet evening with his family and had a great night's sleep. In the morning he snuck out even before Amelia Louise woke up and took a run across town with Lady. Once back, he made coffee and jumped in the shower. When he came out, Amelia Louise was on the bed with Sheila. He played with her and got her dressed while Sheila made them toast and scrambled eggs.

His belly and heart full and his mind clear, he started to drive to work. He stopped along the beach and said his prayers facing out into the ocean. The sun was now high above the endless horizon, and while the morning was bright and clear, he could see the mountains of fog hovering near the island of St. Pierre off in the distance. He watched as the new speedy ferry raced across the water from Fortune and thought that maybe it was time to take little Amelia Louise over for her first visit to the French territory just off the waters of Newfoundland.

His thoughts and prayers were interrupted by a honking horn behind him. It was Fire Chief Hodder. The other man beckoned him over.

"We ran our tests yesterday and sent off our samples. Once we got close enough, we could see where the accelerant had been spread around the kitchen floor, although I'm not sure what caused the explosion that people say they heard. It might be that they had some explosives of some kind, but that will come back in the lab results, too. In any case, there's nothing to shake my initial suspicion of arson. So I guess it's over to you to figure out who did it," said Hodder.

"We've already started looking for the person or persons seen leaving the scene," said Windflower. "But that's as far as we've gotten."

"Don't the Mounties always get their man?" asked the fire chief.

"That's the story," said Windflower with a laugh. "Enjoy your day."

Hodder drove away, and Windflower left the ocean to go to the detachment. He got to his office and started making a list for the day. That included checking in with Ron Quigley about the complaints, talking to Cec Howse about his property in Grand Beach and, if he had time, going over to the B & B to take a look around himself at the damage. He wasn't an expert by any means, but if they were going to invest a lot more money in the place, he wanted to investigate a little further. He was still making his list when Jones showed up at his door.

"Got a second?" she asked.

"What's up?" responded Windflower.

"I was scanning the police reports and found this one that was interesting," said Jones. "I guess our guys in Bay Roberts found some purple bubble gum with traces of narcotics near an overdose victim. There was a whole roll of it. The man recovered, but they think he may have got the gum with the dope in it in the mail."

"That's interesting. Smithson found a piece of purple gum at the trailer out in Grand Beach. He's going to get it tested. Make sure he sees that story. Thanks."

"Geez. I hope we don't have to deal with that here. I thought we had a handle on that file."

"Check with some of the locals," said Windflower. "See if you can find out if anybody has heard anything, or if anyone is selling it."

"I'll talk to Bobby Fox. He owes us one since we let him off on his breach. Plus, he's overdosed two or three times himself. I can't imagine he wants anybody else to go through that."

"Put the article up on the board, too. We definitely need to keep our eyes and ears open about this. And make sure everybody has their naloxone kits with them at all times."

"Will do," said Jones. "We just got a new supply of spray. I'll pass it along."

Windflower was starting to go back to work on his list of things to do when his cellphone rang. "Good morning, Ron. How are you?"

"Somebody's in a better mood," said Quigley.

"A good night's sleep," said Windflower. "'We are such stuff as dreams are made on, and our little life is rounded with a sleep.'"

"That's The Tempest, isn't it?" asked Quigley. "Might be appropriate for the mess you're in."

"I'm not ready to say 'all's well that ends well,' but I'm feeling okay about whatever comes out of this," said Windflower.

"I talked to Majesky. He did clear having Evanchuk stay in Grand Bank, but that's it. He said he had to stay impartial."

"What does that mean?"

"It means that he's been handed the investigation. The good news is that he doesn't like Raymond any more than the rest of us. The downside, especially for Tizzard, is that he's a stickler for regulations and authority."

"Well, I guess we live with that," said Windflower. And while he had Quigley on the phone, he thought he should pick his brain on another matter. "Ron, do you know anything about purple fentanyl?" he asked.

"That's one of the things our task force has been talking about," said Quigley. "Some people call it purple fentanyl and others call it purple heroin. Doesn't really matter what you call it. It's deadly."

"We found a small piece that might be purple fentanyl," said Windflower. "Going for testing today."

"This is a big problem," said Quigley, "because some bad guys are just mixing up stuff now. They take synthetic fentanyl, which they're getting dirt cheap from factories in China, and add it to their heroin. Sometimes they're even adding carfentanil to it, too. In some cases, the paramedics are having to use more than one naloxone kit to try to revive overdoses. It's a big problem in southwestern Ontario right now."

"And it looks like it might be here, too," said Windflower. "There's a story out of Bay Roberts that it may be coming in by mail. Anyway, we're checking on the ground around here to see if anyone knows anything."

"Smaller pieces might be getting in by mail. But we're seeing a large distribution chain in Ontario and Quebec. It's only a matter of time before it starts getting delivered everywhere. Anyway, keep me posted on what's happening down there, and good luck with Majesky."

"'Good luck is often with the man who doesn't include it in his plans,'" said Windflower.

"And 'fortune brings in some boats that are not steered,'" replied Quigley.

Windflower was trying to think of another quote as the phone went dead. Before it could ring again, he grabbed his jacket and hat. "I'm going out for a minute," he called to Betsy as he left the office and walked up to the B & B. The fog had decided to come in and stay, and the top of the beautiful old house looked like it had disappeared. He walked up the broad wooden steps and stood on the porch looking down toward the water through the gaps in the buildings on the waterfront.

This would have been the view of the old sea captain who had built the house over 100 years ago with lumber salvaged by him and his crew from a shipwreck. He might have wandered out in the morning to check the weather, thought Windflower, or to see what boats had arrived overnight. Today he wouldn't have seen much as the fog started to sink further down into Grand Bank.

Windflower opened the door and walked around the main floor. Everything was as they had left it when they shut the place before Christmas. The B & B portion of the business was only operational during peak tourist season, but he and Sheila had kept the kitchen open for dinner on weekends for the fall. If they decided to do the repairs, they could re-open for the peak months of June to September. If not, well that's what he had to figure out. He walked upstairs, and that's where he could see the damage from the leaky roof. There were water stains on many of the ceilings, and in two bedrooms, they had partially collapsed. He was still inspecting the damages when his cellphone rang. He almost ignored it but had to take a peek. He was glad he did.

"Hi, Sheila," he said. "What's up?"

"Hi, Winston. We got a call this morning. Someone wants to buy the B & B."

25

"What do you mean?" asked Windflower. "Who wants to buy the B & B?"

"This American, a guy from Fort Lauderdale. He sailed up the Atlantic last year and came around the coast. He stayed on his yacht but was here for dinner one night. He's retired and looking for a summer property for his family."

"Did you tell him about the roof?" asked Windflower, his heart sagging a little.

"I did. He said he wasn't that worried about it, said that even with replacing the roof and making other alterations, the price would be far better in this area than anywhere else. It might be the answer to our problems."

"It might be. Let's talk when I get home, okay?"

"You don't sound as enthusiastic as I thought you would be."

"I guess I'm realizing how much I like this place."

"We'll talk tonight," said Sheila.

Windflower took one more look around and then went downstairs and locked up. By the time he was walking back to work the fog had taken complete control. Cars passing by, very slowly, were like shadows, and every so often a figure would appear like a ghost walking on the other side of the street. But Windflower knew the way and was soon back at the detachment.

"A little foggy," said Betsy as he came into the building for the second time that morning. "I've got some news for you," she said, following him into his office.

"I've got some, too," said Smithson, who came shortly after. "We've got a match."

"You go first," said Windflower to Betsy.

Betsy beamed. "The results from the pictures that Eddie drew with his dad came back. They say that one of the two men is Everett McMaster. Look, you can compare the drawings to the pictures. Pretty close, eh?"

Windflower peered at the drawing and the printout that Betsy held up for him. "I'd say that's him, for sure."

"And the other guy is likely Marcel Perreault," said Smithson. "Both McMaster and Perreault were in that trailer. Here's Perreault, without the beard, that Tizzard drew." He held up the other picture and its corresponding printout.

"Wow, Tizzard did a pretty good job," said Windflower. "As did both of you," he added quickly.

"We're all part of the same team," said Betsy proudly.

"There's two more matches from the fingerprints I took in the trailer," said Smithson. "I was right. There was a woman in there. It was Daphne Burry."

"That's the lady in the accident, and the one who was here with that guy," said Betsy.

"Yes, with Vince Murray," said Windflower. "Did you find his fingerprints there, too?"

"No, Sir," said Smithson. "It's possible I missed it, but I don't think so. The other prints I found belonged to the dead man you came across up on the trail, Paul Sparkes."

"Isn't that interesting?" said Windflower. "Anything else?"

"Just that there was one series of prints that came back as unidentified," said Smithson. "Maybe they're just not in our system."

"Maybe. But our system captures everything now from every jurisdiction for the last 20 years. If we don't have them, they likely haven't been charged or convicted."

"Yet," piped in Betsy. "Because the Mounties always get their man."

"I keep hearing that," said Windflower. "Great job both of you. Betsy, can you send those pictures out to the media, tell them they're updates from yesterday's sketches and include a note again that we are looking for these two men in connection to the hit and run. If they're still around here, we should be able to find them."

Smithson and Betsy walked away happy, and Betsy was busy

preparing her note to the media while Windflower pondered his next move. The intercom from Betsy jarred him back to reality. "Superintendent Majesky on line two," she said.

"Good day, Superintendent," said Windflower.

"Sergeant," said Majesky. "I need to talk to you about your letter."

"Yes, Sir," said Windflower.

"I need to know if you want to make this a formal complaint or if you think we can resolve this through discussions."

"I'm willing to talk, but it's pretty serious. Evanchuk has some real difficulties with Acting Inspector Raymond's behaviour, as do I."

"Evanchuk will have to make her own decisions."

"What happens to Tizzard if I drop my formal complaint?"

"That's none of your business, Sergeant. I need your answer within 24 hours. You understand the consequences if it is found that your complaint is frivolous or unwarranted?"

"I understand, Sir."

"Off the record, Windflower, I like you and think you've been a good officer. But I am not able to protect anybody once a formal investigation begins. Let me know your answer."

Betsy came into Windflower's office again shortly after his call with Superintendent Majesky. "There's someone here to see you," she said.

"Send them in," he said.

"My name is Cec Howse," said a tall, lanky man wearing a bomber jacket that read Howse Construction. "I hear you were asking about my old trailer out in Grand Beach."

"Thank you for coming in," said Windflower. "Have a seat."

"I haven't used that trailer for years. Bought it at an auction and have rented it out over the years until it got rundown. I was kind of unsure what to do with it, really."

"Who was the last person you rented the place to?" asked Windflower.

"Like I said, that'd be a few years back. Jarge Hickman had it last, I think. He was a distant relative of the people that run Hickman Motors in Burin. He was using it to store car parts, but then he turned it into a bit of a junk pile. By the time I heard about it,

Jarge was gone, and I was stuck with the mess."

"Where did he go?"

"Where we're all goin' eventually," said Howse. "Now if there's nothin' else, I got lots of work on the go."

"No, that's okay for now. Thanks again for coming in," said Windflower.

Betsy came back in shortly afterwards. She had the look that Windflower had seen a hundred times before. She wanted to ask him about his recent guest but didn't know how to begin without appearing too intrusive. "Did you want something, Betsy?" asked Windflower.

Caught in her own web, Betsy tried to pivot away, but somehow knew she was trapped. She couldn't ask directly and finally in exasperation spoke. "Is there anything you need from me?"

"No, I think I'm good right now," said Windflower at first. But then seeing her distress, he decided to ask her what she knew about Cec Howse. That was right in her wheelhouse.

"Cec Howse grew up poor, like most of us," she said. "But he married Cecilia Foote, the merchant's daughter. The father liked him and brought him into the business. That went well for a while until the two of them had a falling out. Cec ended up not only leaving the business but Cecilia, too. He went out on his own and struggled until there was a change in government. After Joey, and once the Conservatives got in, he started to pick up some roadwork and hasn't stopped since."

"He looks like he's been pretty successful."

"Yes, in business," said Betsy. "But he doesn't look very happy. He's been married and divorced three times now. He's also known as a bit of a gambler and a womanizer."

"How do you know that?" asked Windflower.

"It's no secret that he has had a succession of women up in the house with him and on vacation in Florida every year. He's gone to Las Vegas or Atlantic City every other weekend. And they say he's become a hard man."

"What do you mean, Betsy?" asked Windflower. "He was pretty polite when he was in here."

"I don't like to gossip much," said Betsy, which Windflower

knew to be true, at least the much part. "But he let his son go off and nearly kill himself. Refused to help him. What were you talking to him about today, if you don't mind me asking?"

"We were asking him about the trailer he owns up in Grand Beach," said Windflower.

"That's where his son, Michael, was living," said Betsy, "until he moved away last year, up to Hamilton somewhere, I think."

26

Betsy had Windflower's full and undivided attention, though she wasn't sure why. She had learned over the years that she had the most valuable tool that a person in her line of work could have—information—and if she talked long enough about what she knew, it often helped the investigations.

"Can you check our records to see if we have anything on Michael Howse?" asked Windflower. "And see if you can find out where he might be living or a contact number for him."

"You can count on me," Betsy said proudly. Not only did she have helpful information, she was being given the authority to collect more.

"I'm sure I can," said Windflower as he watched her nearly dance away from his office.

Windflower reflected on the pieces Betsy had just added to the puzzle. Cec Howse had been mute about Michael and his living at the trailer, and there were probably no good reasons for the silence. Windflower knew he'd have to have another conversation with Cec Howse and soon. But first, he had to get to the Mug-Up, not that he was particularly hungry, but because a good chat with Herb Stoodley was long overdue, given the situation with Majesky, the B & B and everything else going on.

The lunchtime crowd at the Mug-Up had mostly cleared out when Windflower pushed on the door to the café. He spotted a table of familiar faces and went to say hello to Evanchuk and Eddie and Richard Tizzard.

"Pull up a chair," said Richard.

"How's everybody today?" Windflower asked.

Eddie Tizzard and Evanchuk just looked at each other. Richard Tizzard spoke. "They're pining and moaning about what might never be," he said, "instead of enjoying the day that God gave them. 'If you cry because the sun has gone out of your life, your tears will prevent you from seeing the stars.'"

"That's good," said Windflower. "I can tell you a couple of things. One is that Superintendent Majesky has been charged to look into my complaint. That's good news in my opinion."

"Majesky is a straight shooter," said Eddie.

"He asked me to consider having a discussion about the issues rather than an investigation," said Windflower.

"What did you tell him?" asked Evanchuk. "What happens to my complaint then?"

"Exactly my concerns," said Windflower. "Not to say anything about his issues," he said, pointing to Eddie. "But I haven't made any decision yet. What do you think?"

Eddie spoke first. "I know I screwed up, and I don't want anyone else to suffer because I made a big mistake. I think it would be better for you and Carrie, for your careers, if you cut me loose and tried to deal informally with this."

"I'm not doing this just for you," said Evanchuk. "This man is a bully, and he needs to be called on his behaviour. With all respect, Sergeant, I hope that you continue with your complaint. If you decide to drop it, that's fine, too. I have no problem filing my own complaint."

"Thank you both," said Windflower. "I have a few more hours to think about it. And I'm going to see Uncle Herb about a sandwich and a cup of coffee." He walked away from the table and went to the counter where Herb Stoodley was cashing out one of the regulars. "Be right with you, Sergeant," said Stoodley.

The rest from the table came up behind him as he was waiting. "Good luck with your decision, Sergeant," said Richard Tizzard. "Remember that 'something terrific will come no matter how dark the present.' You are a wise man, Windflower."

Windflower smiled. "I have learned that 'a fool thinks himself to be wise, but a wise man knows himself to be a fool.'"

Richard Tizzard laughed. "I'll pay for our table when you get a chance, Herb," Richard Tizzard said.

"Thanks, Sarge," said Eddie Tizzard, and he reached to shake Windflower's hand. Windflower shook Eddie's hand and was about to do the same with Evanchuk when he noticed she was on the verge of tears. He hugged her instead and whispered in her ear. "It's going to be okay."

Waiting at the counter for his lunch, Windflower watched the Tizzards and Evanchuk walk up the road. Herb Stoodley brought over a cup of coffee. "Go sit down at a table. I'll be over when your sandwich is ready."

Windflower was happy to have a few moments to sip on coffee and relax. True to his word, Herb Stoodley walked over with a sandwich. It was a speciality of the café, a turkey and dressing sandwich made with fresh turkey and stuffing mixed together and a healthy dollop of mayonnaise, all served on whole wheat bread that was so fresh it stuck to the top of your mouth.

Windflower had two sections of the sandwich gone almost before Stoodley had sat down. The other two quickly followed their cousins. "Excellent," said Windflower, wiping his mouth with a serviette.

"Glad you enjoyed it, albeit briefly," said Herb. "What's on your mind today?"

Windflower ran through the discussions he'd had with Sheila about the B & B. Then he told him about Tizzard, Evanchuk and Majesky. Stoodley listened attentively. When Windflower paused, he rose, took his plate and cup and went to the kitchen. He came back with a fresh cup of coffee for both of them. Coming right behind him was Marie with two plates, each with a substantial piece of chocolate peanut butter cheesecake.

"Thanks," said Windflower, taking a bite of his favourite dessert.

"Avoid making important decisions when hungry," said Stoodley, taking a bite himself.

"Shakespeare?" asked Windflower, as he neared the halfway point of his cheesecake.

"I used to think it was Betty Crocker. But it's a variation of a Robert Heinlein quote, you know the sci-fi guy."

"The thought is good, but the cheesecake is even better," said Windflower, forking the last morsel. "So what do you think I should do?"

"It feels like everything is converging, doesn't it?" asked Stoodley.

Windflower simply nodded. "Both for you and for young Eddie and his bride-to-be. But they can make up their own minds. You need to think about where you want to be in five or 10 years from now. It's not likely going to be with the Mounties, unless you're willing to move. And you'll need something when, and if, you leave the RCMP."

"It was always my plan to transition out of the Force. And when I visited the B & B today, it felt as much like home as I've ever felt. I know Sheila would like to stay in Grand Bank. All of that is clear, at least to me. I don't really want to sell it, even if we sink my life savings, meagre as they are, into it."

"Well, that's one place to start. Go home and talk it over with your bride."

"What about all this other mess?"

"Sleep on it. Sometimes the answer comes when we least expect it. And sometimes problems get solved without us having to lift a finger."

"I like that. I could be accused sometimes of making things too complicated. Maybe there is a simple answer to all of this."

"Exactly, my friend. Eat when you are hungry and sleep when you are tired. And things always look better in the morning. 'Let your life lightly dance on the edges of Time like dew on the tip of a leaf.'"

"Thank you, Herb, this has been really helpful."

"See you later, my friend."

27

The rest of the afternoon was a blur for Windflower. Betsy dropped in to say goodnight just after four, and an hour later he called Sheila to make inquiries about supper. She suggested takeout, so he dropped by the fish and chips place and picked up two specials for their supper. He got home and did a quick lap with Lady while Sheila set the table.

Despite his late lunch, he was still hungry for his fish and chips with dressing and gravy. Amelia Louise was eager to try it out as well. Windflower cut up a few french fries and a tiny piece of fish and put it on her high chair tray. She tried to stuff as much as possible into her mouth and then happily grunted back to her daddy.

"She eats like you," said Sheila, putting extra salt and malt vinegar all over her supper.

"That's not a bad thing, to be like her daddy," said Windflower, giving Amelia Louise another french fry and grabbing the malt vinegar for himself.

Sheila laughed and Amelia Louise started squealing, too. "She laughs like her mother," said Windflower. "But that's a good thing," he quickly added.

After dinner Windflower made tea while Sheila gave the baby her bath and put pajamas on her. He played with his little girl until she was tired and then took her upstairs. He sat in the rocking chair and read her a story until he could see her fighting to keep her eyes open. He put her gently into her crib and walked back downstairs.

"I don't want to sell," he said, almost as soon as he sat down.

"Me either," said Sheila. "But why are you so sure all of a sudden?"

"I went by today. And I realized how much I love that old place, how I can see us being together and growing old here in Grand Bank. Yes, it might cost some money, maybe a lot of money. But it just feels right."

"Okay," said Sheila. "I'll call the contractor tomorrow and tell him to get to work. There's a lot to do in a couple of months before we open again in June. I'm glad you got to this place, Winston. I would happily go anywhere with you. But I kinda like it here, and it's a great place for a child to grow up in."

"I agree," said Windflower. "You didn't turn out too bad, except for that stubborn streak."

Sheila feigned outrage and picked up a large pillow to hit him over the head when they heard a knock at the door. Windflower went to answer it. Standing on the step outside their back door were Eddie Tizzard and Carrie Evanchuk.

"Eddie, Carrie," said Windflower. "You don't have to knock."

"We didn't want to disturb you," said Evanchuk meekly.

"Can we come in?" asked Tizzard even more quietly.

"Come in, come in," said Windflower.

"Hi guys," said Sheila. "Want some tea. Dessert?"

"No thanks," said Tizzard. "We just needed to talk to the Sarge."

"I'll just go put this in the kitchen then," said Sheila, picking up the tea tray.

"No, stay," said Evanchuk. "You need to hear this, too."

"I'm quitting the Force," said Tizzard. "As a matter of fact, I already sent my resignation letter to Inspector Quigley. He is still my substantive supervisor."

"What?" exclaimed Windflower. "You can't quit."

"We talked it over," said Evanchuk. "It's been clear that both of us couldn't have a career together in the RCMP. Sooner or later one of us would get transferred and the other one would get left behind."

"This way I can go to law school and follow Carrie around," said Tizzard. "Once I finish my last two courses for my undergraduate degree, I can write the LSAT and apply to law school at the University of Ottawa. Carrie will go back to Ottawa and can probably stick around HQ for a few years. After that, I'll be a lawyer and can practice anywhere in Canada."

"It does sound like you've talked your way through this," said Sheila.

"But the Force is willing to support you through law school," said Windflower. "Are you sure you want to give up being a Mountie?"

"It's hard," said Tizzard. "But ever since I got shot a couple of years ago, I have thought about leaving. Now that we're planning to start our own family, I don't want to take the chance . . ."Tizzard's voice trailed off.

"I'm not leaving," said Evanchuk, a little defiantly. "I think that's what the brass, especially Raymond, would like. If they push me, I'll ask to go back to Ottawa right now. But I'm not backing down."

"Good for you," said Sheila. "I think some of them have got away with too much for too long. I'm glad you're fighting back."

"Okay," said Windflower. "I'm sorry to see you go. But I support you, Eddie, no matter what." He rose and gave Tizzard his second hug of the day.

"Thanks, Boss," said Tizzard. "I guess we should be going." Then he paused. Everyone waited for what he would say next. "I wonder if I could have one of those date squares before I go," he said. That broke everybody up. Sheila handed over the cookie tray, and Windflower went to make fresh tea. An hour later the young couple said goodnight, and Windflower and Sheila watched them drive away.

"They'll be okay," said Sheila.

"Absolutely," said Windflower. "But it won't be the same without having Eddie around."

"Well, he's not dead, and he won't be leaving until at least the fall," said Sheila. "Plus, we can always go visit them in Ottawa."

Windflower smiled at his wife. "You are the best, Sheila Hillier."

"That would be Mayor Sheila Hillier, at least for a few more months."

"Are you sure about leaving politics?"

"I've done my share, and Jacqueline Wilson is quite ready to take over. I want to spend more time with Amelia Louise and get the next phase of my life going."

"Have you decided what kind of business you are going to start?"

"No, but I'm narrowing down my choices. Stay tuned."

"Well, it better be enough to support me and Amelia Louise," said Windflower. "I might be out of the Force soon, too."

"We'll be all right."

"I'm not worried in the least. I have great faith in you."

"Somebody has great faith you're going to take her out," said Sheila as Lady circled them both. "But don't be long."

Windflower wasn't. Lady would have preferred that they stay out longer, but that was the case no matter what. When they got home, Windflower filled up her and Molly's water bowls before turning out the lights and heading upstairs. Later, he kissed Sheila goodnight and drifted off into the kind of relaxing and pleasant sleep that comes after a perfect day.

That was until he woke in his dream.

28

Windflower quickly recognized that he was in a continuation dream. At least it appeared to be in the same location as his last two dreams. There was no fire in this one, but the season had changed, and the snow that was there before was gone. The meadow was still brown and muddy, but there were definitely signs of new life emerging. Another thing that was new was that there was a small house, more like a cabin at the edge of the forest.

Windflower almost missed the cabin at first. It was the same colour as the dull earth, and part of it reached back into the trees. That's interesting, thought Windflower. I wonder what that means?

"It means that part of you lives in this world and part of you resides on the spirit side," said the hawk, startling Windflower from his perch above him. "But you knew that already. I guess you just forgot." With that, Windflower thought he heard the hawk laughing. Then he thought he heard other laughter.

The moose and the deer and the rabbit all came out from the woods and moved closer to him. Behind him was a young man who Windflower thought looked familiar.

"Yes, it's the same boy," said the moose. "He's growing up and is safer now that we have built him a house."

"You helped a little," said the hawk. "By asking for help you have become stronger, and all aspects of you are growing again."

Windflower thought that sounded pretty good.

"It's not that wonderful," said the rabbit. "You were too scared to do anything else. Trust me, I know."

"What do I do next?" asked Windflower, finally finding his voice.

"You have already been given that gift," said the young deer.

"It's in your wallet. Find your courage."

Windflower had many more questions, but he could feel the earth slide beneath his feet, and he fell backwards. He woke with a start but not disturbed as he sometimes did. Instead, he felt calm. He couldn't describe the feeling, but if he could, he would have said it was serene. He fell quickly back to sleep.

When he woke, he could hear Sheila playing with Amelia Louise in the next room. He lay there as Sheila sang and the baby kind of grunted along. Perfect harmony, he thought. With a little effort he pulled himself out of bed and got to the bathroom. After he had showered, he came back out to find Sheila dressing the baby on their bed.

"Good morning, sleepyhead," said Sheila.

He kissed her on the forehead and raised the freshly changed baby over his head. She squealed with joy, and he kept it up until Sheila pleaded with him to stop before they both got sick.

Downstairs Lady was impatiently waiting for him, so he let her out back while he made a fruit bowl and sliced a couple of croissants from a package on the counter. He made a cheese plate and put out an assortment of jams, including his favourite, a red-hot pepper spread. Then he put the coffee on, grabbed his smudge kit and went outside to see what his dog was up to.

Lady was happy to see him and interrupted her backyard exploration long enough to come visit. When she realized that they weren't going for their usual walk, she went back to sniffing the new growth in the backyard.

Windflower unfurled his bowl and put in a small portion of his medicines. Then he lit the mixture and watched as the smoke curled upwards in the foggy morning. He allowed the smoke to waft over him and guided it with a feather to purify his heart and mind and spirit. Then he sat and thought about the people he loved and gave thanks for their gifts. He prayed for their well-being and the strength to go through whatever challenges might face them. He made sure to also acknowledge his allies in the animal and dream worlds who, even if he couldn't always see them, he knew were helping him on his journey.

He was about to end his prayers when the thought came to him that he should also pray for those who he thought of as less than friendly, who might even wish to do him harm. Without being specific he thought about those people and offered a similar prayer for their happiness, peace and serenity.

That's when he remembered his dream. He pulled out his wallet and started to go through the contents: cash, credit cards, identification, pictures of Sheila and Amelia Louise and various receipts. Then he saw what he was looking for. It was a small printed card that Uncle Frank had given him. On one side was a picture of a waterfall and on the other was printed the Serenity Prayer.

Windflower read it out loud. "God, grant me the serenity to accept the things I cannot change, the courage to change the things I can, and the wisdom to know the difference." Uncle Frank had said when he gave it to him that acceptance was about other people, but that change and courage was about ourselves. He also said that the wisdom would come after he made enough mistakes on the first two.

Windflower put the card back in his wallet and went inside. Amelia Louise had already started breakfast and had jam smeared from cheek to cheek. Lady and Molly had started too, each with a piece of croissant that had made it from her tray to their waiting mouths below.

Sheila poured him a cup of coffee, and he spent a wonderful half hour eating his breakfast and watching the antics of his little family. He kissed Amelia Louise and Sheila goodbye and gave both pets a pat, making a special promise to Lady of a run later that day.

"I'm going over to Doc Sanjay's tonight," he said as he headed out the door. "But I'll be back after work to give you a break first."

"Thanks, Winston, have a great day," shouted Sheila as Amelia Louise called out her singsong, "Da, da, da." Even Molly started to purr and mew, and Lady was happy to join in with a few yips and yaps. He was laughing as he got into his Jeep.

He had a lot to think about, but his head was clear, and he felt good inside himself. He remembered something his grandfather had once said to him a long time ago, that it was always a good day to be brave. With that thought and a great breakfast fortifying him, he pulled up to the Grand Bank RCMP Detachment.

Inside Jones was getting ready to leave, and Evanchuk was just starting her shift. He waved good morning to them and went to his office to make his first call.

"Good morning, Superintendent," said Windflower when Majesky came on the line. "I've made my decision. I've decided to go ahead with my complaint, and I would like an investigation."

"Very well," said Majesky. "I will put those wheels in motion. I cleared my schedule just in case, so I think I can come over this weekend. Will you ensure that Constable Evanchuk and Corporal Tizzard are available?"

"Constable Evanchuk will be," said Windflower. "But I'm not sure about Corporal Tizzard."

"Just tell him to be available," said Majesky.

"I will ask him, Sir. But I think that he is resigning his position, if he hasn't done so already."

"What? He can't quit in the middle of this."

"I think he can, Sir, with all respect. But I will tell him that you would like to interview him."

"Okay," said Majesky. "I will be in Grand Bank tomorrow."

29

Soon after Majesky hung up, Betsy came in to say good morning to Windflower and give him some news. "We received another tip about the pickup," she said. "This time it was in Swift Current. Someone saw the news and said they saw the two men at the chip stand. I've alerted Whitbourne and Clarenville."

"Sounds like they may be on the move," said Windflower. "Good work, Betsy."

Betsy looked pretty pleased with herself. "I've also got some news on Michael Howse. He's in rehab in northern Ontario. Elliot Lake to be precise. Opioids," she reported matter-of-factly.

"How did you find that out?" asked Windflower.

"He has a cousin who was married to Margaret Smedley's sister," said Betsy. "Naomi told me."

"Who's Naomi?"

"That's my other cousin on my mother's side, twice removed. She's always got good information, especially about anybody who's gone away. It's kind of her specialty."

Windflower thought about asking Betsy what her specialty was on the information front, but his head was spinning. "Okay, great. Keep me posted on any updates," he said.

The rest of the morning went quickly. Windflower did a couple of media calls about the hit and run, and somewhere along the way thought about the other case that was on his docket: Paul Sparkes, who had been found wrapped in an old rug and left out on the trail. He thought about what he knew, which was a little, and what he didn't, which unfortunately was a lot.

He pulled the Paul Sparkes file out of the pile on his desk and started to go through it. Not much new, he thought, and then he saw under the family listings another section on known associates. He ran his finger down the list, noting some well-known local criminals. He came to one and stopped. It was Michael Howse. Interesting, he thought. Maybe Michael Howse's fingerprints were among those identified from the trailer at Grand Beach.

He called Betsy on the intercom. "Betsy, can you get me the Ontario Provincial Police in Elliot Lake or whichever place is closest to that rehab centre?"

A minute later, Betsy came back. "I've got the number for Ontario Provincial Police Elliot Lake," she said. "Who would you like to talk to?"

"Can you call the desk and ask for their CO?"

Another minute later Betsy was back. "Staff Sergeant Bertrand on line two, Sir," she said.

Windflower punched the blinking light. "Hi there. It's Sergeant Winston Windflower in Grand Bank, Newfoundland. How are you today?"

"I'm well," said Bertrand. "What can I do for you, Sergeant?"

Windflower explained his request to get fingerprints from a patient in the rehab centre in Elliot Lake. "It's in connection with a murder investigation," said Windflower.

"Is the patient a suspect?" asked Bertrand.

"We're not sure yet. He was an associate of the dead guy, and we think he may have been at the murder scene."

"We don't like going over there. Some of the people have serious issues with the police, and the folks that run the place want to keep it safe so that anyone can recover."

"I get that. I guess we could get one of our guys to come up from Sudbury."

"Nah, they're more afraid of you guys than us. Let me talk to the people over there, and if they give the okay, I'll do it myself," said Bertrand.

"Thanks," said Windflower. "His name is Michael Howse. Appreciate it."

He went back to going through his thin file on Paul Sparkes when his cellphone rang.

"Tizzard can't quit," said Ron Quigley.

"You're the second person that's told me that today, and you're the second to be wrong. As I understand it, he has already," said Windflower.

"How could you let him do it?" asked Quigley.

"He had his mind made up when he came to see me," said Windflower. "I think that Raymond was the final straw. He had been planning his exit before all of this came about. This was just the spark. He wants to build a life with Evanchuk and doesn't see how they can do it together inside."

"Well, that is true. I know of a few married couples in the Force, but they all struggled when they were younger. I guess we're not really family friendly. Have you made a decision about the complaint?"

"I'm going ahead. I talked to Majesky. He's coming over tomorrow for interviews."

"Good luck with that," said Quigley earnestly before the men exchanged goodbyes.

Windflower finally got up to stretch his legs and get a cup of coffee. As he was coming back, Betsy stopped him in the hall.

"Acting Inspector Raymond is on the phone for you," she said.

"Tell him I'm busy," said Windflower.

"He said it was about Daphne Burry."

"Okay," said Windflower. This was a call he had to take. He picked up the phone.

"Windflower."

"The woman is awake, and she wants to talk," said Raymond.

"That's good," replied Windflower. "See what she knows about who might be after her."

"She said she will only talk to you."

Raymond sounded particularly glum, and Windflower thought about gloating a little but managed to suck it back.

"I'll go see her," he said. He waited for something else, not a thank you but maybe an acknowledgement. All he heard was crickets. That was okay. If he could get something from Daphne Burry, that would be enough, he decided.

"I'm going over to Burin," he said to Betsy on the way out.

30

While Windflower wanted to talk to Daphne Burry, he also wanted to get out of the office. He enjoyed the drive to Burin. He liked the long stretches of empty lands that were aptly called barrens. On clear days, he could see across the barrens for what seemed like forever. Even when the fog was heavy, like today, and he couldn't see hardly more than a few feet on either side of the highway, a patch of fog would lift every so often, and the wondrous feeling of being alone with nature would overpower him and take him deep inside himself. There was no phone, no music, no people and no noise. It was perfect.

Forty-five minutes later he was feeling refreshed from his solitary drive, and he parked his Jeep and walked into the Burin Peninsula Health Care Centre. He got directions from reception to follow the signs for intensive care. He saw a Mountie sitting on a chair outside the area, playing with his phone. The man jumped when he saw Windflower.

"Sorry, Sir, I was just . . . ," stammered the other police officer.

"Don't worry," said Windflower, looking at his name tag which read A. Bruce. "Constable Bruce, I'm here to see Daphne Burry. Is she in here?"

"Yes, Sir," said Bruce. "She's the bed in the corner."

"Anybody been here to visit her?" asked Windflower.

"Not since I've been here, Sir."

"Good. I'll check back with you when I'm leaving."

He opened the door to the intensive care unit and looked around. He saw the other patient, an older man. Someone was sitting on a chair next to his bed. Windflower nodded to the sitting person and walked over to the corner where Daphne Burry lay, surrounded by

monitors and tubing as she had been in the Grand Bank Clinic. He
pulled up a chair and looked at the woman in the bed.

She was pretty beaten up. Her face was scraped and bruised,
and her head was still bandaged. One leg was in traction and one
arm in a sling. Despite all that, she looked peaceful, almost happy.
Surely the drugs, thought Windflower. But she also had a beauty
underneath all of the damage that had been done to her, mostly by
others but some of it probably self-inflicted from too many nights
in bars and hanging out with the wrong crowd. Windflower imagined what she must have been like before she started, willingly or
unwillingly, on her destructive path.

Daphne Burry's eyes opened as he was staring at her. She
looked frightened at first and then in her foggy state realized who
it was. "Water," she gasped through her cracked lips. Windflower
went outside and asked Bruce to get the nurse. The nurse came in
moments later with a cup of ice chips and scooped up a few in a
spoon for her.

Daphne Burry sucked greedily on the ice. She started to wake
up a little more. Windflower spooned up a bit more of the chips
after checking with the nurse.

"You wanted to see me," he said as the nurse walked away.

"They wanna kill me. They may have got Vince already," whispered the woman.

"Who are they and why do they want to hurt you?" asked
Windflower, omitting the news that Vince Murray was on the
loose from jail.

"I need protection."

"You have security right here, outside the door."

"Long-term protection. I'm not safe, even in here."

"It depends on what you have to say and how involved you
might be in any criminal activity," said Windflower. "Right now,
you're safe."

Daphne Burry started to struggle. It was as though she was
trying to get out of bed, but the protective restraints made sure she
couldn't. The more she struggled, the more pain she was in, and by
the time the nurse came back, she was moaning.

"I think that's enough for now," the nurse said to Windflower.

The nurse gave Daphne Burry a shot, and within a few seconds, her eyes grew cloudy again and she was out. "I gave her an extra one, and it should hold her for an hour, maybe two," the nurse told Windflower. "Did you want to talk to the doctor?" she asked.

"Not really," he said. "What's her prognosis?"

The nurse pulled down the chart. "She's going to be moved into St. John's as soon as they're ready for her. We don't do anything but minor surgeries here anymore. We have the equipment, but not the doctors. Right now, we're just trying to keep her stable."

Windflower left the ICU and went to talk to Bruce. "I'm going for lunch, but I'll be back in an hour or so."

The sun was starting to peer through the fog banks as he left the parking lot at the hospital. That was welcome. So, too, was the drive along the side of the ocean as the road meandered through the many different portions of what was now officially known as Burin. Many places that no longer existed as communities, like Fox Harbour and Salt Pond, or Great Burin and Stepaside in the middle of the bays, lived instead inside of people's hearts and memories.

You really did have to see some of this to believe it, thought Windflower as he pulled up near the wharf that was attached to the boardwalk. He had walked out onto this boardwalk many times, sometimes on sunny days only to nearly be lost in the fog on the way back. But today, he was having a very different experience. The ocean rose out of the fog as he stepped along the wooden walkway, and when he reached the end, he could see out across the blue horizon forever. He stood for a moment motionless and allowed the sea and salt water to wash over him, cleansing him as surely and completely as any medicine smudge.

When he came back to the shoreside, he walked the few steps up the hill to the small café next to the gift shop and museum and craft shop. Only the café was open; all the others were closed until the summer. When they were open, they featured some of the best quality knitted goods, embroidery, crocheted items, woodwork and local traditional artwork around. To his dismay the gallery across the street had been closed, permanently. He had bought a few pieces of art there, but as he peeked through the covered windows, he lamented that he would likely not do that again, unless someone bought the gallery and re-opened it.

Windflower walked back across the street and through the café door. It was warm, cozy and intimate, like someone's fancy dining room, he thought. Everything looked wonderful, and the aromas were exquisite. The room was half full, and even though he knew he wasn't supposed to, he took a quick glance at everyone's plate to see what looked good as he said hello, and then took a seat by the window.

That just made his lunch decision so much harder. He saw one table with pan-fried cod and scrunchions, another with beans and toutons, and still one more with a full turkey dinner. Sitting at a seat by the window, he thought of the old days when people had their big meal at lunchtime. Folks like Richard Tizzard remembered those days well and called that meal dinner. Then they had a smaller version of a meal in the evening that they called their tea. Windflower was ready for his dinner this lunchtime and settled on the pan-fried cod when the waitress came to take his order.

His dinner was wonderful with two pieces of fresh cod, likely caught in the waters nearby, fried to a golden brown and covered in scrunchions, flecks of fried salt pork. Two scoops of mashed potatoes and a portion of canned peas and carrots completed his plate. He sat in peace and comfort enjoying his meal and looking out the window until the returning fog took his view away. He refused the offer of freshly baked pie for dessert but bought one to take home to Sheila.

31

Sufficiently sufficed, as Uncle Frank would say, Windflower drove slowly back to the hospital. Bruce was at his post outside the ICU, looking a little more alert, maybe because he knew Windflower was coming back. The sentry nodded to Windflower as he made his way back inside. Daphne Burry was stirring when he sat in the chair beside her bed, and after a little while she started to wake again. He walked outside to get some more ice from the nurse, who told him he had 15 minutes before she had to do some tests.

He offered Daphne a couple of ice chips, which she greedily accepted. Once she was hydrated and awake, she started to speak.

"The guys were McMaster and Perreault. They kept calling themselves hit men, but they were just goons," said Burry. "They were good at beating people up and collecting money, but they were not in charge."

"Who was in charge?" asked Windflower.

"Am I getting a deal?" asked the woman.

Windflower shrugged. "Depends on what you have to say," he said. He'd been through this before, many times. Everybody in trouble wanted a deal. They watched too much TV. There were a handful of crooks that got immunity and witness protection, but they were certainly an exception and never the rule.

"Whatever," she said. "I'll tell you what I know, and you take it up the line. If you try and frame me with any of it, I'll deny it all."

Windflower shrugged again. She sighed and continued.

"McMaster and Perreault are the guys after me and Vince. Perreault tried to run me over. I was on my way back from Vince's mother's place to get some stuff I left behind when he saw me on the road. What's going on with Vince anyway?"

"He escaped from jail in Marystown."

"Really?" Burry's eyes brightened for the first time that day. "Me and Vince were a good team. We never did people any harm. We were in the insurance racket."

"You mean you stole cars," said Windflower.

"Yeah, but everybody's got insurance," said the woman. "We only did a few around here. Not too many Beemers or Mercs. Mostly in St. John's. Then we got recruited to go to Halifax. That's where the big operations were. There and Montreal."

"Who recruited you?"

"Sparky. He'd been working with the car guys for years. He'd boost 'em and drive 'em right into a container on the dock. It was sweet."

"You mean Paul Sparkes? And who was he working for?"

"Yeah, Sparkes. He was dealing with a Romanian crew. That's who hired McMaster and Perreault. But they were taken over by another group. I don't know who they are, but some of the guys in Halifax spoke Italian. Somebody said that they took over the whole car business in Europe." She looked over at the cup of ice chips by the side of her bed.

"Gimme some more ice," Burry said. Windflower gave her a few more small pieces. "What happened to Paul Sparkes?"

She tried to speak but started to choke on the ice. The nurse was coming in and saw her distress. "That's enough for today," said the nurse.

Windflower protested. "A few minutes more?" he pleaded.

The nurse was firm, and Windflower left as she was settling Burry down. He had many more questions, but they would have to wait. He went to his Jeep to start his drive back to Grand Bank. Before he left, he unmuted his phone and checked for missed calls and messages. Top of the list was Betsy. He didn't bother checking the message.

"Hi Betsy. What's up?"

"There's a man found dead in Clarenville," she said. "They think it's Vince Murray."

"Okay. I'm on my way back from Burin. Find out what you can," said Windflower. "Also, can you let Evanchuk and Tizzard know that Superintendent Majesky is coming tomorrow to interview them?"

Windflower didn't bother with the rest of his messages. There were none from Sheila, and he'd call anyone else back later. He drove up to the highway and turned towards Grand Bank.

It felt like another shoe had dropped. Somehow, Vince Murray's death didn't come as a surprise. And Daphne Burry told a good story, but Windflower was pretty sure she had left out any parts that didn't make her or her boyfriend, that is her late boyfriend, look good. But at least the loop led back to Paul Sparkes, the man whose death had started this whole thing. There was a lot more to ponder, and Windflower thought about spending the next half hour thinking about the investigations. But he decided against that.

Instead, he opened his glove compartment and found a CD that Herb Stoodley had given him a little while ago. It was Piano Concerto No. 2 by Rachmaninoff played by the Royal Scottish National Orchestra. At first, the solo piano wafted over him as he drove along in the fog. Next, the strings came crashing in to join the piano like the ocean's waves to the shore, followed by the familiar second movement that Windflower recognized had been adopted by Eric Carmen in All By Myself. Then came the finale roaring in like a train. It was majestic and wonderful, and for a few brief minutes Windflower forgot all about his problems and cases, the crimes and criminals. It was just Windflower and Rachmaninoff on an open road in Newfoundland.

As he came over a crest in the road, the music died, and Grand Bank came into view. Back to work, he thought. But even with all the stuff he had to deal with, especially Raymond, Windflower was grateful. He'd just had a fabulous lunch and a beautiful drive in the countryside. People cared about him, loved him and were waiting for him just over the next few hills. He was still smiling when he parked his car and walked into the detachment where Betsy was waiting for him.

"It is Vince Murray in Clarenville," she confirmed. "They found him in the parking lot of a hotel. It looks like he stole a car. Stabbed was the first report. I'm still waiting for confirmation on that part though."

Windflower knew that Betsy had got the information from one of her sources, colleagues she called them. He didn't ask questions about her sources anymore. He didn't need to. She was usually 100 percent right. He was grateful to get the almost instantaneous news from her informal network.

"Okay, let me know when you find out anything else." He checked his phone again when he got back into his office. There was one new message that he missed when he was listening to Rachmaninoff. It was from Bertrand in Elliot Lake.

"Good afternoon, Staff Sergeant. Have you got something for me?"

"I do," said Bertrand. "Michael Howse voluntarily decided to let us print him."

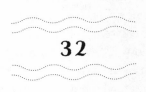

32

Windflower was a little excited by the news. Michael Howse's prints could well prove crucial to the investigation of Paul Sparkes' murder and maybe even the assault on Daphne Burry.

"How did you convince him to let you take the prints?" asked Windflower

"That was the only way the treatment centre would let us do it," said Bertrand. "But he knew we'd just catch up to him when he checked out, anyway. I'm faxing the prints over to you right now."

"Thanks very much," said Windflower. "By the way, when does Howse get out of rehab?"

"Graduation is today. He'll be in Elliot Lake until the bus comes tomorrow at noon."

"Thanks again for your help."

Windflower hung up and then walked out to see Betsy. She met him halfway.

"They look like they're a match," she said, holding up the two sets of prints.

"I know you're good, Betsy. But put both in the system and ask if they're a match."

Betsy went away, a little disappointed that her superior officer wouldn't take her word for it but determined to prove that she was right. That was okay with Windflower. He needed a few minutes to catch his breath. He called Sanjay to make sure they were still on for their Scotch-tasting date and then phoned Sheila.

"How are you today?" he asked when she answered the phone.

"We're all great. Run a little ragged, but it's been a good day. I hear you were over in Burin."

"How'd you know that?"

"My spies are legion," said Sheila. "And 'every man is surrounded by a neighborhood of voluntary spies . . .'"

"Betsy. And that's not Shakespeare."

"Even better. Jane Austen."

"Ah," said Windflower. "I've got a few things to clear up and then I'll be over for an hour if you need a break."

"That would be great. Maybe I'll go over to the Mug-Up for a snack. See you soon."

Windflower shuffled the papers on his desk for a few minutes and was getting ready to go when a triumphant Betsy marched into his office.

"There," she said, laying a printout of the e-mail from HQ on his desk. "The prints match."

"Thanks Betsy," said Windflower as nonchalantly as he could. "I knew you were right."

Betsy smiled from ear to ear.

"We'll need to talk to Michael Howse," said Windflower. "Can you get Smithson to set up that computer link-up we used before? I'll call Elliot Lake and get them to set it up on their end."

"You mean Skype?" asked Betsy.

"Yeah, that's what I mean. I'll try to arrange it for early tomorrow morning, before Majesky gets here," said Windflower. He called Bertrand back and asked him to bring Howse back to the OPP offices for nine in the morning.

On his way out, Betsy told him that Smithson, who would be doing the night shift, was ready to go for the next morning. He'd be at the detachment whenever Windflower would be ready for him.

"Tell him eight-thirty so we're sure everything is ready for nine o'clock. Now, I'm going home to see my beautiful girls."

"Good night, Sergeant. See you on Monday," said Betsy.

"Have a great weekend, Betsy."

Windflower drove home, and when he walked in, it looked like a mini-disaster zone. Toys, clothes, bits of food and fur were strewn all over. But in the midst of the mess, everyone—human and non-human—looked happy. And when they saw him, they got even happier. Sheila hugged him while Amelia Louise, Lady and Molly fought over possession of his ankles. He nearly tumbled over.

"Welcome to my life," said Sheila. "But I wouldn't have it any other way."

"Me either," said Windflower. He gave her a big hug and then sat on the floor to participate in ground-level activities.

Sheila grabbed her purse and snuck out before Amelia Louise could notice, even though the little girl was quite happy playing with her daddy and her two favourite animal friends. Windflower was pretty happy, too, and after their rolling-around-on-the-floor games, he gave her a piggyback ride all over the living room, accompanied by Lady barking and Molly trying to climb up for a ride, too.

After tiring everybody out, including himself, Windflower got a book from the bookshelf and sat with Amelia Louise on his lap and the two pets at his feet. He chose his favourite, The Velveteen Rabbit. He almost cried every time he read it. Amelia Louise loved it, too, and she shouted, "Rabba, rabba," whenever he pulled it off the shelf.

He was about to put the book away at the end of the story, but Amelia Louise pulled it back from him, so he decided to read it again. Why not, he thought?

He was ready to read it for the third time when Sheila returned from her brief time away. All eyes in the room turned immediately to her, and Amelia Louise was insistent on being held by her mamma who had been gone away so long.

"Thank you for tidying up and putting everything away," said Sheila.

"I don't know how you manage it all," said Windflower. "I'm very impressed."

"I hope so," she said. "I can manage a lot, but you'll have to take Lady out. I can't seem to get her out enough with everything else going on here."

"No worries. We'll do a quick spin before I head over to Sanjay's. C'mon girl."

The dog sprung to her feet and was at the door in a flash. Windflower put her leash on and led her out. They did a longish trip around the beach and back up past Sobeys before heading down towards the brook and home. Windflower said a quick goodbye to Sheila and turned back towards the brook. He crossed over the bridge and stared down into the harbour where a small fishing boat was coming in to dock.

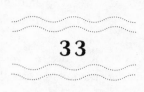

33

There were few real fishermen left in Grand Bank anymore. At one time, Grand Bank had been at the centre of one of the most profitable industries in the province, the Banks Fishery. Recently, the near collapse of the inshore cod fishery had pushed most of the fishermen out of the water. Today, most of the fishers, like those in the small boat Windflower was watching, were only engaged a few weekends of the year for what they called the food fishery, small catches for personal consumption that would be enough to feed their families if they were lucky. The chance to catch a few fish was a far cry from what was once thought to be an endless bounty from the sea.

Windflower walked to Doctor Sanjay's house and knocked on the back door. Sanjay had adopted the local custom of only using the front door as an emergency exit. Everybody from visitors to delivery people went to the back door. Sanjay's wife, Repa, opened the door.

"Welcome, welcome, Sergeant. So nice to see you. How are Sheila and that beautiful child of yours?"

"They are well, thank you," said Windflower.

Vijay Sanjay was close behind his wife to welcome his guest. "Winston, come in my friend. Our house is blessed by your company."

"I will get the food organized," said Repa, and she hurried to the kitchen.

Inside Sanjay's living room was a table with three bottles of Scotch, a tall glass jug of water and six tasting glasses. On another table was a chess board with two facing chairs. "I hope you don't mind. I have arranged the chess board in case you wished to play. I seldom have opportunities since my eldest son has left home."

"I would love to," said Windflower. "I'm hoping you might let me win a game, though."

Sanjay laughed. "To win or lose is not the point of chess. It's the kinship that we create in the playing. But first, let us sample this beautiful Oban."

The doctor poured them each an inch of the Scotch in their tasting glasses. Windflower had been through this process with the good doctor many times before. He had learned to take a look at the colour of the whisky first and then to smell or nose the Scotch. Next, he took a small sip, and then another. He watched as Sanjay did the same. Then he poured a splash of water into his glass to determine if the taste would hold up even when the Scotch was diluted.

"So, what do you think, my friend?" asked Sanjay.

"Wow, that is a smooth Scotch," said Windflower. "It tastes a bit salty and has a hint of smokiness."

"Ah yes," said Sanjay. "I agree. A beautiful whisky. It does taste a little like the sea, and I can sense some fruit as well. Orange, fig maybe."

Windflower finished his drink. "Yes, I can taste that, too."

Repa came into the room carrying a tray. She had a dish of freshly made veggie samosas with several dips; on another plate was a fish curry and a third had steamed rice. "Enjoy," she said, part invitation and part order.

Windflower was happy to oblige and took a samosa and dipped it in one of the sauces. It turned out to be a hot and sweet sauce with a bite at the end. At Sanjay's insistence, he then took a portion of rice and laid some of the fish curry on top.

"It is supposed to be a catfish curry," said Repa Sanjay. "But cod will have to do for today. I hope you like it."

Windflower took a forkful of the fish and tasted the red curries in the sauce. His mouth came alive, and it was all he could do not to scream. The doctor saw his distress and poured him a glass of water.

"Thank you," said Windflower.

"Is it too hot for you?" asked Repa.

"No, no, it just surprised me," said Windflower.

Vijay Sanjay laughed. "It is a surprise," he said. "Bengali food is not known for its spiciness, except for curried fish."

Repa Sanjay left the men, and Windflower helped himself to another samosa and more of the fish and rice. He and Sanjay talked about the weather and Grand Bank and what they were planning for the summer. When they had their fill of food, they moved to the side table and started playing chess. Sanjay was a near master of the game, and Windflower lost the first two games quite badly. But in the third he managed a draw and decided to end the contest on a near-winning note.

Sanjay feigned disappointment but was happy to go back to Scotch tasting. The next bottle was a Highland Park 12-year-old whisky that the doctor described as one of his favourites. The two men followed the same procedure as before. Windflower admired its amber colouring and remarked on its light peaty flavour.

"I like it because it is brilliantly subtle," said Sanjay. "A little citrus and malt and a very nice smoky finish with just a hint of heather. It is everything a Scotch whisky should be in my very humble opinion."

"I agree," said Windflower, draining the last drops from his glass.

"More chess?"

"I think I'll have to pass. We have a busy day tomorrow with Superintendent Majesky on his way."

"And we still have the Macallan."

"Until the next time, Vijay. Thank you so much for your kind hospitality."

"You are very welcome. 'The greatest gift of life is friendship, and I have received it.' And in abundance, I might add. Let me get Repa. She will want to say goodbye."

Vijay Sanjay came back a moment later with his wife who was carrying a foil-wrapped tray. "Just some small treats for your beautiful wife," she said. "Thank you for visiting."

"Thank you both again," said Windflower, taking the tray.

"Do you wish me to drive you home?" asked the doctor.

"No, I think I need the air tonight," said Windflower. "Good night."

The Sanjays stood in the doorway watching Windflower cross over the bridge. He turned and waved goodbye before he disappeared into the fog as he made his way back to his house.

Sheila was sitting in the living room, reading her book. Molly was wrapped around her ankles. The cat woke to survey Windflower but realized she was better off where she was and closed her eyes again. Lady, however, was quite a different story and galloped to greet him.

"How was your evening?" he asked Sheila.

"It was more of the same," she said. "Absolutely wonderful and totally exhausting. It's not even nine o'clock and I'm ready for bed. How was your time with the Sanjays?"

"Wonderful, as always. They spoiled me and sent me home with a doggy bag for you. I hope she put in some of the fish curry we had. It was so spicy!"

"Excellent. I assume you're taking the dog out. So I'll see you upstairs when you get back."

"I won't be long. Majesky is coming to interview us all in the morning. And I have to do one of those computer calls with a guy in Ontario," said Windflower.

"What guy?"

"Michael Howse."

"Cec's son? What's he done now?"

"You know him?" asked Windflower.

"More that I know of him. He was the pain-in-the-bum child of Cec and his last wife. He was always on the edge of trouble, but his dad would talk or buy Michael's way out of it. Stealing cars was his big thing and then dealing drugs. He would move away with his mother when things got too hot around here, but sooner or later he'd be back in Grand Bank. Last I heard of him, Michael Howse was living in an old trailer out in Grand Beach."

"That's what I hear. But his father didn't say anything about that when I talked to him."

"I don't think his dad wanted him around. It interfered with his lifestyle. He saw himself as a bit of a playboy."

"But Cec Howse has a successful business."

"Some of that is optics. His company has been losing money for years. They had a good run until the Liberals got back in, and then his contracts dried up. He's been bugging the town council for work for years. But we have a competitive process, and his price is always too high. Plus, the rumour is that he is a big-time gambler. But I don't know that for a fact."

"Interesting," said Windflower. "I'll need to have another chat with Cec Howse, and my list of things to talk to him about has just got a lot longer. But first I have a Lady that's demanding my attention."

Lady had got her leash and was swinging it against Windflower's leg. He reached down and put it on. "See you soon," he said.

Windflower and Lady wandered all over the quiet streets of Grand Bank as the fog hung eerily just above their heads. Every so often a car's headlights would appear in the darkness, and he would pull the dog closer to him and away from the road. There was no real danger since it would be difficult if nigh impossible to speed in the narrow, winding streets. But it wouldn't look good if a Mountie and his collie got run over while taking an evening stroll.

When they got back, Windflower looked after the pets and turned off the lights downstairs. The bedroom light was on, but Sheila was fast asleep with her book underneath her arm. Windflower extracted the book and turned out the light. Seconds later, he was gone, too.

34

The morning came early, too early for Windflower's liking. But he rolled out of bed before Sheila and went to check on Amelia Louise. She was still sleeping, too, a rare morning occurrence. He slipped quietly downstairs and whispered to Lady who was all ready to go. He pulled on his RCMP hoodie and slipped into his runners. The pair were out the door in a flash and soon speeding down towards the wharf. He stopped to let Lady do her business and watched as the fog lights in the lighthouse swung out to sea and back over them.

It was another peaceful morning on the wharf. People were starting to arrive at the factory on the other side of the harbour for their morning shift and were gathering in the parking lot for a chat and a smoke. Windflower could barely see their shadows, but it was so quiet that he could almost hear their conversations. Even the ever-present seagulls were subdued on this Saturday morning.

He pulled gently on Lady's leash and led her all the way through town and up to the trail at the clinic. They continued on to the top, paused briefly at the lookout, where the fog made sure there was nothing to see, and then went down the trail to the bottom. Windflower stopped at the place where he had discovered the dead man's body and took a quick look around. The area had been disrupted since his last visit, probably by curious townsfolk who wanted to see if they could decipher their own clues from the scene.

For Windflower, there was little of interest left here. There was just the memory of the slight shock he had felt when he realized he was lying next to a dead person. In some ways he had become inured, numb to such grim findings. But another part of him had been scarred by the sudden and unexpected violence that he witnessed as part of his job. The near death of Eddie Tizzard, missing children and just being close to the evil that people do to their fellow humans had an impact on him. Of that he was sure.

Luckily, he had a kind and gentle woman, a beautiful baby girl and four-legged friends like Lady and Molly to keep him on the light side, the right side of life. He smiled at Lady and called her to join him for the last part of the run home.

There still was no movement from upstairs, so Windflower started the breakfast preparations. He ground the coffee and put it into the percolator. Then he took a package of frozen fish cakes out of the freezer, placed them on a cookie sheet and put them into the oven to thaw. He cracked a half dozen eggs, dropped them in a bowl and added a splash of milk, heavy black pepper and a little salt. He sliced a honeydew melon and placed it in a bowl on the table. Once he heard activity from above, he would finish the preparations.

For now, he was on his own, so he grabbed his smudge kit and with his two pets in tow, went out to the back. Molly sat on the steps watching the still-brown grass for pests and rodents like the tiny voles that lived in the area. Lady went for her inspection tour of the perimeter. Everything secured, she came and sat beside Molly on the patio. That was amazing, thought Windflower. Once mortal enemies, the two were now able to sit in peace with each other. Well not quite total peace as Molly gave Lady a swat when she tried to get too close. But it was a stable ceasefire.

Windflower smudged and prayed at leisure this morning, acknowledging all his family, friends and allies, and thinking about all of them before asking that they be given strength and good winds to carry them on their journeys. He even had time to pray for what some would call the bad guys. He asked that Acting Inspector Raymond's heart be filled with gratitude and good things because it didn't appear to be that way right now. He also prayed for the criminals and suspects and those lost people who were causing pain to so many others. In his deepest heart he knew they were suffering, too, or they wouldn't need to be so mean.

When he and his pets came back in, he could hear the joyful signs of life coming from upstairs as Sheila and Amelia Louise went through their own morning routines. He came up to get a kiss from both and to bring Sheila her coffee. Then, he quickly went back downstairs where he got the scrambled eggs going in one pan and transferred the now-warm fish cakes to an iron skillet. He started toast and set the table, and by the time Sheila made it downstairs, everything was ready.

Sheila placed Amelia Louise in her high chair, and Windflower put a small portion of eggs and a little cut-up melon on her plate. He dished up breakfast for himself and Sheila and finally sat down to eat.

"These fish cakes are nice," said Sheila.

"Yeah, not bad for frozen, aren't they?" said Windflower.

The pair didn't say much more as Windflower in particular paid close attention to his breakfast and in playing little games with Amelia Louise that mostly involved her throwing things on the floor. What Lady and Molly didn't get, he put on a side plate for the garbage, except for her favourite toy, a little stuffed rooster which he wiped and returned, again and again.

Sheila picked up the dishes and started to clean up while Windflower took the baby upstairs to change her and get ready for work. He came down a few minutes later and kissed Sheila on the forehead.

"I should be back sometime after lunch," he said.

"We're going over to Marystown," said Sheila. "Do you want me to pick anything up?"

"See if they've got any fresh halibut. Maybe I'll barbeque tonight."

"Mmm, that would be nice."

"Mmm," parroted Amelia Louise.

Windflower laughed and waved goodbye as he headed out the door for work.

Smithson was in the small boardroom and had the speakers and large monitor set up when Windflower arrived.

"We're good to go when you are," he said. "The connection is strong and should be fine."

"You look pretty wide awake for someone who's been up all night," said Windflower.

"Good living," said Smithson. "Listen, Boss. Can I talk to you for a few seconds before the call?"

"Sure," said Windflower.

"Why did Tizzard quit?" asked the younger cop. "I mean I know he was in trouble for jumping Raymond, but why didn't he stay and fight it?"

"There's a lot of factors," said Windflower. "But for Tizzard, I think this has been coming for a while."

"You mean like after he got shot?"

"That's another piece of it. I think we all wonder about our future on the Force from time to time."

"Even you?"

"Even me," said Windflower. "Now, I'm going to get a cup of coffee while you double check this infernal system, okay?"

"Yes, Sir," said Smithson.

When Windflower came back, the screen was live. Sitting in front of the camera was an OPP officer and another man that Windflower surmised was Michael Howse.

At Smithson's urging, Windflower said hello. "Good morning, Sergeant," said the OPP officer. "My name is Wilfred Bonnefield, and this is Michael Howse."

Howse glared at the other officer and looked perturbed at being named.

"Good morning, Mr. Howse. I'm Sergeant Winston Windflower from the Grand Bank RCMP. I'd like to ask you a few questions."

"They told me I had to if I wanted to get out of this hellhole town," said Howse.

"We understand that you were living at a property in Grand Beach," said Windflower.

"I stayed in that piece of dirt trailer 'cause I had nowhere else to live," said Howse.

"Are you familiar with Vince Murray?" asked Windflower.

"I know him, yes."

"Daphne Burry?"

"His girlfriend."

"How about Paul Sparkes?"

Howse hesitated and finally said, "Grand Bank is a small town, Sergeant. I know just about everybody, except for the police." Howse laughed at his own joke.

35

owse was still laughing, but Windflower decided to press on with the video interrogation.

"What about Everett McMaster? Marcel Perreault?" asked Windflower.

"Never heard of them," said Howse.

"What if I was to tell you that they were at the trailer in Grand Beach?"

"Not when I was there."

Windflower noticed that Howse was starting to look a little less confident on the monitor. "We think Paul Sparkes may have been killed out there," said Windflower. "Do you know anything about that?"

"Nope," said Howse. "Nothing. Are we done now?"

"I'm going to talk to Daphne Burry later today. I'll see what she has to say. Are you sure there's nothing you want to tell me?"

"Listen, that streel will say anything to keep herself and her greasy boyfriend out of jail. You got nothing on me."

"Constable Bonnefield," said Windflower, "I'm going to need you to hold our guest for the weekend in connection with the murder of Paul Sparkes. Would that be possible?"

"You can't do that. I'll get my lawyer," screamed Howse.

"No problem, Sergeant. Please send along the paperwork," said Bonnefield. "We can find accommodations for our friend here in Elliot Lake."

"Thank you, Constable," said Windflower as he heard Howse yelling in the background. He turned to Smithson who was now shutting down the system. "Can you do up the forms to hold Michael Howse as a material witness in the murder of Paul Sparkes and send them to Elliot Lake?"

"Yes, Sir," said Smithson.

"Then go home and get some rest."

Windflower was still processing what he'd heard from Howse, which he realized wasn't a lot, when Jones came into his office.

"Everything's pretty quiet out there. How did the interview go?"

"Hard to say," said Windflower. "The only thing that seemed to bug him was when I mentioned Daphne Burry and Vince Murray."

"Does he know Vince Murray is dead?" asked Jones.

"I don't think so," said Windflower. "Can you check with Clarenville to see if they've got anything else on his death? I'm waiting for Superintendent Majesky to show."

"Absolutely," said Jones. "Are you worried about talking to Majesky?"

"No. I'm more concerned about Evanchuk."

"She was pretty upset last night. She feels responsible for getting you in trouble and for Eddie quitting."

"I'll talk to her," said Windflower.

"I'll call Clarenville," said Jones.

Windflower was sitting in his office when he heard the door open and somebody call out. He walked to the front and met Superintendent Wally Majesky at the door.

"Pretty lax security," said Majesky.

"It's normally a quiet place," said Windflower.

"Oh yeah, I heard that. Except you've got a dead body and a hit and run underway, and another guy who was in your custody is now dead, too."

Windflower shrugged. "I didn't say we didn't have crime or problems. Just quiet. Usually."

"Don't worry. I'm not here to bust your chops on security or your police work. That's never been a problem. Where can I set up?"

"You can use the small boardroom if that's okay. Evanchuk should be here soon."

"And Tizzard?"

"I'm here, Sir," said Eddie Tizzard who had come in with Evanchuk while they were talking. "I'm ready when you are."

Majesky walked down the hallway to the boardroom, and

Tizzard followed behind.

Evanchuk looked a little stunned. "Come in and sit down," Windflower told her. "This is not your fault. This has been coming for a while. I would have had to deal with Raymond sooner or later. He is a bully."

"I know that on one level," said Evanchuk. "But I still feel responsible. Especially for Eddie."

"Eddie did make a big mistake with his actions. But that's on him. He understands and accepts the consequences."

"But he's giving up the Force."

"Yes. He's giving it up but only because he wants to build something better for himself and for you. Now, go get a cup of coffee and relax. This will all work itself out."

Evanchuk gave him a weak smile and went to the back to get her coffee and to collect herself for her interview.

Fifteen minutes later Tizzard came into his office. "I'm starving," was all he said.

Windflower laughed out loud and then caught himself. "How did it go?"

"The super asked me to reconsider. Said he was going to throw the book at me. But that considering my record, he'd recommend they take me back."

"What do you think?"

"I dunno. I said I'd think it over, but I'm starting to like the idea of a new life, a new adventure. I guess some of it depends on what happens to you and Carrie."

"Don't worry about me," said Windflower. "I'm not."

"Well, I don't mind taking my lumps," said Tizzard. "But if they're not going to deal with someone like Raymond, that will make my decision real easy."

Windflower almost said that he agreed but decided to hold his tongue.

"Anyway, is it okay if I get a snack in the back? I know I'm technically not working here, but my stomach is growling."

"Go ahead," said Windflower. "We'll make an exception for today."

Jones came in shortly after Tizzard left. "Nothing more from

Clarenville," she said. "But we got a call from Bruce. He's the guy assigned to the hospital. He says that Daphne Burry had a visitor. Her sister. She told her that Vince Murray was dead. Burry freaked out and started yelling about how she needed protection and wanted a deal."

"She suggested that to me, too," said Windflower.

"She told Bruce that she wanted to name names, that she had nothing left to hide now," said Jones.

"Can you talk to Bruce and tell him that I'll come back over once I get freed up here?"

"Will do. Oh, and Bruce also told me that the hospital is planning to ship Burry into St. John's. He is going to escort her, but as far as he knows, there's no plan for security when she gets to the Health Sciences in St. John's."

"Tell him I'll check on that, too. Thanks."

Jones went to make her call, and Windflower ran through some of the papers on his desk. He glanced up at some point to see Tizzard leading Evanchuk out. He was going to go after them when Majesky called out to him. "I'm ready for you," he said.

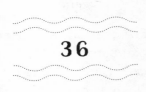

36

Windflower walked into the boardroom and closed the door behind him.

"I want to check a few things with you," said Majesky. "Then I'd like to hear what you have to say. Is that okay with you?"

"Fine with me," said Windflower.

"I haven't talked to Raymond yet. But if what Constable Evanchuk told me is true, this is a very serious situation. Do you know what happened to her?"

"Not all of it, Sir," said Windflower. "Only that it was difficult for her."

"She says that he didn't just bully her. She claims he wanted to date her, that he was persistent. While she tried to put him off, she said that he became aggressive and that he tried to grope her when they were alone."

"I didn't know any of that, Sir."

"I think that's why Tizzard jumped him. Because Evanchuk told him about it," said Majesky. "I don't know that for sure. Do you?"

"No, Sir. I can't say that I have direct knowledge of that."

"But you're not surprised."

"If he knew, I'm not surprised."

"That doesn't condone what he did, and I'm still going to have to nail him, if he comes back. But it might explain one thing. Now, what's your involvement in all of this, Sergeant?"

Windflower spent the next 20 minutes running through his relationship with Raymond and detailing as many incidents as he could remember. "I felt undermined and disrespected," said Windflower as he started to wrap up. "I work hard, I try to do my job in the right way, and I don't deserve to be treated like this. Nobody in the RCMP does."

Majesky asked a few more administrative questions and then thanked him for his contribution.

"What happens next?" asked Windflower.

"First of all, I am going to talk to Inspector Raymond. But in the interim, Evanchuk stays here until further notice. I will advise the people who need to know. After I have all the information, I will write my report with recommendations. This will happen quickly, Windflower. I can promise you that."

"Thank you, Sir. Before you head back, can I talk to you about a case?"

"If you buy me a coffee at that nice café you can."

"No problem, Sir," said Windflower.

He followed Majesky over to the Mug-Up and was slightly surprised that most of the parking spots had been taken. Then he remembered it was Saturday and time for pea soup and por' cakes at the café. Even though it was not quite noon, the place was nearly full. Windflower and Majesky snagged a table just as people were leaving.

"What's going on here today?" asked Majesky.

"It's a bit of a Grand Bank tradition," said Windflower. "People come Saturday morning for pea soup and por' cakes."

"What are por' cakes?"

Windflower couldn't help but smile. He loved explaining local traditions to visitors. "They are kind of a fat little potato pancake baked in the oven," he said. "There's minced pork, pork back fat and potatoes along with some baking powder and flour to bind everything together. You eat one or two, dipping them in molasses."

"You like them?"

"As the locals say, they're sum good b'y."

"Okay. I'm game," said Majesky. When Marie, the waitress, came to take their order, Majesky ordered two por' cakes and a cup of coffee.

"And pea soup?" asked Marie.

"Why not?" said Majesky. After Windflower ordered the same, Majesky asked him about the case he was interested in.

"It's about the body we found up on the trail. We think he was murdered, and one of the people's prints we found at the possible murder site was this woman, Daphne Burry. She was the victim in another case, a deliberate hit and run," said Windflower.

"So you think the cases are connected?" asked Majesky. "That's often the case in small towns, isn't it?"

Windflower nodded and continued. "Anyway, this woman says she has information but wants protection. Right now she's in the Burin hospital, but she's getting transferred to St. John's. That's the other thing. Raymond hasn't made any arrangements to get security for her in St. John's."

"Let me deal with that last part first," said Majesky. He got up from the table and walked outside to make a call.

When he came back, Marie was putting down their pea soup and por' cakes.

"Just in time," said Majesky. "The woman will have protection in St. John's."

"Thank you, Sir," said Windflower.

"And why don't I go with you to Burin? It's on the way to Marystown, and if she is the real deal, maybe I can expedite things. Now let's eat our lunch."

After lunch Windflower went to pay at the register, which was being run by Herb Stoodley. "Got the big brass with you today," said Stoodley.

"Superintendent Majesky," said Windflower. "Here to check some things out."

Majesky came up behind him as he was paying.

"Are you the owner of this place?" asked Majesky.

"My wife is the owner," said Stoodley. "I'm just part of the hired help."

"Well, pass along my compliments to her and the chef. Those por' cakes were sum good b'y," said Majesky.

Stoodley laughed out loud and winked at Windflower. "I'll be sure to pass that along, Superintendent."

Majesky followed Windflower on the highway over to Burin and parked beside him in the hospital parking lot. The pair went down the hallway to intensive care, where Bruce was sitting on a chair outside doing a crossword puzzle.

Bruce jumped to his feet. "Sergeant, Superintendent," he started to stammer.

Windflower held up his hand. "Relax, Constable. Can you bring us up to speed?"

"Yes, Sir," said Bruce. "I don't know for sure, but I heard the nurses talking. One of them said that the doctor was coming soon to sign the transfer papers. I was waiting to talk to her to get an ETA."

"And Daphne Burry's sister was here?" asked Windflower.

"Yes, Sir," said Bruce, pulling out his notebook. "Hannah Burry. I asked for her identification and went inside with her."

"She told her sister about Vince Murray?" asked Windflower. "What was her reaction?"

"Daphne Burry went into hysterics. Before they could sedate her, she alternated between sobbing and screaming."

"What else did she say?" asked Majesky.

Bruce looked at his notes again. "She said that she knew who did this. She said they were going to pay, that she would make them pay. She was yelling at me for a deal. I didn't know what to say."

"Is she awake now?" asked Windflower.

"She was sleeping when I checked on her earlier. She is probably due to wake up soon. She goes in and out because of the meds. But she's a lot calmer now," said Bruce.

"Let's go see her," said Majesky.

37

Windflower and Majesky walked inside the ICU and towards Daphne Burry's bed. She was moving around and moaned a little as they got closer.

"Daphne," said Windflower. "Daphne, it's me, Windflower. From Grand Bank. I've got someone with me who wants to talk to you."

The woman opened her eyes and looked groggily at the two men near her bed. "Ice," she croaked. Windflower took the cup of ice from the table near her bed and lifted it to her mouth until a small chip came out. Daphne Burry sucked on the chip loudly and started to wake up even more.

"Who's he?" she asked. Majesky introduced himself.

"Can you make a deal?" she asked him.

"Why don't you tell me what you know, and we'll go from there?" said Majesky.

Daphne Burry rolled her eyes and looked again at Windflower. He shrugged and nodded. "He's your best chance," he said.

"I was at the trailer the night that Paul Sparkes died," she whispered.

"Who else was there?" asked Windflower.

"Vince. McMaster, Perreault and Michael Howse, too. Sparky had received the payment, and we were all there for our share."

"What was the payment for?" asked Majesky.

"Opioids," said Burry. "Sparky was the middleman. He would receive the product and the money from the top and parcel it out. Except that he had found a way to cut the product with carfentanil without telling anybody. Everybody was upset."

"So, what happened?" asked Windflower.

"The goons McMaster and Perreault beat him up. Me and Vince had nothing to do with it. We just wanted our money. After he was knocked out, McMaster gave him a needle. Then they said he was dead. Vince and me got out of there as fast as we could."

"Sounds like you were part of this right up until Sparkes died," said Majesky. "Why should we make a deal with you?"

"Because I know who was paying the shot for all three of them," said Burry. "More ice."

Windflower gave her another sliver. "McMaster and Perreault were working for old man Howse," she said after getting some liquid in her throat.

"How do you know that?" asked Windflower.

"Michael told us. That's why he took off."

"He went to rehab in Ontario," said Windflower.

Burry laughed. "He went there to hide out. Even his old man couldn't touch him in there. So, do I get a deal?"

Windflower looked at Majesky. He nodded. "We've got protection arranged in St. John's. We'll get a full statement. If your story holds up, I'll make the call," said Majesky.

There were many more questions for Burry, but the officers' time with her was up. Two nurses came into ICU with a doctor. They were polite but moved the Mounties out of the way to examine their patient. Windflower and Majesky waited outside until the doctor came back out.

"Are you transferring her to St. John's?" asked Windflower.

"Yes," said the doctor. Windflower noted her name tag: Dr. R. Forsey. "She will need reconstructive surgery that we can't do here. She's also particularly unstable because she is diabetic. We don't have the people or the equipment to help her through the next stages of her recovery."

"Thank you, Doctor. We'll have someone going with her," said Windflower.

Doctor Forsey nodded, and Windflower and Majesky left the building and debriefed in the parking lot.

"Interesting stuff," said Majesky.

"Yes indeed," said Windflower. "She just implicated one of the best-known citizens in the community. But I have to say that nothing in what she said doesn't match up with what we know, which I admit isn't a lot."

"I'm sure it's part of the truth, at least the part that serves her. I'll get someone into St. John's to do a full interview with her, and then we'll see what happens after that. We'll keep you in the loop."

"Thanks. It feels like we have a few more facts to work with."

Majesky got into his car and drove away to Marystown. Windflower watched him go and realized that the superintendent was on his way to interview Raymond. Oh, to be a fly on that wall, he thought.

He was still thinking about Majesky and Raymond, Daphne Burry and both Michael and Cec Howse when he saw Grand Bank appear out of the fog in front of him. He parked in front of the detachment and met Jones who was coming out.

"Great, you're back," said Jones. "I'm just leaving. Carrie is here to take the overnight shift. She's pretty upset."

"I'll talk to her," said Windflower.

"I've got some news from Clarenville. Someone saw a black pickup leaving the scene where Vince Murray was found dead. They've put out another note on that," said Jones.

"Maybe the same guys from here," said Windflower.

"Yeah," said Jones. "I passed that along. How'd it go in Burin?"

"Daphne Burry says that Cec Howse is involved, along with his son Michael and the two creeps we've been tracking."

"Wow. If that's true, it would shake things up around here."

"If it's true. We'll bring Cec Howse in for questioning on Monday. I hear he's away right now."

"People say he's a gambler and a bit of a playboy. But what's his interest in all of this?"

"Still to be determined," said Windflower. "Stay tuned."

Jones jumped into her cruiser and drove away. Windflower went inside where Evanchuk was sitting in the back room cradling a cup of tea.

"How are you?" he asked.

"I've been better," said Evanchuk.

"I think you're very brave. I'm proud of you for coming forward."

"Thank you, Sergeant. But it feels like I'm taking a big risk, not just with my career but with Eddie's as well."

"Well, that might be true. But the great Bengali poet, Tagore, once said, 'Let me not pray to be sheltered from dangers but to be fearless in facing them.'"

Evanchuk tried to smile but looked like she was going to cry. Windflower went closer to her and asked her if she wanted a hug. She said yes through her near tears, and he held her close until he felt her pull away.

"It will be okay," he said. "Because it already is. Have a good night and be safe. If you need me, you can call."

"I'll be okay," said Evanchuk. "Eddie will come by later, and I'm fine when I'm working. Takes my mind off everything. Have a good night, Sir."

Windflower waved goodbye and went to his Jeep to drive home.

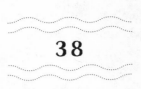

38

Windflower's house was in its usual chaos, and as always, everybody was happy to see him. After paying suitable attention to Amelia Louise and his two favourite animals, Windflower went to the kitchen to examine the halibut steaks Sheila had purchased in Marystown.

"Perfect," he pronounced when he saw the pale slabs with their pinkish glow. "Great job, Sheila."

"Glad it meets your standards," she said as she, the baby and both pets came to examine him and his cooking skills. "We'll leave the master to his work. The baby may have a quick nap before dinner if you take the other two out with you."

"No worries," he said as he scrubbed two baking potatoes and put them in the oven. Then he chopped up tomatoes and half a cucumber to go into the salad. He didn't have time to make a salad dressing, but there was a great bottled raspberry vinaigrette in the fridge. Next, he made his sauce for the fish. A little butter went into a saucepan along with some brown sugar, garlic, lemon juice and soy sauce. Next came an extra helping of cayenne pepper to give it a little spark.

While the sauce was heating, he got two handfuls of green beans from the fridge and cut the edges off. Then he put them in tinfoil, added a dash of salt and pepper and a dollop of butter and closed it up. He turned the burner off and spooned a little of the sauce over the halibut.

"C'mon guys," he said to Molly and Lady who followed him outdoors. Molly took her perch near the barbeque, while Lady went off to explore her territory. Windflower turned on the grill to heat it up. Medium-high would be good for the halibut. Any more than that would dry it out. He went back inside and came out with his halibut, sauce and vegetables, as well as some olive oil for the grill. He lightly oiled the grill and put the green beans on. He spooned another portion of sauce on the halibut, placed the fish on the grill and closed the cover.

Two minutes later he turned the halibut and checked the green beans. The green beans were steaming perfectly, and he closed up the foil packet. The halibut was browned very nicely on the side that had been down and smelled delicious. He closed the cover and sat back to wait another two minutes. After that, he checked the food and it was still doing great. The halibut flaked a little when he touched it with his fork. He turned it and poured the remaining sauce over the top. He turned off the grill and closed the cover again while he went inside to get everything else ready.

Sheila had beat him to it and had the table set. "Amelia Louise is having a catnap. Usually I would try to keep her going 'til bedtime, but it's the weekend. I don't mind if she stays up a little later. Do you want some wine?"

"I'll pass on the wine. But I'll have some Perrier, thanks," said Windflower. "This is almost ready. Hey, we'll have an adult meal tonight."

"I'm ready for it," said Sheila as she poured herself a glass of Zinfandel and got Windflower his sparkling water.

Windflower went back outside and took everything off the grill. He looked down to see Lady and Molly sitting straight up beside him. He laughed and called them in with him. He laid the fish and vegetables on the counter and took the baked potatoes out of the oven and laid them on their plates. Then he placed a piece of halibut and a portion of green beans next to them. Lady was sitting at his feet, alternating between panting and drooling. Molly pretended she didn't care but stationed herself next to the dog, just in case.

Sheila took a forkful of halibut. "Oh my God," she said. "This is sooooooooooo good."

Windflower tasted his. "Oh yeah baby, the king's still got it."

"I salute you, master of the grill," said Sheila.

The couple ate and chatted their way through their fish and potatoes with sour cream, steaming hot green beans and the cool green salad. Windflower brought Sheila news about Majesky and the interviews and about Evanchuk, too, though he omitted the sexual overtones, since he felt that was not his story to tell. But when Sheila commented, she mentioned that Carrie had already talked to her about all aspects of the treatment she had received from Raymond.

Sheila also told him about the roofer's plans to start on Monday at the B & B because the forecast called for a rare week without precipitation.

"That is rare," said Windflower as he finished off the last few scraps of food on his plate. When he looked down, he could see that Lady and Molly had both drifted off to sleep, probably in sheer despair because the humans had kept all that great smelling food for themselves. Windflower got them both a treat and went out to clean off the grill and put everything away. As he was doing that, he noticed that the evening was clearing and the fog was drifting upwards and maybe even away from Grand Bank.

He went back in to tell Sheila the good news, but he could hear from the monitor on the counter that Amelia Louise had woken and was being attended to. Sheila brought a still sleepy-eyed baby downstairs and handed her to Windflower. "Look outside," said Windflower.

Sheila saw the sun starting to set, which she hadn't seen in almost a week and smiled.

"I saved her a little potato and a few green beans. Feed her while I finish up, and then we'll go for a walk."

"Great idea," said Windflower. He put Amelia Louise in the high chair and spooned a little potato into her mouth. Before he knew it, the baby had grabbed the spoon and fed herself a little bit before throwing the rest on the floor. Lady was happy to help clean that up.

"Did she get any?" asked Sheila.

"A little," said Windflower sheepishly as he wiped her mouth and lifted her out of the high chair. "Let's go before the weather changes its mind."

Soon the couple with the baby in the stroller and Lady happily by their side were winding their way through Grand Bank. Along the way they met and said hello to most of the downtown inhabitants, and Lady reacquainted herself with all the Grand Bank canines. It was just getting dark when they got back home, and Windflower took Amelia Louise upstairs for her bath.

They were playing with some of her bath toys when Sheila came up with a cup of tea for him.

"Thank you, my dear," said Windflower as they watched their little girl express her joy with splashes of water.

"Thank you," said Sheila. "That was a wonderful dinner. After we get her to bed, let's watch a movie. We haven't done that in forever either."

"Great plan," said Windflower. He dried Amelia Louise off and dressed her in her pajamas. Then he got a book from her shelf and sat in the rocking chair. The book was called Babies in the Forest, and it was a chunky board book that had lots of flaps that Amelia Louise loved to lift to reveal a series of baby animals in the forest. She loved this story and playing the game, and she got Windflower to read it three times before she started to drowse off.

He put her into her crib and tucked her in with a kiss goodnight. He went downstairs where Sheila had the movie all ready to go along with fresh tea and a slice of apple pie for each of them. He kissed her on the cheek and snuggled up next to her on the couch. While the couple preferred the older, classic movies, Sheila was shaking it up by choosing some newer movies as well. Windflower was happy just to be relaxing and hanging out with his wife. Tonight, the feature she had selected was Green Book.

Green Book was based on the true story of a black professional pianist hiring a very uncouth Italian-American bouncer for a concert tour in the still-segregated American South. It was both funny and sad to see the two men's cultures and personalities interact as they faced a series of racist actions towards the celebrated artist. There were great performances by Viggo Mortensen as Tony Lip and Mahershala Ali as his black boss. They learned to understand each other and develop a true friendship along the way. The movie had won a number of Oscars, including Best Picture and one for Ali as Best Supporting Actor. Both Windflower and Sheila thoroughly enjoyed the movie, and both felt that Mortensen should have won Best Actor.

After the movie Windflower took Lady for one more spin and was still in bed by half past ten. Sheila was reading her book when he came upstairs but put that on the bed stand and came closer to him when he got into bed. It was the perfect ending to a great day, and Windflower fell asleep that night full of love and gratitude. His was a wonderful place to be in.

39

Sunday morning was Windflower's special time with Amelia Louise. Sheila got to sleep in, and he would look after the baby. It was his favourite time of the week. She was waiting for him when he came into her bedroom, and the light was starting to fill her room. She was watching the light play with the mobile above her crib and gave him a big smile when she saw him.

He picked her up and grabbed her clothes and stuff for changing and brought her downstairs so they wouldn't wake her still-sleeping mother. He changed her and warmed up a bottle of expressed milk that was in the fridge. Sheila was still breast feeding, so they were using her milk as they introduced solids to the baby's diet. Amelia Louise liked holding the bottle herself now as she drank and that gave Windflower an extra hand to make some coffee.

When the baby had finished her bottle, Windflower put her coat and hat one her for the second part of their Sunday morning, a walk with Lady. The collie loved this walk. She knew that Windflower was not in a big rush and that he wouldn't mind if she stopped regularly to do her investigations. Amelia Louise seemed to enjoy it, too. Maybe for her it was a special time with her daddy, thought Windflower, which was a very pleasant thought indeed.

The small, quiet town of Grand Bank was super quiet on Sunday mornings. Later, many of the locals would rise and head to church or go for little walks just like Windflower was doing. But for now, Lady, Amelia Louise and Windflower had the streets to themselves. They walked along the oceanside and down to the beach. It was too rough for the stroller, and Lady didn't like the smooth beach rocks on her feet, so the trio just watched the waves roll in for a few minutes.

Then they walked down to the brook where both Lady and the baby got very excited at the arrival of an army of ducks that came looking for their breakfast. Luckily for them Windflower had brought a small bag of stale bread from the house and scattered pieces in the water while Amelia Louise and the dog screamed and barked their enthusiasm at the feeding frenzy. Windflower held the dog so that she didn't jump in after the ducks, and Amelia Louise alternated between feeding herself, the dog and the ducks. It was a scene that always brought Windflower great joy.

They finished their walk and went home, where Windflower made himself and Amelia Louise a bowl of fruit, and he finally got to enjoy a cup of coffee. He made sure to pay some extra attention to Molly so that the cat didn't feel completely left out. She certainly looked disappointed, thought Windflower, but maybe that was her natural cat look. He sat on the couch and watched the baby fend off the pets, who were now wanting the remainder of her fruit. He absent-mindedly turned on the TV and switched to the local news.

It was yesterday's late-night edition being replayed this morning. He only got a glimpse of the two men being led into the RCMP detachment in Gander. But one had a Maple Leafs hat and the other had a beard. The piece of the story he heard didn't identify the men but said they were arrested in connection with a murder in Clarenville. These were his guys; he was sure of it. Automatically, he thought of phoning the office but told himself to delay that. He needed to appreciate his Sunday morning and could always call later.

That gave him a few more hours of family time and enjoyment. Sheila woke shortly afterwards and offered to make him waffles. That was an offer he gladly accepted. Amelia Louise sat happily in her high chair with maple syrup smeared across her face and strawberries squished on her plate. She was waving a large piece of waffle above her head when she accidently or deliberately dropped it over the side. Lady and Molly each came away with a portion.

Sheila and Windflower watched with pleasure, although Windflower had much more pleasure enjoying his own waffles and strawberries. They were listening to CBC's Sunday Morning in the background and making small talk when Windflower's cellphone rang. He looked at Sheila. "Go ahead," she said. "Otherwise, you'll just be thinking about it all morning."

Windflower wiped up the last of the maple syrup with his final piece of waffle and took his phone to the living room. It was Jones.

"Hi Sarge," she said. "Sorry to bother you, but I thought you'd want to know we got McMaster and Perreault."

"Yeah," said Windflower. "I saw the news."

"I guess there was a car chase, and their pickup ran off the road. But of course, they weren't hurt," said Jones.

"They never are. Like vermin."

"The guy I talked to from Clarenville said he knew you. Sergeant Bill Ford."

"Fordy. He used to be my boss."

"Really? Must've been a while ago."

"A few years back," said Windflower. Jones waited for Windflower to say more, but he was reluctant to open up. "Bill Ford is one of the good guys," he finally said. "He just ran into some difficulties he couldn't manage."

"Okay," said Jones, sensing that he didn't want to go any further into it. "Sergeant Ford said to call him when you get a chance."

"Thanks very much. I'll call him later."

Windflower walked back into the kitchen where Sheila was wiping up the baby and tidying up the kitchen. "I'll clean up in here if you want to get her dressed," he said. "I thought maybe we could go out to the T. It's such a nice day."

"That sounds grand," said Sheila. "Everything okay at work?"

"Yeah, things are good. Bill Ford is in Clarenville now."

"Oh, how's he doing?"

"I don't know, but I'll call him later."

"I always liked Bill. He and Uncle Frank got along pretty well, didn't they?"

"They did indeed," said Windflower as Sheila left with the baby.

They got along because of what they had in common, thought Windflower, like drinking too much and being unable to stop when they wanted. That had cost Bill Ford a lot, including his job as inspector a few years ago. But it sounded like he was back on track. Windflower hoped so. He would check in with Ford later, but now he had a kitchen to clean. Lady and Molly both volunteered to help, but he shooed them into the living room while he wiped and mopped the floor.

Sheila came down with Amelia Louise who called for her da, da, da all the way down the stairs. He grabbed her in his arms and swung her above his head. She squealed from that moment until he strapped her into her car seat in Sheila's car. Lady and Molly were led in beside her in the back, and Windflower took the co-pilot position as Sheila drove them through town and out to the L'Anse au Loup T.

All of Windflower's family loved the T. For Sheila, it had always been a part of her life growing up in Grand Bank. People had cabins on the other side of the road, and she could remember coming out here with her parents as a young child to walk along the beach and collect tiny stones for her rock collection. Lady loved the freedom of being outside and so near the water. She would see the seals basking on rocks close to shore and bark at them while they seemed to bark back. Molly was content to sit in the window in the back of the car and survey the world from her throne.

Windflower looked down at Amelia Louise, noticing how happy she seemed to be. He handed her some tiny flowers, which she either clutched onto tightly or tried to eat, only to have her father take them back. But mostly she just seemed content to be here, like her dad. The T usually made Windflower feel perfectly serene, except when four-wheelers would come tearing down the fragile shoreline. Then he would have to put on his stern Mountie look and glare at the joyriders until they slowed down. But today, it was just the Windflower crew on the T, enjoying the sun on their faces and the wind in their hair.

40

When they got back from their walk on the T, the whole Windflower family had a nap, Amelia Louise in her crib, Sheila with her book as a very hard pillow on her bed and Windflower on the couch with Lady at his feet and Molly as close as possible to his head. It was Amelia Louise who made sure they didn't sleep all day.

Windflower heard her first, changed her and played with her on her bedroom floor until Sheila woke as well. Then, he handed her over to her momma and went to call Bill Ford in Clarenville while Amelia Louise had her mid-afternoon snack. He found the number for the Clarenville RCMP and wasn't surprised when he was told that Ford was at the office on a Sunday. When there was an investigation, especially a high-profile one, weekend work was the norm.

"Bill, how are you? It's Winston Windflower."

"Winston, it's so nice to hear your voice. I was meaning to call, but you know how it is, I got busy and . . ."

"I understand, I hear you've got some peeps we may be interested in as well."

"Yeah. We're trying to piece together exactly what happened. But these guys are connected, that's for sure."

"We were looking at them for a hit and run on Vince Murray's girlfriend," said Windflower. "And they might be involved in a murder here as well, a body found on the trail."

"That's what Constable Jones said this morning," said Ford. "I've been trying to talk with them, but so far neither is co-operating. And they've each asked for a lawyer."

"Not surprising. Maybe I should come over and see what I can get from them. They're not going anywhere, right?"

"Nope. They're both on probation, and I'm pretty sure they've violated their conditions. So, they're our guests until we decide to transfer them back."

"Where are their files?"

"Ontario. McMaster's case is in Hamilton and Perreault is with Kitchener-Waterloo. By the way how is your uncle doing these days?"

"Frank is good," said Windflower. "He's mostly in Alberta but has been down here at least once since you were here. How about you? I kinda lost track of you for a while."

"I'm well," said Bill Ford. "I was on administrative leave for a while and then spent a long year at HQ while they kept a close eye on me. As soon as I could, I got back into the field. I was in Fredericton for a year, and finally this slot opened up."

"Are you still fishing?"

"Every weekend. You should come up when the salmon season opens, and we'll do the Gander River."

"I'd like that. But in the meantime, I'll come by tomorrow to see our two new friends if that's okay."

"See you in the morning," said Ford.

"Who were you talking to?" asked Sheila as she came into the living room with Amelia Louise. "Bill Ford," said Windflower. "I have to go to Clarenville tomorrow. They picked up the guys who we think did the hit and run."

Sheila laid the baby on the floor, and the little girl immediately made her way to Windflower to pick her up. "Daddy's girl," said Sheila, smiling.

"You betcha," said Windflower.

"Do you have to go into work?"

"Nope. This is my family day." Windflower took out Amelia Louise's toy box and laid some toys on the floor in front of her. She sorted through the toys and settled on one of her favourites, a set of big, soft blocks.

"Those are really good for her, you know," said Sheila. "They're improving her motor skills, mental stimulation and creativity."

"And her chewing ability," said Windflower as the baby tried to put one of the largest blocks into her mouth.

"Speaking of food. Why don't we go over to the diner in Fortune for supper tonight?"

"Fine by me. How do you think she'll do?"

"Well, I can feed her a little in the car when we get there and then put her in the snuggly until she wakes up."

"Sure, we'll take a few toys, and she'll be okay in a high chair over there for a few minutes after she wakes up. Sounds like a plan."

"Okay, I'll do some laundry while you play your games."

"Absolutely," said Windflower as he extracted one block from Amelia Louise's mouth and pulled another away from Lady who was claiming it as her own. They were still playing on the floor when Sheila returned with a basket of laundry, but they had moved on to a puzzle that Moira and Herb Stoodley had given Amelia Louise.

It was a fuzzy, chunky puzzle that featured four animals that stood up and that could be inserted back into their slots. There was a mirror in the middle, which absolutely fascinated the baby, and she loved trying to put the kitten, bunny, puppy and bird back into their right spots. Each spot had a picture of the animal on it to guide her, but Amelia Louise relied on her own sense of taste and touch and a little help from her daddy to get it right. When she did, both she and Windflower squealed.

"It's hard to tell who enjoys that game more," said Sheila.

"That would be me," said Windflower. "Is it suppertime? I'm starving."

"Let me put this stuff away, and we can go if you're sure you can tear yourself away from that puzzle."

A few minutes later Sheila bundled the baby up, and Windflower topped up the animals' food and water before going to the car for the quick trip to Fortune. It was fast but scenic as they drove along the ocean. The ferry was just coming back from St. Pierre, the island ceded to France in one of the numerous wars for territories in the so-called New World many years ago.

"We should go over again sometime soon," said Windflower.

"We haven't been over since we had one of our first dates," said Sheila.

"I think it was our first," said Windflower. "I was so nervous."

"I was just excited to be on a date, thinking about maybe starting another relationship."

"I remember you were absolutely gorgeous. I knew that night that I would have to marry you, if you would have me."

"Then you made me have to ask you," said Sheila, faking outrage.

"But I said yes," said Windflower as they pulled into the diner's parking lot.

"Hand me my blanket, and then I'll take the baby," said Sheila, thinking about how much her life had changed for the better since that awful day her first husband had died.

Windflower gave her the blanket and raised Amelia Louise out of her car seat and put her into Sheila's arms. Sheila covered the baby and fed her while Windflower waited patiently. When they were finished, Windflower took the dopey baby and helped Sheila with the snuggly. Once Amelia Louise closed her eyes, they went inside and were seated at a table near the back of the restaurant.

Windflower ordered the fried cod, while Sheila opted for the full turkey dinner. Amelia Louise slept pleasantly in her snuggly next to her momma. Their food arrived, and Windflower regretted his choice when he saw Sheila's mound of turkey with dressing and all the vegetables covered in a thick, brown gravy. But once he tasted his cod with little flecks of scrunchions, he was in heaven.

"This fish is so fresh," he proclaimed.

The waitress passing by overheard him. "That was caught this morning," she said.

Windflower smiled at Sheila as if to say that he knew that already. She smiled back. "I think this turkey was caught this morning, too. It is so tender."

The couple enjoyed their supper in relative peace until Amelia Louise awoke near the end of their meal. Windflower took her from Sheila and found a high chair to put her in. He gave her the last of his french fries, and she happily chewed them to a pulp until it was time to go.

After getting home, Windflower took Lady for a walk around town and was back home soon after to read Amelia Louise her bedtime story. He and Sheila had a couple of games of crib and shared one more pot of tea before calling it a night. Windflower stayed downstairs while Sheila had her bath, and once he heard the water drain, he went upstairs to join her. They were in bed by ten o'clock, and not long after, he could tell Sheila was drifting off. He soon followed, but then he could feel himself being pulled awake inside a dream.

He was in the familiar meadow of the previous dreamscapes. The meadow was filled with patches of brilliant wildflowers, which meant that the seasons had changed again. There was a house at one end, and Windflower started walking towards it. He was expecting to see more of his animal allies and certainly not what happened next.

41

G ood day, Winston. How's she going b'y?" asked Uncle Frank.
"Uncle Frank! What are you doing in my dream?"

Uncle Frank laughed. "Sometimes that happens," he said. "I'm here to give you a message."

"I thought only dead people could communicate in the dream world," said Windflower, still trying to make sense of what was happening.

"Stop trying to make things fit into your understanding. You don't even know what you don't know."

Windflower thought about that for a moment. "I'm not going to argue with somebody in a dream," he finally said. "Give me your message."

His uncle laughed again. "You are still stubborn, but gaining in wisdom, most of it by making mistakes," said Uncle Frank. "That's how we all do it, eventually. Pain is a great motivator. My dream world message to you is to be careful. I see a fire. I see people running, some towards you and some away. You will have to choose."

"What does that mean?" asked Windflower. "Choose what? Am I in danger? Is my family?"

Uncle Frank started to answer, but he faded away into noth-ingness like fog drifting off into the atmosphere. Windflower screamed at him, but Uncle Frank appeared powerless to stop his disappearance, and seconds later Windflower was standing alone in the meadow.

Windflower woke bathed in a cold sweat. He took a long, warm shower and went back to bed, still feeling a little shaken. Sheila woke a little and reached for him. He held her until she fell back asleep and then a little longer until he did the same. Before it was light, he was up and out of bed. He snuck downstairs and let Lady out into the back while he got his smudge kit.

In the stillness of the early morning, he lit his mixture and performed his ritual. He asked only to be guided with a pure heart and that his family, friends and allies be given smooth waters to travel upon. He felt his heart lift a little, but there was still a heavy burden on his shoulders. After he finished, he took Lady on a brisk walk. When he got back home, there was no noise or sign of life from upstairs, so he left a note on the kitchen table asking Sheila to call him later in the morning on his way to Clarenville.

It was just starting to get light when Windflower got to his detachment. The lights were on, but there was no one there at the moment. He went to the back and made a fresh pot of coffee. While he was waiting, he heard the front door open and someone coming down the hall.

"Morning, Boss," said Smithson.

"How're the roads this morning?" asked Windflower, pouring them both a cup of coffee.

"Quiet," said Smithson. "I love being out there, almost by myself. It's like just me and nature."

"I know what you mean," said Windflower. "I'm going to Clarenville this morning."

"I heard about McMaster and Perreault. Did they kill Vince Murray?"

"Suspects. I want to see what they have to say about being in that trailer in Grand Beach. Michael Howse wasn't much help."

"What about his old man?"

"What about Cec Howse?" asked Windflower.

"Don't you think it's strange that he didn't tell us his son was living up there?" asked Smithson as a reply.

"Let's bring Cec Howse in for a chat," said Windflower. "Daphne Burry says he's mixed up in all of this. I hear he was out of town this weekend. See if he can come in around five. I should be back by then."

"Will do, Sarge."

Windflower filled his thermos. That would hold him until the Tim Hortons in Marystown, where he could pick up a breakfast sandwich. He said goodbye to Smithson and went to his Jeep. He put his phone on hands-free and turned on CBC to get the news. There was more news from Clarenville, this time naming the two suspects who had been arrested. There was a clip of Bill Ford saying that the two men were being questioned in the death of Vincent Lloyd Murray of Grand Bank, but little else. Windflower knew that drill really well. Give as little information as possible while maintaining good relations with the media and the public.

Traffic was light, and Windflower was making good time. There were many more cars as he neared Marystown and the usual lineup at the drive-through. He got a refill for his thermos and an egg and sausage sandwich to go. He was munching away on his breakfast when his phone rang.

"Hi Sheila," he mumbled with his mouth half full.

"Good morning, Winston," she said. "You were up and out early."

"I'm trying to get to Clarenville and back today. Two and half hours each way. How are you this morning?"

"We're all good here. I'm going over to the town office later, and Levi is coming by to walk the dog. Nothing too exciting."

"Be careful today, okay?"

"I'm always careful, Winston. Did you have another dream?"

Windflower paused. "You know me too well," he said. "Yes, I had a dream. Something about a fire. Uncle Frank was in it."

"Your uncle was in a fire?"

"No, no," said Windflower, pausing again. "It's probably nothing. Be careful, okay?"

"Okay, drive safely and watch out for the moose."

"I will. Bye."

After he disconnected, Windflower thought again about his dream and what it meant. It was too early to phone Alberta, but he made his mind up to phone Uncle Frank later on. He turned off the radio and enjoyed the scenic drive out of Marystown. On his right was Mortier Bay. It was quiet down there now, but when they had built the oil platforms for the offshore rigs, it had been more than a beehive of activity, and at night it had looked like a spaceship was in the middle of the bay.

He drove up Highway 210 past the Spanish Room turnoff and then up towards the Terrenceville exit. He climbed a series of hills and crossed over the vast barrens of empty land abutting the ocean. It was a quiet and meditative journey that was only broken by the jarring sound of his phone.

"Good morning, Doc," said Windflower as the doctor's name came up on his screen.

"Good morning, Sergeant. Your assistant tells me you are travelling today," said Sanjay.

"On my way to Clarenville. How can I help you today?"

"You are very kind," said the doctor. "But perhaps I can help you or at least give you some information. I have the preliminary tox report on the late Paul Sparkes. In addition to the presence of insulin, which I believe may have ultimately killed him, our dearly departed friend had some other interesting chemical additives."

"Pray tell, my dear doctor," said Windflower, knowing that Sanjay loved being dramatic about his work.

"Cannabis, heroin, morphine, fentanyl and minute traces of carfentanil. None of it was enough to kill him. It's like he was out to sample the whole range of mood-altering substances."

"That is interesting. Have you ever heard of purple heroin?"

"Only anecdotally. I saw an alert on it, from Ontario I think. Isn't it a mix of heroin and other substances?"

"That's what I understand. It may be here. We found small amounts of it at a trailer that we think might be where Paul Sparkes died."

"That's not good."

"Nope. Thank you for the information. At least now we're getting a few more facts to go along with the speculation."

"True," said Sanjay. "'Facts are many, but the truth is one.' Remember that, my friend."

"Thanks, Doc. We'll talk soon," said Windflower as he ended the call. More facts, and more problems, he thought. And still a long way from the truth.

42

Windflower followed the highway as it traversed across land without any real signs of human or even animal activity. There were a few passing cars that slowed noticeably when their drivers saw his RCMP insignia. Then he came to the winding section that signalled the approach to Swift Current. This was one of his favourite parts of the drive. His Jeep seemed to cling to the curves in the road as it wound its way closer and closer to the little fishing village. Though it was still alive, Swift Current was like many other small communities now on life support and dying off along with their aging populations. But it remained a highlight of Windflower's journeys, nonetheless. It felt magical, like he was trapped in time somehow, and he hoped he was.

Fifteen minutes after passing Swift Current, he was pulling into the parking lot of the gas station and restaurant at Goobies when his phone rang again. It was Ron Quigley.

"Morning, Ron," said Windflower.

"Good morning, Winston. I hear you're on the road."

"Pulling in for gas at Goobies," said Windflower. "I'm going to Clarenville to see two guys they picked up. We think they're the same ones from the hit and run, and they may be connected to our murder, too."

"I love it when things come together," said Quigley.

"I'm not sure they're all together yet. I'm hoping to know more after I talk to them. Did you know Bill Ford was in Clarenville?"

"I did not. Once you leave, even temporarily, you're forgotten about, I guess."

"We would never forget you."

"That's good, 'cause I'm coming back for a while, hopefully for good."

"How'd you swing that?" asked Windflower, delighted.

"I told them about the purple heroin you found, and they want me to do some more digging down there," said Quigley.

"Great news," said Windflower. "You going to Marystown?"

"Yeah, I should be there tomorrow night. I'll be over to see you."

"Okay, I'll see you then," said Windflower. He liked that news. Maybe it was a signal that things were getting back to normal, at least on the work front. That pleasant thought kept him in a good mood as he filled his tank and his coffee thermos for the rest of the trip to Clarenville.

Clarenville was one of the prettiest little towns on the island. Situated in the Shoal Harbour River Valley, it was also near three eastern peninsulas: Avalon, Burin and Bonavista. There were great trails and coastal towns nearby, and a lot of tourists came to see the whales and many sea birds, which were part of the natural wonder of the place. Clarenville was long known as the Hub of the East Coast, and it had a large RCMP detachment and thriving service industry economy. Windflower knew a little about the history of the place because Richard Tizzard, having worked as an apprentice in shipbuilding there many years ago, had told him about it.

According to Richard, a sawmill owned by a man named William Cowan in the mid-1800s became the core of a growing community of fishermen. The name Clarenville was attributed to many sources and stories, the most popular one being that it was named after the Duke of Clarence, eldest son of the then Prince of Wales, later King Edward VII, who died in 1892.

When Windflower went to Clarenville, it was mostly, as it was today, to go to the RCMP offices, which were conveniently located right off the highway. He exited the highway, parked his vehicle and waved good morning to the other officers who were coming and going. Once inside he asked the administrative assistant for directions to see Sergeant Bill Ford.

"You must be Sergeant Windflower," she said. "I'm Mary Sceviour."

"Nice to meet you," said Windflower, a little puzzled as to how she knew his name.

"Betsy said you were coming. If you need anything, anything at all, let me know," said the woman.

"Thank you," said Windflower. Betsy was looking after him, even from a distance.

He followed instructions through the maze of offices until he came to Bill Ford's. Ford was on the phone but waved him in. Windflower could hear his side of the conversation, and it sounded like he was trying to calm the person on the other end.

"We have not laid charges because we are still questioning your client," said Ford. "You can apply for bail, but if you do, it will still take a couple of days to process, and we'll keep him here until the paperwork is done." Ford listened for a few more minutes and then said, "You can see your client anytime. Have a good day."

"Lawyers," he said to Windflower after he had hung up. "How are you, my friend? It's been a while." He got up from his desk and went to shake Windflower's hand.

"It has been," said Windflower. "Too long," he added as he shook Ford's hand back.

"We'll get a chance to catch up later," said Ford. "You want more coffee?"

"No, I'm running on a full tank. What are the lawyers saying? McMaster's and Perreault's, I'm assuming?"

"Yeah. You know, the usual. Although what's interesting here is that they both asked for separate lawyers. I guess they're not that close."

"Have you interviewed them yet?"

"I tried, but they wanted their lawyers. Now the lawyers are trying to get them out. We delay as long as we can while we're collecting evidence."

"What have you got so far?" asked Windflower.

"There's blood in the pickup. We suspect it's Vince Murray's. And we have a witness that saw all three of them together in town," said Ford. "This morning we got a call from the Marystown jail. They've got some video of one of them. Looks like he was cutting the fence in back and Murray was coming through."

"So they might have sprung him? Then why did they kill him, if they did kill him?

"Good question. Maybe he had something they wanted and

wouldn't give it to them. Do you know what these guys were doing in Grand Bank?"

"It's a bit fuzzy. Did you hear about our case?"

"Two cases, isn't it? A body in a carpet and a hit and run. Are they connected?"

"Maybe all three are," said Windflower. "McMaster and Perreault are the common element. We found their prints at what we think is the first guy's murder scene, the one in the carpet. We've got a witness who's looking for a deal, and she's all over them."

"That might get their attention," said Ford. "Why don't we see if one or both will talk to us?"

"What about the lawyers?"

"They can have them there if they want. They're both local guys, so they can get here quickly."

"Okay, let's try it."

43

Windflower followed Ford downstairs to the holding cell area. Ford signed them both in and led him to a cell where a man with a beard was lying on his bunk.

"Good morning," said Ford. "Marcel Perreault, this is Sergeant Windflower from Grand Bank. We'd like to ask you a few questions."

"Talk to my lawyer," said Perreault. "I got nothing to say."

"Well, you might want to hear what Daphne Burry had to say about you," said Windflower.

The bearded man sat up on his bunk. "I still got nothing to say."

"She says you were at the trailer in Grand Beach," said Windflower. "She's fingering you and asking for a deal." He could see he had the man's attention now. "Why don't you tell me your side of the story?"

"I got nothing to say," said Perreault, lying back down. "Talk to my lawyer."

Ford looked at Windflower and motioned him to leave. "Dead end," he said. "Let's try the other guy."

Windflower followed Ford down another corridor. They stopped in front of a cell with a man pacing inside.

"Are you here to let me out? Did my lawyer get a bail hearing?"

"Not yet," said Ford. "I do have somebody who wants to talk to you, though."

"Good morning, Mr. McMaster. I'm Sergeant Windflower from Grand Bank. I don't have a lot of time to waste, but I might be able to offer you something if you cooperate."

"Whaddya mean?" asked McMaster. "Can you get me out of here?"

"That depends on how cooperative you are," said Ford.

"We have a lot on you right now, the hit and run in Grand Bank, the murder of Paul Sparkes in the trailer in Grand Beach and now Vince Murray," said Windflower.

"None of that was me," said McMaster. "If I testify against Marcel, can you get me a deal?"

"Maybe," said Windflower.

"Let me talk to my lawyer."

Windflower and Ford walked away and went back to Ford's office where he called McMaster's lawyer. "He'll be here in an hour," Ford told Windflower. "You hungry?"

Windflower's stomach grumbled a little at that question. "I could eat something."

"Let's go to Rod's. Best fish and chips in town."

"Sounds good to me," said Windflower.

A few minutes later the two men were sitting in a beautiful little local restaurant sipping on some of the best seafood chowder ever and waiting for their fish and chips. When it came, it was perfect, too. At Ford's suggestion, Windflower had only ordered the one-piece fish and chips but was happy when he saw the size of their servings of fresh, local cod fried in a crispy batter with golden brown french fries.

The RCMP officers got caught up on their lives as they ate. Mostly, it was Windflower talking about Amelia Louise, but Ford seemed as happy to listen as Windflower was to talk about his daughter. Ford picked up the check with a promise from Windflower to reciprocate the next time around. They drove back to the RCMP offices, where Mary Sceviour smiled at Windflower again and told Ford that a lawyer, Al Penney, was waiting for him in Boardroom D.

Ford led the way to the boardroom. Al Penney was a criminal defence attorney, well known to Ford and the RCMP in Clarenville. Some lawyers were known as ambulance chasers, but Penney's reputation was that of paddy wagon chaser. Nobody came through the prisoner entrance at the detachment whom he wasn't aware of or who failed to receive a copy of his business card. How that happened remained a small mystery, but it continued because there always seemed to be people needing his services and it helped facilitate the justice system.

Al Penney was a middle-aged, pudgy man whose suit had fit him better when he was 20 pounds lighter. His tie looked like it had been hastily retied in a random manner never seen before by Windflower or probably anyone else. But Al Penney talked a good game. That's what Ford had told Windflower on the way down the hallway.

"Al, this is Sergeant Windflower from the Grand Bank detachment. He wants to talk to Everett McMaster about a couple of incidents that we believe your client has some involvement with."

"Thank you, Sergeant," said Penney. "Nice to meet you, Wildflower."

"It's Windflower. Nice to meet you, too."

"My client says you have a deal to offer him," said Penney.

"Not yet," said Windflower. "Maybe if he tells us what he knows, I'll see what I can do to mitigate his situation."

"Ah, I see," said Penney, "a fishing expedition." Windflower started to speak, but Penney held his hand up. "I've been around the block before, and while I know that Sergeant Ford is an excellent angler, I'm not sure of your capacity, if you know what I mean."

Ford interjected. "Sergeant Windflower has great connections," he said, "including with the superintendent in Halifax."

"Well then," said Penney. "I've talked to my client. He has some things that I believe will be of interest to you. Why don't we allow him to talk to you informally? With me present and off the record, of course, and see where it goes."

"Absolutely," said Windflower, who then looked at Ford.

"I'll have him brought up," said Ford.

44

Minutes later a shackled and still-agitated Everett McMaster was led into the boardroom and sat beside Al Penney. "You don't have to answer any questions you don't want to," said Penney. "And this is off the record, so they can't use it against you if it doesn't work out. Understand?" McMaster nodded.

"Why don't you tell us what you were doing at the trailer in Grand Beach," said Windflower.

"We were there to collect money from Sparky," said McMaster.

"What was the money for?" asked Windflower.

McMaster looked at his lawyer who gave him the go-ahead. "He owed people some money. We were there to collect."

"Drugs?" asked Windflower.

McMaster checked with his lawyer again before nodded.

"What happened?"

"Sparky said he didn't have it, so we had to convince him a little. It wasn't hard, there were five of us and only him."

"Why did you kill him then?"

"Listen. I didn't kill nobody. We softened him up. We didn't know he was even dead until it came out in the news. That's when we came back to see Murray and his girlfriend. If anybody killed him, it was them."

"Who were you working for?"

"That's where the dealing comes in," piped in Al Penney. "If he tells you that, he wants something for it."

McMaster smiled and folded his arms.

Windflower decided to shift gears. "What about running over Daphne Burry?" he asked.

"That was Marcel's idea. He was still upset about not getting anything from Sparky, and we heard that she and Vince had got stuff out of him."

"What kind of stuff?"

"Howse told us that they got dope and money after we left. She was running from us. I told Marcel to just scare her, but he ran her over. Then we took off."

"What about the fire?"

"I don't know anything about a fire. After he hit the girl, we were gone. We knew it was too hot for us around here. We went to Marystown. Marcel knows a girl there."

"You got Vince Murray out of jail?" asked Windflower.

"That wasn't that hard," said McMaster. "A few bucks the right way and a set of wire cutters," he said with a smirk.

"But then you killed Vince Murray."

"That was Marcel, too."

"He's not giving me much," said Windflower. "All he's doing is blaming other people when he was there and likely part of the whole deal."

"That's where who he's working with comes in," said the lawyer. "My client is not a nice man; he hangs out with all the wrong people, and they hurt each other. There are no innocents here. But he has a big fish on the end of his hook if you're interested. If not, good luck with your investigation."

This time Windflower looked at Ford as if to ask if he could trust the lawyer. Ford nodded to go ahead.

"What do you want?" asked Windflower.

"Okay, wise decision, Sergeant," said Penney. "My client would like immunity from prosecution in return for his testimony. And he, of course, will need protection once he turns."

"I don't have the authority to make that deal. But I will make the call," said Windflower.

"Make the call," said Penney.

Windflower and Ford left the room and went back to Ford's office. He called Superintendent Majesky. He wasn't there but called back soon afterwards. Windflower gave him the update on the speaker phone.

"It feels like he has something," said Windflower.

"Okay, tell him we'll plead him out as an accessory and that he still has to deal with whatever he has outstanding," said Majesky. "You'll have to process this with the Crown down there."

"What about the protection?" asked Windflower.

"Tell him we can offer segregation and maybe relocation. But no witness protection. I already got my knuckles wrapped for suggesting that for the Burry woman. Seems the budget is more important than justice these days."

"Thank you, Superintendent," said Windflower.

"I think I'll have something from my inquiries on those other matters soon," said Majesky discreetly. "I'll let you know."

Windflower turned to Ford. "Let's see what happens."

45

Windflower and Ford went back to the boardroom where Everett McMaster and his lawyer Al Penney were waiting for them.

"I have good news," said Windflower. "I have authorization to continue our discussions."

McMaster confidently smirked at his lawyer, who was not as excited as his client. "What are the parameters of your authorization?" Penney asked Windflower.

"We're off the record here," said Windflower. "Why don't you have your client tell us what he knows, and then I'll make my offer. If it's good, we keep talking. If not, we lock him up again."

This time Penney looked at his client for approval.

"We were working for Howse," said McMaster.

"Michael Howse?" asked Windflower.

"No, that douchebag is a loser. His old man, Cec Howse. He hired us to collect money that he said Sparkes owed him."

"Are you saying that Cec Howse was involved with some drug deal?" asked Windflower.

"All I know is that Cec Howse was financing his son Michael and Sparky. They were running the drug operation along with his brother."

"Whose brother?"

"Sparky's brother, Big Billy," said McMaster.

"Anything else?"

"Because I want you to know I am fully cooperatin', I can tell you who killed Sparky, too."

"Who?"

"Daphne Burry. I heard her talking to Vince before we left. She said they should kill him so he doesn't turn on them. She said she had a needle that would do the job."

"My client has given you plenty," said Al Penney. "What's your offer?"

"We can lower the charges on all this to accessory," said Windflower. "He does the minimum, plus whatever else he has back in Ontario, if he testifies in court."

"What about protection, man? They'll kill me in the joint."

"We can offer segregation and then perhaps a relocation package," said Windflower.

"We'll have to talk about it," said Penney.

"Let us know," said Windflower. Ford rose and called the guard to take the prisoner back to his cell, and the police officers walked back to Ford's office.

"You were good," said Ford. "But I'm not surprised. You were always good."

"Thank you for your help, Bill," said Windflower. "Can I leave this all with you, now? I'll talk to the Crown if things move along."

"No worries," said Ford. "We'll take most of it from here. We'll still have to investigate and prosecute on the Vince Murray case anyway."

"Okay, let me know what Al Penney has to say. I'm heading back. I'm supposed to see Cec Howse when I get back."

"That should be interesting. Let's stay in touch."

"I'll call," said Windflower.

He had lots to think about now, but fortunately there was plenty of time to do just that. He stopped at Goobies for a cup of tea and then hit Highway 210 on the way back home. The drive was pleasant and relatively uneventful as he sipped his tea and listened to another CD that Herb Stoodley had provided as part of his ongoing classical music education. Today it was Franz Liszt's Hungarian Rhapsody No. 2.

Stoodley had told him that Liszt was as popular in his day as Lady Gaga is in today's modern music. This particular piece was one of Liszt's most requested and most famous. Windflower loved it the first time he heard it and enjoyed it even more with every playing. The piece was a little slow at first but very melodic. Stoodley explained that the second section, the friska he called it, featured alternating tonic and dominant harmonization, and its energetic rhythms always had Windflower's toes tapping, even as he drove along the highway.

He was almost sad to hear the crescendo of octaves rising and falling across the entire range of the keyboard, bringing the rhapsody to a conclusion. He was sad but also very relaxed. He thought about a quote that Doc Sanjay had once told him, from Tagore of course: 'The world speaks to me in colours, my soul answers in music.' He was still thinking about that when his phone chirped at him. It was Betsy.

"Good day, Betsy. How are you?" he asked.

"I'm well, Sergeant. I hope they treated you well in Clarenville."

"Yes, Betsy. Your colleague was very nice."

"Mary said you were on your way back. I wanted to let you know that Mr. Howse will be coming at five. You will be back by then, or should I get him to come later?"

"That should be good. Who is there this afternoon?"

"Constable Evanchuk, Sir. Shall I ask her to wait for you? I'll have to go home to get Bob's supper ready."

"Yes, that would be great. See you tomorrow, Betsy."

Windflower hung up from Betsy and immediately made another call.

"Majesky," came the voice through the speaker.

"Superintendent, I thought you should know my perp in Clarenville says that Daphne Burry may have killed Paul Sparkes," said Windflower.

"That's the guy you found on the trail," said Majesky.

"Yes, and he says that he and his buddy were working for Cec Howse."

"What do you think?"

"Well, it's possible that Burry was involved with the murder. Didn't I hear the doctor say she was a diabetic?"

"I think so, easy enough to confirm?" asked Majesky. "But what difference does that make?"

"Doctor Sanjay said that Sparkes died from an insulin overdose," said Windflower. "It's not proof, but it's a theory. As for who they were working for, I'm seeing Cec Howse when I get back to Grand Bank this afternoon."

"Let me know what he says. It's a real bag of snakes, isn't it?"

"Good description, Sir. I'll let you know," said Windflower.

What was that verse by Shakespeare? Windflower racked his brain. Finally, he remembered:

> You spotted snakes with double tongue,
> Thorny hedgehogs, be not seen;
> Newts and blind-worms, do no wrong;
> Come not near our fairy queen.

But who was the fairy queen? Not likely Daphne Burry, he thought as he parked his Jeep in front of the detachment. He checked his watch. Right on time. But there was only one vehicle alongside his, an RCMP cruiser.

He walked inside. Evanchuk was sitting at Betsy's desk reading a report.

"Hi, Sergeant. I was waiting for you. Mr. Howse hasn't showed yet. Should I call him?" she asked.

"No, give him a few more minutes," said Windflower. "How are you?"

"I'm okay," said Evanchuk. "Can we talk for a minute while we're waiting?"

46

Windflower settled down across from Evanchuk and nodded that he had time to talk. Evanchuk paused, and Windflower waited patiently until she was ready.

"I'm not the only one," she finally said.

"What do you mean?" asked Windflower.

"There is another woman who says she was harassed by Raymond. She called me, and she said she heard of at least two more from his earlier days in New Brunswick. But they're afraid to come forward. The woman said that Raymond heard she was going to speak out and that he threatened her. The women felt intimidated by him."

Windflower stood staring at Evanchuk for a few seconds and was about to reply when the door flew open and in came Cec Howse. "Stay here," said Windflower. "We'll talk before I go home, okay?" Evanchuk nodded.

"What's all this about, Sergeant? I'm a busy man," said Howse.

"I'm sure you are, Mr. Howse," said Windflower. "We're all busy these days. Come in my office, please."

Cec Howse glared at Evanchuk but followed Windflower.

"Why didn't you tell us that your son, Michael, was living at your trailer in Grand Beach?" asked Windflower.

"Michael is a druggie and a flake. I never know where he is," said Howse. "He comes and goes like the wind, usually more like a storm. I end up cleaning up after him."

"What about Everett McMaster and Marcel Perreault? Do you know them?" asked Windflower.

"I know everybody," said Cec Howse. "And everybody in this town knows me."

"What was your relationship with those two men? One of them told me that they were working for you."

"I hired them to collect some money for me, that's true. But they are not my kind of people. They serve a purpose. I don't have a relationship with them."

"They were hired by you to collect money from Paul Sparkes, is that correct?"

"Listen, Sergeant, most of this town owes me money. I'm like the local Money Mart. They can't borrow money from the bank, so they turn to me. I'm doing them a favour," said Howse.

"Did you know that Paul Sparkes was financing a drug deal?"

"What people do with the money is up to them. I did not commit a crime, and I have no knowledge of any criminal activity. Now, if you'll excuse me, I have a dinner engagement with a beautiful woman." Howse rose to leave.

"I'm going to ask you not to leave the area," said Windflower. "We are now investigating two murders and associated crimes, and your name has come up more than once."

"Don't mess with me, Sergeant. I know you think you are the authority around here. But money is the real power. I was here long before you, and I will be here long after you're gone."

"Are you threatening me?" asked Windflower, trying unsuccessfully not to raise his voice.

"That's not how I do business. I'm sure we can come to some mutual arrangement. Think about it. And your young family." With that, Howse was up and out the door, leaving Windflower speechless.

He was still sitting there with his mouth open when Evanchuk came to see him a few minutes later.

"Are you okay?" she asked.

"Yeah, yeah, just surprised a little," said Windflower. "So tell me what's going on with you. I should tell you that Majesky told me about the seriousness of your complaint. I'm sorry you had to go through that, and I still think you're very brave."

"Thank you," said Evanchuk. "I've processed most of it now. I'm angrier about letting it go on as long as it did. Mad with myself."

"It's not easy to come forward," said Windflower.

"I know," said Evanchuk. "That's why I wanted to talk to you. The woman I spoke with wants to tell her story but doesn't know how to do it or who to go to. I suggested the superintendent, but that seemed too much for her. I think if she talks, the others might come out, too."

"This is big," said Windflower, thinking about what she had said for a moment. "What about bringing Ron Quigley into this? You can vouch for him with the others, and he's a pretty square shooter."

"That would be great. But he's in Ottawa."

"He's coming back to take a look around at the opioid situation in Newfoundland as part of his work with the task force. They want to check out the possibility that purple heroin is in the province."

"That would be great," said Evanchuk, looking visibly relieved. "I actually thought about calling him before."

"Great. He'll be in Marystown tomorrow. We'll get him to come over."

"Thank you so much again, Sergeant. You don't know how much I appreciate your help."

"No worries. Now, if you'll excuse me, I'm going home to see my beautiful wife and even more beautiful daughter."

"Have a good night, Sir. See you in the morning."

Windflower started to drive home and remembered he had one more call to make. He sat in the parking lot of the detachment and called Uncle Frank.

His Auntie Marie answered the phone. "Frank's not here," said his aunt. "He's gone out again on the land with his apprentice. I don't think he'll be back for a few days. He has a cabin up there and provisions for a week, plus whatever fish he can catch."

"That's too bad," said Windflower. "I wanted to talk to him. He was in my dream."

"That is powerful medicine," said Auntie Marie. "To have someone you know, someone who is still living, show up is a big sign. Tell me about it."

Windflower told his aunt about the brief but vivid dream, including Uncle Frank's warning about the fire. "Does that mean I'm in danger?" he asked.

"One step at a time, my little rabbit. Haven't you been having other dreams as well? Tell me about those, too."

He told Auntie Marie about the other dreams and how he felt better after listening and paying attention to what he had heard and seen.

"That's very good," said his aunt. "Now, think carefully. Was there a fire in this dream, or did Uncle Frank only talk about a fire?"

"There was no fire," said Windflower. "That's interesting because in all the other dreams there was a fire with my allies around it."

"Hmm, fire can mean many things in a dream, everything from destruction to desire, illumination to transformation, enlightenment to anger. The fact that you are afraid, and I can hear that in your voice, might mean that it is simply a warning to be alert and careful. Maybe you are underestimating your risks in some part of your life."

"That is interesting. It does feel like I'm on the cusp of something, maybe a new beginning."

"Stay vigilant then. More will be revealed. I do not believe you are in imminent danger, but watch for the fire in your next dream. That should tell you more."

"Thank you, Auntie. You are very helpful, as usual."

"Fire is also our male energy. But it must be balanced with water, our female side. Like Grandfather Sun and Grandmother Moon, everything needs to be in balance. Look for the water in your dream, too. And seek it out in your life as well."

"Is that female energy outside of me? Do I have to get it from a woman?"

"There are some things that you can only get from a woman. Otherwise we wouldn't be here," Auntie Marie said with a hearty laugh. "But we are all things together. You have that part, that energy in you. You should find it and use it. Now, go home and kiss my angel for me, and your lovely partner. I will get Frank to call you when he returns."

"Good night, Auntie."

Feeling much more relieved, but now a little tired and more than a little hungry, he pointed his Jeep towards home and his perfect little family. Everyone was pleased to see him, and after greeting them all appropriately, he and Sheila enjoyed a wonderful dinner of homemade macaroni and cheese with fresh, hot garlic bread and a nice evening at home.

That night he was a little anxious about having another dream. But that quickly passed when he snuggled into Sheila and felt the warm, happy glow of tiredness wash over him and lull him to sleep.

47

Windflower woke refreshed and relieved. He slept through the night and didn't have any dreams to disturb him, although a smaller piece of him would've liked to have had a dream. That way, he'd have more clarity about the lessons he was supposed to be learning. He thought about that a little more, but not for long because he soon heard Amelia Louise calling for attention.

It was a very nice start to his day as he changed the baby and brought her to her mother. He ran downstairs and put the coffee on before jumping in the shower to clean up. He got coffee for himself and Sheila, telling a waiting Lady that he would be right back, and went back up for a few minutes of early morning playtime with Amelia Louise.

Sheila sipped her coffee and watched while her favourite people in the world fully enjoyed each other's company.

"How do you feel today?" she asked.

"I feel good," said Windflower. "Lots of stuff spinning around at work, but I'm okay. I talked to Auntie Marie last night. That helped."

"It's always good to connect with family," she said.

"Uncle Frank is away for a few days, but Auntie Marie helped settle me down, told me to focus on balance. I think that was good advice."

"Balance is good. You're getting better at it, you know."

"Thank you, Sheila. Auntie Marie says I have to work on my female side, my water."

"Now that you need a lot of work on," teased Sheila.

Windflower faked mock outrage and then threw a pillow at her. Amelia Louise screamed, "Da, da, da."

"Encouraging your daughter in such behaviour is despicable," said Sheila as she picked up another pillow and hurled it at Windflower's head, just missing him as he ducked.

"Oh yeah," said Windflower, and he laid the baby on the bed and jumped on top of Sheila. Soon all three of them were tangled up completely and laughing out of control.

"I better go walk the dog," he said, extracting himself from the pile.

"Want some eggs?"

"That would be great."

"Gate," said Amelia Louise. When her parents looked at her and laughed, she repeated, "Gate, gate, gate."

"She'll have eggs, too," said Windflower. "I'll be right back."

Windflower took an eager Lady out into the bright sunshine of the morning. It was a glorious day, and because he was a little later than usual, Windflower got to say hello to many of his neighbours and the regulars down at the wharf. There were fewer of the old guys these days at the wharf because the ongoing construction of the waterfront beautification project was making it noisy.

"Why is it so loud and dirty when they say they're trying to make it beautiful?" asked one old codger.

"That's a good question," said Windflower.

"Seems to me it were pretty beautiful to start with, eh b'y," said the man.

"I agree," said Windflower as he pulled Lady away and headed home for his breakfast. Amelia Louise had already started hers, and as usual Lady was happy to help clean up what the baby had thrown overboard. Amelia Louise laughed at Lady when she saw her eating up the food on the floor, laughed at Molly who had come to inspect and laughed at Windflower as he sat next to her high chair.

"Somebody's pretty happy today," said Windflower.

"She's always happy," said Sheila, handing him a plate with fruit, scrambled eggs and a piece of raisin toast. "I think the reason we have kids is to show us how happy we can be with the smallest things."

"We have lots to learn from children, especially before they get to school and start picking up everybody else's anxieties and worries."Windflower smiled at Sheila, which caused Amelia Louise to laugh again.

He could still hear her laughing when he closed the door and went to his Jeep. He had a lot to do this morning, but he also needed time to think. He drove down to the beach and parked his vehicle. He walked along the beach and felt himself unwind as the water flowed in and out in a steady but peaceful current.

He thought about all the things going on with him at home, at work and maybe even in his head. His family life was better than good, and the decision to make the repairs to the B & B felt right. Expensive, but right. When he started to look closer at his life, it seemed that more of his anxiety and ill ease was coming from work. Part of it was because of Raymond, but more of it was because of something stirring deep inside. What was it? As he walked along the beach, it came to him. For the first time in a long time, maybe ever, he wasn't proud and happy to wake up as a member of the Royal Canadian Mounted Police.

That was a disturbing revelation. So now he had a choice, or maybe he had a few choices. He could do nothing. That was certainly a choice, he thought, but that would make him even more frustrated and ungrateful. He knew from experience that what he was not grateful for, he would lose. Not right away. Things didn't work that fast usually, but over time they would slip away. Another choice was to embrace the change that he felt was coming and consciously work to make the best of his final period as a Mountie. Or he could change his attitude and keep a job that had given him so many gifts for so long. Wow, that was a lot to think about right there.

But that wasn't all he had to grapple with. What about all the other Mounties like Evanchuk and his two beat cops, Jones and Smithson? They both needed his advice and guidance, to say nothing of Eddie Tizzard, whom he loved like a brother. But quite possibly Tizzard wasn't a Mountie anymore. And anyway, neither he nor Tizzard had to be on the Force so they could be friends.

And he wanted answers to the many questions he still had about the Sparkes and Murray murders and the hit and run of Daphne Burry. Technically, the Vince Murray case wasn't his, but he counted it on his list of unresolved matters. It fit in somewhere, but where? And who killed Paul Sparkes? What was the operation that was of so much interest and, apparently, had so much money? What roles did Michael or Cec Howse have in all of this? And had Cec Howse tried to threaten or bribe him, or both, the day before?

Despite all of the questions, his head started to clear even as he noticed the fog coming back over the Grand Bank Cape to ruin the perfect morning. Well, that was good while it lasted, he thought both of the walk and the fine weather. Now it was time to go to work. First up, he needed to talk to Ron Quigley about the other women that were having problems with Acting Inspector Raymond. As he drove into the RCMP offices, he realized that was going to be easy since Quigley's SUV was in the parking lot.

48

Quigley was sitting in the back talking with Smithson. Windflower said good morning and poured himself a coffee. "We should chat," he said to Quigley. He turned to go to his office.

"Boss, I need to tell you something if you have a minute," said Smithson.

"Sure," said Windflower.

"We got a call last night from somebody who lives down near where the fire was," said Smithson. "He said he thinks he knows who was driving away in the pickup before the explosion. It was Billy Sparkes."

"Big Billy? The brother to Paul Sparkes, the dead guy I found wrapped up on the trail?" asked Windflower. "Is he sure?"

"He says he thought it might have been but wasn't completely sure. That's why he didn't come forward before now. But I guess he saw Billy Sparkes in Marystown with his pickup yesterday, and he's sure now."

"Interesting," said Windflower. "Can you ask Mr. Sparkes to come and see us? Tell him we have a few questions. If he's reluctant, can you go and pick him up? Take someone with you, though. Big Billy is, well, big."

"Yes, Sir," said Smithson.

"A break in the case?" asked Quigley as he settled in a chair in front of Windflower.

"Who knows at this point?" said Windflower. "We keep following our noses and hopefully something turns up. Anyway, I want to talk to you about Evanchuk."

Windflower ran through what he heard from Evanchuk about the other women. "They're afraid," said Windflower, "and with pretty good reason."

"You know, I heard rumblings about Raymond before. So did others. That's probably why it's Majesky on this case," said Quigley. "I should talk to Evanchuk first."

"That would be good. I don't know what her schedule is. She was here last evening. But call her. I'm sure she'd want to talk to you."

"How's Tizzard doing? You must miss him around here."

"I was thinking just that when I came in this morning. He would have had his feet up telling some yarn from his dad and eating, that's for sure."

Quigley laughed. "Well, he's not dead. Do you think it's worth asking him to reconsider?"

"Maybe," said Windflower. "But I might wait until this Evanchuk stuff gets sorted and see what Majesky is going to suggest."

Quigley paused for a moment. "That's why I need to talk to him," he said. "Majesky asked me for a recommendation."

Windflower's eyes grew big, and he wanted to ask Quigley what he was thinking about, but he resisted that urge. "I still think you should talk to Evanchuk first," was all he said.

"I'm going to call her now," said Quigley. "I'll let you get on with your day."

After Quigley left, Betsy came in to say good morning and to give him his messages. There was one from Bill Ford in Clarenville and another from Fire Chief Martin Hodder. He called the fire chief.

"Good morning, Chief. How are things?" asked Windflower.

"Things are good b'y," said Hodder. "I was calling you because you might want to take a look around over at the fire scene. They've knocked down the structure and are waiting to cart it away. But there was a finished basement, and most of it looks like it might be intact. One of my guys went down there, and he says there's some kind of equipment, like a mechanical mixer or something."

"Wow. That survived the fire?"

"There was a concrete slab on top of it. That's good protection. Plus, we managed to get the fire out pretty quickly once it started to rain. I'm going back over there right now."

"Great. I'll meet you there."

Windflower walked to the back where Quigley was finishing a

phone call. "Evanchuk," he said. "She's coming over around noon."

"Super," said Windflower. "Can you come with me? I have a feeling you want to see this."

They both got in Windflower's Jeep and drove to Coronation Street where the fire had been. It was easy to spot. A large pile of charred timber and random pieces of furniture were piled in a mountain of rubble. It still smelled like a fire. Hodder was getting out of his vehicle. Windflower did the introductions, and the fire chief led them to the back of the site where a narrow stairway led to the basement.

There was little light, so Hodder turned on his industrial flashlight and laid it on the floor. He used another smaller torch to shine a light around the room. Quigley took one look around and shouted out loud. "We need to get out of here. Now!!"

The three men scampered up the stairs. "If I'm right, this is a fentanyl production lab. Or it was. If that's the case, everyone who comes close could be in danger," said Quigley. "I saw at least two pill presses. That large machine that looks like a mixer, that's an industrial one. I saw a video on how it works."

Once they were away from the basement, Quigley started barking out orders. "We need to close off this scene. No one can get in," he said to Windflower, and then to Hodder, "Who's been down here?"

"Just my deputy, Marty Foote, and the three of us," said Hodder.

"Good," said Quigley. "Both of you need to get checked at the clinic. Exposure to the chemicals that might be present here could be fatal. It's a good sign that you haven't got sick yet, but this could be really serious."

"I'll have the entrance sealed and guarded," said Windflower. "Are you going to call forensics?"

"First, we'll need the lab techs," said Quigley. "They're in Halifax, but I'll see if they can chopper over. Then forensics can take a look around."

"Is this really where they were mixing up drugs?" asked Chief Hodder. "In the middle of Grand Bank?"

"It looks like it," said Quigley. "I saw a similar set-up out in Edmonton that was capable of producing 120,000 fentanyl pills a day."

"Holy . . . ," said Windflower, leaving the second part of that exclamation hanging in the air.

"Yeah, two people, a middle-aged couple in a quiet neighbour-hood in Edmonton. Pretty scary stuff. Some of the first responders got exposed, and one of them got really sick. That's why the first step is to secure and clean the scene. Even minuscule amounts of fentanyl can cause an overdose or death."

"I'll stay here, and we can handle the scene until you get your guys here," said Hodder.

"Thanks, Chief," said Windflower. "I'll send somebody over."

Quigley was already on his phone talking to Halifax. "Okay, let me know," he said as he hung up. "They think they can come over tonight."

"That'll be good," said Windflower. "Is anybody around here in danger?"

"Not unless they go downstairs," said Quigley. "But they were all in great danger while that lab was in production. It looks like they left in a hurry. They don't usually leave their pill presses and equipment."

"Where do they get that stuff anyway?"

"You can buy anything you want on the Internet. But those industrial pill presses are illegal and just having one can bring a massive fine and jail time."

"I guess the risk is worth the reward."

"They seem to think so. Every day they'll produce 100,000 or more pills. At even five dollars a pop, it's pretty good money. It's what makes dealing with this so difficult. It's cheap and relatively easy to get into, and there's bags and bags of money to be made."

"Enough money to get people killed."

"Absolutely, and enough to not worry about the thousands of people that die from overdoses."

"Okay," said Windflower. "I'll find Smithson and get him on security detail. Will you look after everything else?"

"Yeah, I got it," said Quigley. "I'll call forensics while I'm wait-ing for Evanchuk."

Windflower waved goodbye as he left Quigley to make his calls.

49

Windflower found Betsy waiting for him at the office. "Good morning, Sir," she said. "Looks like you've been busy already this morning.

"Good morning, Betsy," said Windflower. "Yes indeed. Will you call Smithson and ask him to go over to the fire scene on Coronation Street? The fire chief will give him directions. He'll be there until a technical crew arrives sometime tonight."

"Goodness," said Betsy. "Sounds serious."

"It is serious. There might be some chemical contamination in the basement. But that's between us for now. We don't want to get people alarmed."

"Absolutely. You got a call from a lawyer, David Williams from St. John's. He would like to talk to you about his client, Cec Howse."

Windflower took the slip from Betsy as she went back to her office. He noticed she was smiling as she left. That was because she knew a secret that everybody in town would soon be calling her about. She wouldn't tell them anything, of course, except what her boss had intimated—that there was nothing for people to get upset about. Mission accomplished, thought Windflower as he called the St. John's number.

"Williams, Williams and Green," answered the receptionist.

Windflower knew of this law firm. It was one of the best and most connected in the province. They had a Liberal on staff, who was once party president, and a former Conservative member of the provincial legislature. Windflower wouldn't be surprised to learn they had lawyers from the NDP or even the Green party in their ranks, too. They covered all the political bases.

"David Williams," said the lawyer.

"Good morning. It's Sergeant Winston Windflower from the Grand Bank RCMP."

"Good morning, Sergeant," said Williams. "Thank you for calling me back. My client Cec Howse tells me you have been making enquiries about some of his business arrangements."

"We're involved in a murder investigation," said Windflower. "Your client's name has come up a few times now. We were asking him about his loans to a deceased person. We still have questions about that."

"Are you accusing my client of any particular offence?"

"We're simply seeking his co-operation in this investigation. Perhaps you can help to clarify his relationship with the deceased in this case, Paul Sparkes, and the full nature of his business with him."

"It is my understanding that this was a perfectly legitimate business loan to Mr. Sparkes," said Williams. "Mr. Sparkes was seeking capital to enter the recreational cannabis market."

"There's also the question of how a trailer at Grand Beach, which is owned by your client, came to become a murder scene."

"That property is owned by my client, but as you can tell from its appearance, it has been neglected for some time. That might make it an eyesore, but that's not a crime. As I understand it, you have individuals in custody who are the primary suspects in this case. I might suggest that you focus your attention on them."

"Thank you for the suggestion," said Windflower, beginning to tire of the St. John's lawyer's style. "But there is also the involvement of Michael Howse in all of this. He was at the trailer at the time that the murder occurred."

"That is speculation, Sergeant," said Williams. "But now that you raise Michael Howse, I want to inform you that my firm will be representing him as well. You have 12 hours to charge him or release him before our associates appear in court in Sudbury on his behalf."

Windflower was stuck now. He really didn't have enough to charge either of the Howses. The lawyer sensed his hesitation. "Sergeant, far be it for me to tell the RCMP how to do their jobs. But I would suggest that you cease what could be perceived as harassment of my client in Grand Bank and get on with your usually excellent police work."

Windflower hated the condescending tone but, at least for now, had to admit to himself that the lawyer was right. He had no intention of telling Williams that. "Thank you, Mr. Williams. We will continue to follow all leads and interview witnesses as appropriate to resolve our case," he said.

He thought he could hear David Williams start to say something else but hung up the phone. He was more than a little irritated and replayed the conversation in his head, trying to think how he could have handled it any better. While he was pondering that, he saw Evanchuk walk by his office. He thought it looked like she was going to see Quigley, but Quigley popped his head into his office.

"I've talked to forensics, but they're all tied up. So, I checked with the technical crew, and they've got forensics capacity and will check for evidence and prints," he said. "I'm going to talk with Evanchuk now. We should go for lunch afterwards."

"That sounds great." While Windflower waited for Quigley, he busied himself with his increasing mound of paperwork. A half hour in, a flushed Evanchuk hurried by his office and out the front door. He could hear her vehicle rush away.

Quigley came by a little later. "Let's talk over lunch. I've already got a call into Majesky."

Windflower rose and was walking out with Quigley when Betsy called him over. Quigley went outside to wait. "Constable Smithson has gone over to Coronation Street," she said in a whisper.

"Why are you whispering?" asked Windflower.

"I didn't want anyone to overhear us," said Betsy. "You know, about the situation."

"There's nobody here but us."

"You can never be too careful. Constable Smithson also said to tell you that Billy Sparkes had agreed to come in and will be over this afternoon."

"Thank you, Betsy," said Windflower. "I'm going for lunch with Inspector Quigley."

50

Quigley and Windflower decided to walk down to the Mug-Up despite the dark and dreary day that had developed. Windflower had been right to fear the fog's re-emergence. It was back with a vengeance. It was thick, soupy and wet and hung over everything like a gray blanket. Windflower had come to expect fog after so many years living in Grand Bank, and Quigley had grown up in the east end of St. John's where he claimed he'd not just lost his way home in the fog many times but had lost several small pets to the fog as well.

"What did she say?" asked Windflower as they approached the café.

"She told me her story and what she'd heard about others," said Quigley. "But she said she couldn't tell their story, that was up to them. She agreed to contact the woman in Marystown and ask her to relay the message that I was open to helping them get their concerns up the line."

"Fair enough."

"I agree," said Quigley, opening the door to the Mug-Up for Windflower. "I said I was going to tell Majesky what she had told me, and she was fine with that. Now we'll see what they and he want to do about it."

Windflower said hello to Herb Stoodley, who was chatting with a customer at the cash. A few moments later he approached their table with two cups of coffee. "Good day, Sergeant, and welcome back, Inspector. Hope you're back for good now."

"Not quite," said Quigley. "But it's nice to be here, even with the fog."

"Well, if Shakespeare lived here," said Stoodley, "he wouldn't say, 'it raineth every day,' although that would be close. He might say that it foggeth every second one, and he'd be right on. Now would you gentlemen like some lunch?"

Both men laughed. "I'll have turkey soup and a bun, please," said Quigley.

"I'll have a turkey and dressing sandwich on whole wheat," said Windflower.

While they were waiting for their lunch, Windflower told Quigley about his interactions with Cec Howse and now his lawyer. "Unless I come up with something soon, we'll have to let the young guy go, too."

"You could charge him with something and bring him back," said Quigley.

"That's tricky. I'd have to get Raymond's approval for the expense, and he's not likely going to go for that."

"True, but Majesky might. Let me run it by him. It sounds like Michael Howse might have something pivotal to say about all of this, and if he goes free up in Ontario, he'll be gone."

"Okay, thanks Ron," said Windflower as Herb Stoodley returned with their meal.

"Thank you, Herb," said Quigley. "You know, I don't mind this kind of weather."

"You're from St. John's. That explains everything," said Stoodley as Quigley blew on his soup to cool it down.

"It's more than just that," said Quigley. "'Clouds come floating into my life, no longer to carry rain or usher storm, but to add colour to my sunset sky.'"

Herb Stoodley laughed and walked away. The two officers ate their lunch and resisted the urge to add cheesecake to their meal. Quigley even paid, which pleased Windflower almost as much as his lunch. The pair strolled back together. Quigley stopped just before the detachment door when his cellphone rang. "Majesky," he mouthed to Windflower.

Windflower nodded and started to go inside. Then he stopped and stared at a vehicle in the parking lot. It was a black pickup, a Ford F-150. He went inside where Betsy greeted him immediately.

"Billy Sparkes is in your office," she said.

Windflower squeezed by the bigger man, who, based on the whiff Windflower got as he went by, hadn't changed his clothes or washed in a week.

"Waz all dis about?" asked Sparkes.

"Thank you for coming in," said Windflower. "Were you around Grand Bank last Tuesday night?" he asked.

"No b'y," said Sparkes. "I wuz 'ome wid da missus."

"Somebody saw you here," said Windflower. "Somebody saw you driving away in your pickup truck, just after the big fire started."

"No b'y," said Sparkes. "Dey must be mistaken. And I resents da fact dat yer accusin' me of sumtin. Me brudder is dead. Murdered and ye does nuttin about dat. Now ye wants to blame me fer sumtin else. I wants me lawyah."

Sparkes started speaking louder with every interjection he made, and by the end he was standing up screaming at Windflower. Ron Quigley came running in to see what was going on.

"Everything okay?" he asked.

"Fine," said Windflower. "Sit down, Mr. Sparkes. We're just having a conversation. But we're not communicating very well. Do you want to tell me what you were doing in Grand Bank last week or do you want me to arrest you?"

"I wants me lawyah," said Sparkes.

"Okay, come with me," said Windflower. "We'll help you call your lawyer. Then I'm putting you in the back."

"Ye 'restin me?" asked Sparkes.

"Not yet," said Windflower. "You are being held on suspicion of arson. Let's go."

He took the large man to the boardroom where he made his phone call. He put him in a cell, locked the door and came back to his office.

"Is he the guy?" asked Quigley.

"I don't know yet, but we've got a witness putting him and his truck at the scene, both heading off in a hurry just before people heard an explosion."

"So he's got some explaining to do."

"Exactly. We'll see what he and his lawyer can cook up. What did Majesky say?"

"He said to bring Michael Howes back from Sudbury."

"Great, I'll call the Crown and get that moving," said Windflower. "And what did the superintendent say about Evanchuk?"

"He said he wasn't surprised. Someone slipped him a note when he got to Marystown, and he's been doing some digging on Raymond from his time in New Brunswick. There were complaints, but they all got dropped or buried somewhere."

"Geez. I thought that stuff was in the past with all this talk about dignity in the workplace and everything else we hear now."

"I think it's changing. But some of the older guys are still clinging on to bad behaviour as if it's their right."

"Listen, if a sergeant like me can get bullied, we haven't moved the needle very far," said Windflower. "I'm like Evanchuk now. I'm angry about all this."

"Give it a few more days and let's see where the dust settles," said Quigley. "I still have faith in Majesky."

51

The rest of the afternoon flew by in a bit of a blur for Windflower as he dealt with the Crown Attorney's office to get charges drawn up against Michael Howse and then relayed to Elliot Lake. He was pleased when he got a call back from Assistant Crown Attorney Lauren Bartlett telling him it had all been squared away.

"Thank you very much for your help with this," said Windflower.

"No problem, Sergeant," said Bartlett. "I thought you should know one more thing, though. We have an active investigation on his father, Cecil Howse."

"Oh, that's interesting," said Windflower. "Can you tell me anything about that case?"

"Well, it's public record that we're investigating fraud and embezzlement of funds from his company. The fraud relates to some of the government contract work that they've been engaged in. The embezzlement is a personal case against Cecil Howse. No decisions yet, but we're getting close."

Windflower thanked Bartlett for the information and then hung up. Very interesting, he thought. But he didn't have much more time to think. Just then, Billy Sparkes started kicking up a fuss because, according to him at least, he was hungry. He was shouting something about cruel and inhumane punishment until Windflower sent Betsy out to get him a fish and chips from the takeout.

Soon after, Sheila called Windflower to let him know that she had to take Amelia Louise over for her checkup and to see if he was coming home for supper. When she heard that Ron Quigley was there, she suggested he join them.

Windflower was happy to have Quigley go home with him at the end of the day. They were good friends, and Sheila liked him. Windflower often thought that she might have ended up with Ron if he hadn't been around. That's Ron's loss but certainly my gain, he thought as they pulled into his driveway.

Amelia Louise crawled right up to her daddy when he opened the door, followed closely by Molly and Lady. They all inspected Quigley to see if he was friend or foe. Once they discovered he was friendly, they were all over him. That gave Windflower a chance to go say hello to Sheila and give her a peck on the cheek and a hug.

"That smells wonderful," he said.

"Yes, what have you got going in the kitchen?" asked Quigley.

"It's ravioli," said Sheila. "I made a double batch the last time we had it and froze it. And garlic bread, the very hint of which makes my knees weak."

"Mine too," said Quigley.

"Winston, why don't you take Amelia Louise and Lady around the block?" asked Sheila. "Neither of them have been out all day. Ron and I will have a glass of wine while we're waiting for supper."

Windflower bundled up Amelia Louise against the fog and got Lady's leash. Soon they were out making their way through town. Windflower took a detour to go to Coronation Street. Smithson was sitting in his cruiser out front.

"Evenin', Boss," said Smithson.

"Things quiet?" asked Windflower.

"Except for everybody on the street asking me what's going on, it's pretty dull."

"Good. I like dull. Is Jones on tonight?"

"Yes, she should be there now."

"Can you call her and arrange to do a switch with her? We need someone to stay overnight at the detachment with Billy Sparkes and still maintain security here. One of you can nap over there when you're not here."

"Perfect. I'll call Jones."

"Have a good night," said Windflower as he tugged Lady and the three finished their walk.

When they arrived, the kitchen table was set and Quigley was playing with Molly. "I see you've become acquainted with another of our family members," said Windflower. He took Amelia Louise's coat and hat off her, picked her up and swung her in the air before setting her down in her high chair.

Sheila gave the baby a small, cooled portion of food and started serving up the ravioli and salad. Windflower pulled off a chunk of still-steamy garlic bread and popped a piece in his mouth. When he tasted the ravioli, he purred. So did Quigley.

"I forgot how good home-cooked food tasted," said Quigley.

"This is wonderful, Sheila," said Windflower. "What's your secret?"

"You know what, nothing really special," she said. "But I found this recipe that called for a dash of nutmeg. I think that makes a difference."

"It is grand," said Quigley, holding up his plate for more, with Windflower close behind.

Even though everyone was stuffed full of ravioli, evidenced by the mere spoonful remaining in the baking dish, there was still room for a dessert of cherry pie and ice cream. After the meal was finished, Windflower let Quigley read a bedtime story to Amelia Louise and watched as her little eyes fought to stay open. Eventually, she shut her eyes completely, and she was gone. He brought her upstairs and put her to bed.

Quigley stayed for one more cup of tea and soon headed off to the motel so he would be wide awake for the technical crew's early arrival the next morning. Sheila and Windflower also had an early night, and before Windflower knew it, he heard Amelia Louise playing in the next room, her way of greeting the morning. He walked over and picked her up. She smiled at him, and everything was good in both their worlds.

After coffee he had a mini-walk with Lady. While they were out, he heard a noise like thunder over his head. Lady was so startled she pulled away from him and started running home. He chased after her and, looking up, noticed a helicopter. Then he heard the noise subside and guessed it landed at the RCMP detachment.

He managed to finally catch up to Lady and grab her before walking the last few steps to home. He still had time for some toast and cheese for breakfast with Sheila and Amelia Louise and was then off to work. He had a feeling that the day was going to be a big one. He was right.

As soon as he got there, he could hear Billy Sparkes yelling and Smithson trying, unsuccessfully so far, to calm him down.

"What's going on in here?" asked Windflower.

"Mr. Sparkes wants his lawyer and would like to get released," said Smithson, breathing a little easier now that his boss was there.

"Now," thundered Sparkes.

"Have you called the lawyer's office?" asked Windflower.

"He's on his way," said Smithson. "Frederick Hawkins," he added after reading his notes.

"Freddy will get me out," said Sparkes. "'E'll see dat youse 'ave set me up."

"Get Mr. Sparkes a fresh cup of coffee," said Windflower. "I'm going over to Coronation Street. Call me when his lawyer gets here."

Windflower ignored the yelling and the stream of profanities that followed him as he left the building and drove over to the fire scene.

52

Quigley's vehicle was parked outside along with the fire chief's. He was talking with Jones when Windflower arrived.

"You can go home," Windflower told Jones. "Our part is done here, at least for now. Get some rest."

"Thanks, Boss. See you, Inspector," said Jones as she left.

"Any news yet?" asked Windflower.

"They just started a little while ago," said Quigley. "We commandeered the fire chief's vehicle to transport their equipment over. They've set up a mobile lab in the back. There's three of them. Here comes O'Neill now."

A tall man wearing an RCMP baseball hat and an opened hazmat suit came strolling towards them. "Phil O'Neill," he said, holding out his hand to Windflower. "Technical services."

"Nice to meet you. Winston Windflower. Welcome to Grand Bank."

"Well, there's certainly presence of some chemicals. We set up our test lab in the van. It's not exact but will give us an indication," said O'Neill, holding up a number of clear plastic bags with what looked like swabs inside. "And my guys are starting to do the prints right now. We'll know more by lunchtime."

"You guys are fast," said Windflower.

"We have to be," said O'Neill, disappearing into the back of the van.

"Are you staying here?" Windflower asked Quigley.

"Yeah, I'll stick around and make my calls from here," he said.

"Great. In that case, I'm heading back. I think there's a lawyer in my future, Freddy Hawkins. You remember him?"

"Fat Freddy. Is he still kicking around?"

"Defender of the downtrodden and those who claim to be falsely accused."

"It's not his conscience that guides him, but his pocketbook," said Quigley. "As long as he gets paid, he's happy."

Windflower's cellphone rang. "I bet that Freddy has arrived," he said.

Frederick Hawkins was waiting for him when he returned to the office. Windflower said hello to Betsy and walked to the boardroom where Billy Sparkes was sitting with his lawyer on one side of the table. Smithson was on the other side, closest to the door, looking like he was ready to outrun the others if need be, something he'd easily be able to do. If Big Billy Sparkes could be considered merely large, thought Windflower, then Hawkins would be at least an XXL.

"Sergeant," said Hawkins. "Nice to see you again. It's unfortunate that it always seems to be under unpleasant conditions."

"Indeed, Mr. Hawkins," said Windflower, waiting for the lawyer to speak his mind.

"Well, it seems we have a misunderstanding," said Hawkins. "We think you've got the wrong man."

"We've got an eye witness who claims your client was here on the night of the fire, and he was seen driving away after other people heard an explosion. The fire chief believes that the fire was deliberately set. That's a pretty serious situation," said Windflower. "So maybe your client can start by telling us what he was doing in Grand Bank that night?"

"I told youse, I wasn't 'ere," said Sparkes.

Hawkins gave him a 'shut up I'm talking' look. "There are lots of vehicles that look exactly like my client's," said the lawyer. "It was dark, and maybe your witness was confused."

"They weren't confused about your client," said Windflower. "They confirmed his identity after they saw him again in Marystown. I can bring the witness over to verify again if you wish."

"Give me a few moments with my client," said Hawkins.

Windflower walked to the back with Smithson to get another cup of coffee.

"It's him, isn't it?" asked Smithson.

"Probably," said Windflower. "But having him near the scene doesn't prove anything. I think Hawkins knows that, too. We'll need more evidence."

While they were waiting, Betsy came in to tell Windflower that there was a call for him. It was the Ontario Provincial Police.

"Good morning, Sergeant. My name is Len Ryan. I'm an inspector with the OPP Drug Enforcement Unit. I'm calling you about Michael Howse."

"Good morning, Inspector. What can I do for you?" asked Windflower.

"It's more that I wanted to let you know that we have an ongoing investigation into Michael Howse. He's been connected with a fentanyl ring that's operating out of southwestern Ontario, Kitchener-Waterloo and Hamilton in particular. We want to make sure that we don't lose track of him while we're still working on our case. He's being shipped down to Newfoundland this morning, isn't that right?"

"Yes, Sir," said Windflower. "We're looking at him for his involvement in a murder investigation, but it's starting to look pretty clear like they've been running some kind of drug operation out of this area as well. We have our lab guys checking out a location right now, and Inspector Ron Quigley, who's on the RCMP Opioid Task Force, is here looking after that."

"I know Ron," said Ryan. "I met him at a conference in Ottawa a few months ago. Good guy. Why don't you get him to give me a call? Here's my number. We'll work through him."

Windflower wrote down the number and put it in his pocket. When he hung up, Smithson came in to tell him that Sparkes and his lawyer were ready to talk.

"My client was in Grand Bank the night of the fire, but he had nothing to do with it. He was otherwise engaged," said Hawkins.

"What do you mean?" asked Windflower.

"He has a friend that he visits on occasion. He was visiting her that night."

"I assume that she will confirm that if we ask her."

"Absolutely."

"Okay, bring her in."

Billy Sparkes jumped up. "Ye tol' me dat she wouldn't 'ave to come," he shouted at his lawyer. "I did nuttin, nuttin."

"Take Mr. Sparkes back to his cell," Windflower told Smithson. "I'll talk to your witness when she gets here," he said to Hawkins.

Hawkins shrugged as Sparkes was led back to lock-up and left the RCMP offices, presumably to call the girlfriend. If there is a girlfriend, thought Windflower.

53

Windflower was sitting in his office when Ron Quigley came in.

"We got samples of fentanyl, heroin and likely carfentanil, too," reported Windflower. "And we got some prints that I'm getting Smithson to run through the system. We also got a call from the OPP, Inspector Len Ryan. He said he knew you."

"Yeah, he's with the drug squad. What did he want?" asked Quigley.

"Here's his number," said Windflower, pulling the paper out of his pocket. "He wants to talk to you. They're looking at Michael Howse in connection with a group dealing fentanyl in southwestern Ontario."

"That's interesting. I'll call him. When is Howse getting here?"

Betsy poked her head in Windflower's doorway. "Michael Howse is on the 4:20 flight in St. John's. We need to send someone to pick him up."

Quigley looked at Windflower after Betsy had left. "Can I have her?" he asked.

"She's mine and keep your hands off," said Windflower.

Smithson came in while the two men were still talking about how amazing Betsy was. "We've got some matches," said Smithson, holding up a handful of printouts. "Paul Sparkes and Vince Murray."

"Not surprising," said Windflower.

"Billy Sparkes, too," Smithson added.

"Is that the guy in back?" asked Quigley.

"Yup, mournful brother of the deceased," said Windflower. "Better call Freddy Hawkins and get him back," he said to Smithson.

"Tell him the girlfriend alibi won't be enough."

Smithson started to leave. "When you're finished that, can you go to St. John's? We have a prisoner transfer. Michael Howse."

"I would like to, Boss, but I just worked all night," said Smithson. "So did Jones. And Evanchuk is coming on at noon to do the overnight."

"Fair enough," said Windflower. "Call Hawkins and then hang around here for a while if you can."

Smithson nodded and went to make his call.

"Can I have permission to engage a private contractor to pick up Michael Howse?" asked Windflower. "They'll have to use an RCMP vehicle."

"Who are you thinking about?" asked Quigley.

"Eddie Tizzard."

Quigley thought for a moment. "I guess we haven't got a lot of choice. Why not?"

"Thanks," said Windflower.

Tizzard was surprised to hear from Windflower but pleased to find out that his services might be required. He was at the RCMP detachment minutes after the phone call. He was also happy to see everybody and to get access to his RCMP Jeep again.

"You're not on active duty. You are a private contractor," said Windflower. "Sign the forms with Betsy before you go to make sure you and the vehicle are covered for insurance. And you are not to talk to, interact with or in any way interfere with the prisoner. Is that clear?"

"Yes, Sarge. Thank you, Sarge. I was going out of my mind sitting around. I'll be careful, and I'll even drive slow," said Tizzard.

"Now you've gone too far," said Quigley, coming into Windflower's office as Tizzard was leaving. Tizzard laughed and waved goodbye before seeing Betsy and starting out for St. John's.

"He'll be okay," said Quigley.

"But he won't drive slowly," said Windflower. "That would be a stretch. They don't call him Fast Eddie for nothing."

Quigley laughed. "I talked to Len Ryan. He's sending me over a copy of the file. We'll get a chance to review it before Michael Howse gets here."

"Here comes Freddy Hawkins," said Windflower, looking out the window as the portly lawyer crept along. "Do you want to sit in?"

"Sure. It sounds like Billy Sparkes had some intimate knowledge of the equipment inside the house. Speaking of which, the lab guys are done over there. They've taken the equipment and packaged it up to take back with them. And they've sealed the basement with plastic and are putting a layer of cement over the hole."

"Fast and thorough. Did they bring cement powder over with them?"

"Home Hardware. They're going back tonight if the helicopter can get through the fog. If not, I said I'll drive them to Gander."

"Let's go see Freddy and his client," said Windflower.

"We haven't been able to contact our witness yet," said Hawkins when Windflower and Quigley came into the room.

"No worries," said Windflower.

Smithson brought Billy Sparkes into the room and sat him beside his lawyer. "We have some more evidence," said Windflower. Both Hawkins and Sparkes became remarkably and suddenly alert.

"We now have proof that your client was in the house on Coronation Street. We have his fingerprints," said Windflower.

"How does that connect him to the fire?" asked Hawkins.

"It may or may not," said Windflower. "But it does connect him to a fentanyl lab that was operating in the house. His fingerprints, the traces of fentanyl and other drugs and the machinery to produce the illicit product are all connected. We will continue to pursue the arson charge, but things just got a whole lot more serious for your client. Just possession of the pill press is pretty serious, right Inspector?"

"Penalties range from fines between $50,000 and $70,000 and up to a year in jail," said Quigley. "That's without the presence of drugs."

"None of dat is mine," said Sparkes. "Youse guys are settin' me up."

"Billy, please stay quiet," said Hawkins. "We will need to talk again," he said to Windflower.

"Take your time," said Windflower.

54

Windflower got an apple and a chunk of cheese from the kitchen for his lunch while Quigley went to check on the technical crew. When he came back, Freddy Hawkins came to tell them he and Billy Sparkes were ready to talk. They all went into the boardroom again.

"Well, Sergeant, my client would like to offer you some information. But he would like something in return," said Hawkins.

"You're not really in a position to bargain," said Windflower.

"We are not in the most advantageous position, that would be true," said the lawyer. "And you can proceed with some flimsy charges against my client that would likely keep him in jail for a short period of time. But is that truly in the interest of justice, when others may be guilty of even greater crimes against the state?"

"That's a great speech, but what exactly are you talking about?" asked Windflower.

"My client is a small player in a big game," said Hawkins. "He is willing to testify against the people who ran this operation, the big fish."

"And in return?" asked Windflower.

"He would like immunity from prosecution."

"I don't have that kind of authority."

"But your inspector might," said Hawkins, turning his attention to Quigley. "We hear he has been doing great work in Ottawa on that task force. Since this matter directly affects the opioid issue, we thought he might be particularly interested in what Mr. Sparkes has to say."

"I'm interested," said Quigley. "But Sergeant Windflower is running this investigation, and I'm sure he'd like to hear the nature of your client's evidence before making any recommendation to me or anyone else."

"You are driving a hard bargain, but we're willing to throw ourselves at your mercy," said Hawkins. Sparkes sent him a dagger look at that last remark but managed to hold in his emotions. "Go ahead," said Hawkins.

"I wuz only da middleman," said Sparkes. "Michael Howse set all dis up. 'E 'ad da product and 'e brought in da equipment. I got Paul and den Paul brought in Vince and dat girl. Dey would make up da pills and 'is fadder would arrange to transport dem."

"Who is the father?" asked Windflower.

"Da old guy, Cec Howse. Sometimes 'e would put dem in one of 'is trucks to St. John's and udder times 'e would bring dem hisself when 'e went on a trip. Dis went along great 'til Paul dought 'e could cut da product again and keep some fer hisself. I didn't know 'e wuz doin' it 'til dose udder guys showed up."

"McMaster and Perreault?" asked Windflower.

"Yeah," said Sparkes. "Cec found dem somewhere. I guess Michael found out what Paul was doin' and told 'im to fix it. Next ting I knows Paul's dead."

"So my client is prepared to testify about the involvement of both Michael and Cecil Howse," Freddy Hawkins jumped in. "And we have one more request. My client would like to be transferred to Marystown. He doesn't feel safe here."

"We can accommodate that last request," said Windflower. "But, honestly, I don't know what we're going to do about the other stuff."

"I know you will do your best," said Hawkins. "I have confidence in you, Sergeant."

"Thank you, Mr. Hawkins. Let's see where this goes."

Windflower then asked Smithson to drive the short distance to Marystown to deliver prisoner. "Then go home after you get back, okay?"

Smithson nodded and left the boardroom with Sparkes to get him ready for the trip. Hawkins shook hands with Quigley and Windflower and left the building.

"That was all for you," said Windflower.

"Absolutely," said Quigley. "But you're right. Let's see where this goes. It will be interesting to see what Michael Howse has to say when he gets here."

"The father looks like he's getting pulled in deeper, too," said Windflower.

They could hear a thundering noise outside, and when they went to look, they saw the RCMP chopper landing in the parking lot. Its blades slowed and came to a stop as the technical crew loaded their gear and climbed aboard. Then, with another roar and a great whoosh of air, the chopper started up again and rose above Grand Bank, sending the crew and their evidence back to Halifax.

The afternoon was relatively quiet, and Windflower was about to go home when Ron Quigley came back into his office.

"I just talked to Majesky," he said. "Things are moving fast on his end. He has spoken to two more women and is getting affidavits from others. He's spoken to Raymond and suspended him indefinitely. Raymond wanted to resign, but Majesky thinks he might have to face criminal charges if what the women are saying holds up. He wants me to go back to Marystown and take over, at least for the short term."

"Wow, that was fast," said Windflower.

"There's more," said Quigley. "He's also mulling over Tizzard's case. He ran his ideas by me. I wanted to get your take on it before I let him know."

"What's he suggesting?"

"A three-month suspension and busting him back to constable."

"That's tough."

"He did physically attack a superior."

"Still, it would be a big blow to his pride," said Windflower. "But I'm not sure he's coming back anyway. I guess I understand it, but it's tough."

"My thoughts, too," said Quigley. "But it sounded like Majesky was giving me advance warning rather than asking my opinion. I'll tell him that I think it's too tough and suggest he could trade off the demotion for a longer suspension, but I have a feeling he's set on a lesser rank."

"Thanks, Ron. I guess we'll see what Tizzard has to say about it. Are you going back to Marystown tonight?"

"Going to pack my bags and move back home, for now, anyway. See you later and say goodbye to Sheila and my little friend."

"See you, Ron."

After Quigley left, Windflower closed his computer and left for home. It was still foggy, but there were signs that it might be lifting as he could actually see past the coastline out to sea. A nice night for a walk, he thought.

Sheila agreed with that idea when he got home, and shortly afterwards he and Sheila were pushing Amelia Louise while Lady happily sauntered along beside them. They walked down to the brook where Sheila pulled a packet of torn-up bread out of her purse and scattered pieces on the water. The baby screamed and the dog barked as the parade of ducks, large and small, swam furiously towards the bread. Windflower laughed so hard that tears fell down his face, and Sheila kept the entertainment going as long as her supply of bread lasted.

Afterwards they walked along the brook up towards the sports field where a few hardy youngsters were kicking a soccer ball around. In a few weeks, they hoped, there would be dozens more of them on these fields and more playing softball on the nearby diamonds.

"That's a sure sign of spring," said Windflower.

"Let's hope so," said Sheila. "It's been a long, long winter. Oh, by the way, Carrie Evanchuk came by today. She said Eddie was driving over to Marystown to pick someone up."

"Yeah, we had a prisoner transfer and no one to go. Ron Quigley approved it."

"Does that mean he's coming back?"

"I don't think so." Then Windflower told her what Quigley had said.

"That's awful," said Sheila. "Being a corporal meant the world to Eddie. That would devastate him."

Windflower shrugged and kept pushing Amelia Louise along. "It's not up to me," was all he said.

55

Windflower, Sheila and Amelia Louise were ready for the warmth of their house. When they got back, Windflower made everyone grilled cheese sandwiches and spicy tomato soup. He didn't really make the soup. He just added a ton of cayenne pepper to a can of Campbell's soup. But the grilled cheese was his specialty. He used three kinds of cheese on a fluffy egg bread cut into thick slices and fried the sandwiches to a deep brown on each side so cheese would ooze out at the first bite.

They all loved his grilled cheese sandwiches, maybe especially Amelia Louise. She loved them because she could hold a big piece in her hand and wave it around as she was eating it. Lady and Molly loved them because the baby inevitably dropped some for their eating enjoyment. After dinner and a little playtime, Sheila gave the baby a bath, and Windflower read her a bedtime story. Tonight, it was a book that was appropriately called Time for Bed. Amelia Louise loved, loved, loved the book. It had different baby animals getting ready for bed with big yawns, snuggles and getting tucked in. Windflower loved it too.

Once Amelia Louise was in bed, Windflower joined Sheila in the living room where she was watching an old movie on TV. He settled in beside her when his cellphone rang.

"Sorry," he said, and he stepped into the kitchen to take the call.

"Hey, Sarge, sorry to bug you at home, but I'm here with Michael Howse. There's nobody else around. I think Carrie must be out on her rounds. Do you want me to stay?" asked Tizzard.

"Yes, that would be good," he said.

"Howse also asked to phone his lawyer. Is that okay?"

"Yes, it is. When Evanchuk gets back, can you ask her to get you both food?"

"Oh, we already ate. I got us sandwiches from the drive-through at Tim Hortons. We'll be okay. So I'll stay with our guest?" Tizzard asked again just to be sure.

"Might as well," said Windflower. "But Eddie, remember, you are not on duty."

"Yes, I understand."

Windflower hung up his phone and went back to sit beside Sheila. "Tizzard," he said. "He's going to stay over tonight with the prisoner."

"That's good, isn't it?" asked Sheila. "Given how hard everyone else is working."

"It is good," said Windflower. "It's funny, though. He asked me if I wanted him to stay. He meant overnight. I thought he meant long term."

"Maybe you should have told him," said Sheila, turning off the TV. "Take the dog out, and let's have an early night. Our lives have been so busy, lately."

Windflower kissed her and went to the kitchen where Lady had anticipated him and was standing at the door. They did another quick trot around the neighbourhood, and Windflower was back and upstairs not much longer afterwards. When he finally turned off the lights and snuggled into Sheila, he was happy and grateful. Soon he was also peacefully asleep.

The peace didn't last long, though. Windflower woke in a dream. He looked around, remembering he had to look for a fire. That wasn't hard. There was a gigantic fire rising 20 feet into the air in the middle of the meadow. He could barely see across to the other side, but when he did, he saw the little boy from his previous dream frantically waving to him.

There was fire behind the boy, too, coming from the forest, and it looked like he was trapped. He was calling out to Windflower to help him. Windflower didn't know what to do. He looked around for water to put out the flames but couldn't see any. He scoured the surroundings looking for his allies, but they were not to be found either. Then, he realized what he had to do. He raised his arms above his head and ran screaming into the fire. He picked up the boy, and together they screamed as he ran back.

He fell to the ground as he felt the heat and fire singe his hair and his body and rolled around until he was sure that the fire was out. He paused for just a moment to think, and then it was darkness. He didn't see or hear anything else until he woke up to Amelia Louise in the morning.

He quietly got the baby changed and dressed and brought her to Sheila. Then he went to the backyard with Lady and his smudge kit. This was a morning for prayers and meditation. He wasn't sure exactly what had happened in his dream world, but he knew enough to be grateful that he had survived some kind of ordeal, some kind of test. He also knew that his prayers today should be of gratitude because he learned that after great challenge, more great things were coming. His grandfather, a Chief of his nation, had once told him to open his heart and give thanks because the gifts were always coming. If people were always asking, they would just always be waiting.

So he smudged and offered his thanks to Creator for the beautiful morning and to his fellow travellers on his journey. He listed the many things that he had in his life like a family, good health and his four-legged friends, and he offered thanks for them all. He also acknowledged the people and things that were helping him even if he couldn't see them or they didn't live here with him. Then he prayed for all those in his circle and even those outside who needed love in this lifetime. He asked Creator to help them as he had been helped along the way.

Then he went back inside to show the people he loved the most just how much he did love them.

He made coffee, scrambled some eggs and put together a large fruit bowl. Sheila was suitably impressed when she came down and so was Amelia Louise who smashed strawberries into all parts of herself and her chair. It was so much fun that when Windflower replaced her damaged goods, she did it again. After breakfast he cleaned her up, did the dishes and kissed Sheila and the baby goodbye. Lady was mildly disappointed but was soon solaced by a Milk Bone biscuit. Molly had to then show her disappointment, too, in order to get her treat.

Everybody satisfied with his efforts, Windflower drove to work and was the first of the morning shift to arrive. Tizzard, however, was in the back with his feet up eating the second last of a package of muffins.

"I saved one for you," he said to Windflower.

"I think I arrived just in time," said Windflower, taking the muffin. "A few minutes more and my share would be gone."

Tizzard pretended to be shocked that his boss would think he would do that and then smiled. "Our guest is sleeping like a baby."

"Quiet night?" asked Windflower.

"Yeah, he made his call. Says his lawyer is coming this morning from St. John's. Williams. I don't remember his first name."

"David Williams. I've spoken to him once before. He says he represents both son and father in the Howse family."

"I don't know what kind of mess the kid is in, but it looks like his old man has plenty of trouble."

"What have you been hearing?"

"That his business is in trouble and that he has some difficulty maintaining his version of a jetsetter lifestyle."

Windflower decided to change the subject. "So how does it feel to be back here?" he asked. "Temporarily," he decided to add quickly.

"It feels comfortable. This was my first real job, and I've managed to hang around Grand Bank, well Marystown for a little while, too, for all this time. I like the rhythm of the work, even the long nights. Of course, I had a little nap in the middle."

"Of course. I've missed having you around."

"Thanks, Boss. I have to say that I've missed being on the job."

"I want you to come back," said Windflower. "I know that you've got lots to think about and go through, but I thought you should know that. I don't know how much longer I'll be doing this, but I'd like you to be part of it."

Tizzard looked like he was going to cry and was saved when they heard the door open. It was Evanchuk coming in from her last highway tour.

56

Evanchuk walked to the back where she heard the two talking. "Good morning," she said. "Any muffins left?"

Windflower burst out laughing. Tizzard started protesting about not knowing she wanted one, and then he pointed to Windflower.

"Don't blame me, I just got here," said Windflower. He grabbed a cup of coffee and went to his office to let the other two sort this one out. A while later both came to his office door.

"I hope you settled the muffin dispute," he said.

"He's buying me breakfast after Jones gets here," said Evanchuk. "I want to thank you again for helping me with my complaint. I don't think we could have got the same result without you."

"Did Ron call you?" asked Windflower.

Evanchuk nodded. "He said Superintendent Majesky is bringing in the Constabulary to do the investigation and to work with the Crown on possible charges. I don't really care what happens to Raymond. I just wanted him out of the Force."

"Agreed," said Windflower. He smiled as he thought about Majesky's wisdom of handing the complaints against Raymond over to another police force, the provincial Royal Newfoundland Constabulary. A police force could hardly investigate its own wrongdoings objectively, let alone work with the Crown on them.

"Now we have to wait and see what they say about Eddie," said Evanchuk.

"I'll be okay no matter what comes out of it all. I have you and the Sarge here, and Inspector Quigley will help if he can," said Tizzard. "But thank you, Sergeant. I really appreciate . . . uh, we really appreciate your support."

"No worries," said Windflower. "Now get out of my office. I've got paperwork to do."

He smiled as he walked to his office. They will be okay, he thought. Good people always come out okay.

The morning passed quickly as he worked his way through the stack of paper that Betsy kept replenishing as fast as he initialled or signed it. He was about to go get another cup of coffee when she paged him on the intercom. "Superintendent Majesky on line one."

"Good morning, Sir," said Windflower.

"Good morning," said Majesky. "Can you give me an update on what's happening with your investigations? I'm trying to get a handle on where Daphne Burry fits in. Her lawyer is still looking for some kind of arrangement."

"Here's what I know so far," said Windflower. "Daphne Burry, Vince Murray, the two guys in Clarenville—Everett McMaster and Marcel Perreault—and Michael Howse were likely all at the trailer on the night Paul Sparkes got killed. Daphne Burry says it was McMaster and Perreault who killed Sparkes, but when I talked to McMaster, he said she was the one with the insulin. And Doc Sanjay says the insulin killed him."

"So, it could be any of them?" said Majesky.

"Exactly," said Windflower. "Quite honestly, I'm not sure that we could find a strong enough case against any of them that would hold up in court."

"Or we could take our pick?"

"That's true. I don't want to sound crass, but there are no good guys in this gang, and they all seem prepared to throw each other under the bus."

"That's actually helpful, at least in terms of offering anything to Daphne Burry. But what else is going on here?"

"It looks like a fentanyl operation. And one by one, they're all getting implicated, including Michael Howse and his father, Cec. I'll be talking to both of them later today."

"Okay, let me know what happens on that," said Majesky. "Now, I want to talk to you informally about your complaint and Corporal Tizzard."

"Yes, Sir," said Windflower.

"In regards to your complaint, I am going to uphold it. Based on my interviews with others, it is apparent that Acting Inspector Raymond's behaviour as your supervisor was unacceptable. I will record this on your file and am recommending that you receive an apology, not just from Raymond, which may or may not be forthcoming, but also from the RCMP. Thank you for bringing this issue forward."

"Thank you, Sir."

"As you are aware Acting Inspector Raymond has been removed from his duties, and there are other investigations and actions pending. That would not have happened without your intervention. Now, in terms of Corporal Tizzard, I wanted to let you know that I intend to recommend a suspension and demotion to constable. This is a very serious incident, and some may have considered a full dismissal."

Majesky paused.

"I have spoken to Ron Quigley about this, and I wanted to share it with you before I talk with Tizzard," he said. "Comments?"

"Thank you," said Windflower. "Corporal Tizzard is a good cop, Superintendent. This incident is an aberration in a long period of not just unblemished, but often outstanding, police work as an RCMP officer. He was even shot in the line of duty."

"All true. But you can't attack a superior officer and get away with it. It goes against all standards and sets a dangerous precedent for the ranks."

"I understand that, Sir. But, for the record, I want him back, and I don't believe he will come back as a constable. With all respect, Sir."

"Thank you, Sergeant. I have noted your concerns. Keep me informed of any developments with your investigation."

Well, I've done my best, thought Windflower after the call had ended. "Now I leave the outcome up to someone or something with a much higher rank than mine," he said out loud.

"Excuse me, Sergeant, did you say something?" asked Betsy who had wandered into his office when she saw that his call with Majesky was finished.

"No, nothing," said Windflower.

"David Williams is here to see you. Should I bring him in?"

"Yes please, show him in," said Windflower.

57

The word that came to mind when Windflower saw David Williams was dapper. He was in his sixties with well-groomed white hair and a tan that looked like it cost him a lot of money. He wore a dark gray suit that fitted him so well it must have been specially made, and his silver tie pin glittered on top of pale blue silk. He oozed money and authority, and Windflower already didn't like him.

That opinion didn't improve when Williams opened his mouth to speak.

"You have transferred my client without his permission and are detaining him against his will without any formal charges. I give you one hour to release him before I see Judge Prowse and have him order you to do so," said Williams.

"Good morning to you, too," said Windflower. "Your client is being held in relation to a murder investigation and other matters which have come to light as a result of our enquiries. We have not yet had the chance to interview him. Would you like to see him before we do?"

Williams almost snarled when he spoke again. "You don't know who you're dealing with here, Sergeant. Watch your step." Then composing himself he added, "Yes, I will see him now."

Windflower walked to the back with the lawyer and told him he could talk with his client through the cell's bars.

"I need a boardroom," said Williams.

"We're just prepping it for our interview now," he replied. "Let me know when you're ready and I'll bring you there."

A few minutes later Williams was standing in his doorway. He didn't say a word. "Oh, are you ready now?" asked Windflower. He brought the lawyer into the boardroom and then went to get

Michael Howse out of his cell.

He was a little surprised at Michael Howse's appearance. One would think that after being in rehab and then being flown in from Ontario and driven from St. John's he would look dishevelled or disassembled. Instead, he looked like he'd just arrived for a social occasion. He wore nice brown Italian shoes with designer jeans and a lighter brown leather jacket over a baby blue sweater.

His demeanour was pleasant, too. He didn't speak, but when Windflower opened the cell door, he smiled at him politely as if he were the doorman at a posh hotel. He certainly didn't look like a man in trouble with the law. In fact, thought Windflower, he didn't look like a man with any worries at all.

He brought Howse in and sat him beside his lawyer. The men nodded briefly as Windflower turned on the tape recorder and introduced the people in the room.

"Mr. Howse, can you tell me again what you were doing at the trailer in Grand Beach on the night that Paul Sparkes died?" asked Windflower.

Williams interjected. "That has not been proven."

"We have his fingerprints, and he has acknowledged that he has lived in that trailer," said Windflower.

"It hasn't been proven that he was there on that night," said the lawyer.

"We have witnesses who say he was there," countered Windflower. "Some even say that he was responsible for the death of Paul Sparkes."

Howse sat silent for a moment. Then he spoke. "I was there that night. But I had nothing to do with killing Paul Sparkes. He was beaten up by Marcel Perreault and McMaster. But when I left, he was still alive."

"Well, that should settle things. You have your statement from my client. Will you release him, or do I have to see the judge?" asked the lawyer.

"There are a few more matters that we'd like to discuss," said Windflower. "We now believe there was a drug ring operating out of Grand Bank and that your client may have been involved."

"My client is a drug addict. That is no crime," said Williams.

"He's been trying to get help for that for years. In fact, he just came out of a rehabilitation program. This is discrimination and stigmatization." He seemed particularly pleased with himself at that last word and looked to see if his client was impressed.

He wasn't, and neither was Windflower. "We have a witness who says that your client was one of the key players in this operation, that he may have been the ringleader. That's not an addiction issue."

The lawyer started to protest when Betsy came running into the boardroom. "There's been some kind of accident at Cec Howse's place," she said. "The fire department is getting organized right now."

Michael Howse looked stunned, and the lawyer started stammering. Windflower grabbed the prisoner by the arm and started pulling him down the hall. The lawyer stood in his way. He was talking, but Windflower ignored him.

"Interview is over for now. I'm putting him back in the cell. You can join him or go for a cup of coffee. Your choice," said Windflower. The lawyer moved, and Windflower put the younger Howse in the cell and locked the door. He ran out of the detachment and drove as quickly as he could to Cec Howse's home, which was located just near the highway. It was a massive new house that was intended to show how important the owner felt himself to be.

When Windflower arrived, the fire chief was in the driveway, and he had a shivering woman sitting in the back seat of his vehicle. "She made the call," he said to Windflower. "She's not making any sense. I think she may be in shock. She says he's dead. Something about a package and an explosion."

"Have you been inside?" asked Windflower.

"No. I just got here, and she was standing in the driveway, screaming."

While they were waiting, Jones showed up, and soon behind her was Evanchuk. Windflower left Fire Chief Hodder and went to talk to them.

"We don't know anything yet," he said. "There's a witness in the chief's vehicle. She looks like she's in shock. Evanchuk, put her in your car and wrap her in a blanket until the paramedics get here.

Jones, you secure the scene. I'm going inside."

"Do you want me to go with you?" asked Jones.

"Let me go first," said Windflower. "Call Doc Sanjay."

He walked away as his team went into action. He walked up the driveway and put on his gloves. He opened the door and could smell it right away: a chemical scent followed very closely by something burnt or burning. He didn't know if there was still any danger, so he moved in very slowly. Then he saw the lifeless body of what looked like Cec Howse on the vestibule's marble floor.

58

Windflower checked for a pulse and felt nothing. He took a quick look around to assess the scene and then walked back outside Cec Howse's place. This property was a mess, and he didn't need to see any more right now.

The paramedics arrived, and Windflower directed them to wait outside until Doctor Sanjay arrived. The volunteer firefighters had also come with their truck, but they had no real role here now.

"There's a man dead inside but no identification yet," said Windflower. "We'll take it from here." Martin Hodder nodded and went to talk to his guys. A few minutes later he and the volunteers left.

Windflower went to see Evanchuk who was sitting in the back seat of her cruiser with the woman. She came out when Windflower approached.

"She's in bad shape," said Evanchuk. "From what I can tell, she was staying overnight with Cec Howse. She was upstairs and heard the doorbell ring. She saw a woman at the door with a package. Cec Howse went to open the door, and the next thing she heard was the explosion. She went downstairs. That's all I got from her."

"Okay," said Windflower. "Why don't we have the paras take a look at her? She may have to go to the clinic." Evanchuk nodded and walked to the paramedics. While they were talking, Doctor Sanjay arrived, and Jones backed up her vehicle to allow him into the long, curved driveway.

"Somebody said there was an explosion," said Sanjay.

"Let's go inside together," said Windflower. "Cec Howse is dead. But you should confirm that. And there's a mess all over the place."

Windflower opened the door and followed Sanjay into the house. "What's that smell?" he asked.

"Likely hydrogen peroxide," said Sanjay, looking around at the debris that had been scattered all over. "It's the most common oxidant you find in homemade explosive devices."

"Is that what this is?" asked Windflower.

"When I worked in London as a resident, we had a crash course when the IRA were blowing up cars and people," said the doctor. "You don't think about hydrogen peroxide being an explosive, but when you mix it with other substances, they interact to create a powerful explosion. The terrorists' favourite type is acetone peroxide which is an organic peroxide and a primary high explosive. It usually comes in a white crystalline powder that has that distinctive bleach-like odour we are smelling."

"And that could easily fit into an envelope or package?" asked Windflower.

"That's how they do it," said Sanjay. "Cec Howse is most certainly dead," he added as he rolled the body over gently. "We will need a forensics team to deal with the scene. There is both physical and human evidence to collect."

Sanjay walked to the living room, took a throw off a leather couch and placed it over the deceased. "No one else needs to see that. The paramedics can move the body now. I'll examine what I can, but I can tell you almost certainly that the cause of death is the close proximity to an incendiary device."

Windflower walked back outside with Sanjay who went to talk with the paramedics. Evanchuk came to him.

"The paramedics think she should get examined. Can I take her over?" she asked.

"Sure," said Windflower. "Stay with her. Once she calms down, we'll need to talk with her. What's her name, by the way?"

"It's Amanda Noseworthy, Mandy. She's 28, lives in Red Bay."

Windflower thanked Evanchuk and then called Betsy to have her phone forensics. But she'd already done that. They would be there in the morning. He also went to see Jones and instructed her to stay on the scene until Smithson came over to set up his camera operation again.

"What happened here?" asked Jones.

"It looks like there may have been a bomb of some sort, maybe delivered in a package. The good news is that we have a witness. The bad news is that Cec Howse is dead."

Those last words hung in the air as the paramedics wheeled the gurney out with a shape still covered by the throw from the couch and with one of their blankets on top and tucked in. That was good, thought Windflower. Nobody should have to see what was underneath. They loaded the stretcher into the back of the ambulance and drove away slowly. Doctor Sanjay got into his vehicle and followed behind.

Windflower said goodbye to Jones and got into his Jeep to go back to the detachment. He put his phone on hands-free and called Ron Quigley.

"There's been another development," he said. "Cec Howse is dead."

"What happened?" asked Quigley.

"Looks like a bomb, probably a package. We have a witness who saw the package being delivered. But she's in shock right now. The place is a mess."

"I can imagine. You need anything from me?"

"Nah, I'll get Betsy to send over a note to go out to the media. I've got forensics on the way. The interesting thing is that his next of kin is in our cells right now."

"Michael?" asked Quigley. "How's that going?"

"As expected. He denies everything, and he's got a lawyer who's really starting to bug me, David Williams from St. John's."

"I know him. The best mouthpiece that money can buy. A real pain in the . . ."

"Yeah, well maybe this might shake the younger Howse up. I'll let you know."

"Thanks, and good luck," said Quigley, not even bothering to try to add a pithy quote at the end.

Windflower took the good luck wishes anyway. He needed all the help and luck he could get. As he approached the door to the detachment, he noticed the lawyer in the parking lot, sitting in a brand new, silver Audi A6 and talking on his cellphone.

Windflower was speaking with Betsy when Williams stormed in.

"I demand you release my client," said the lawyer.

"Come into my office," said Windflower. He almost pushed Williams along as they got to his office. He closed the door and directed the lawyer to sit.

"Cecil Howse is dead," he said. "There was an explosion at his house."

"Was it an accident?" asked Williams.

"We don't believe so."

The lawyer looked surprised and shocked.

"I'm going to tell his son right now," said Windflower. "Then, I'm prepared to release him on the condition that he stay in this area until we complete our investigations. Will you agree to that condition and provide a guarantee for it?"

"Yes," said the subdued lawyer.

"Good. You stick around until the paperwork is done. I'm going to talk to him now."

Windflower left Williams in his office and walked down the hall. Michael Howse was lying on his bunk with his arms behind his head. He looked quizzically at Windflower.

"Come on," said Windflower, unlocking the door to the cell. "Let's go back to the boardroom."

"I'd like to have my lawyer present if you're going to interrogate me again," said Howse.

"That's not what I want to talk to you about," said Windflower. "Your father is dead." Windflower knew that sounded tough, but it was always better to be straightforward about bad news.

"What? What do you mean, dead?"

"There was an explosion at his house, and I'm very sorry, but your father is dead."

"No, there must be some mistake."

Windflower shook his head. "No mistake. I saw him, and I'm sorry."

"What happened?"

"We don't know yet. But we're treating it as suspicious."

"So it wasn't an accident?"

"We don't think so. We're not finished with our other investigations, but I'm going to let you out of here, as long as you agree to stay in Grand Bank for the next while."

"Whatever."

"Is there anybody else we should notify about your father's death?"

"Nobody else cares, not his ex-wives and not my mother, although I suspect they'll be coming around to see what they can scavenge. And he hasn't spoken to his brothers in years."

"Okay, you can stay in my office until we get the paperwork done. One more thing, do you know anyone who would like to hurt your father?"

Michael Howse laughed a dry, sardonic laugh. "Who didn't want to hurt him? Listen, he was not a nice man to anybody, not even me. We had a relationship based on need, not on blood or family. Everybody else was someone to take something from."

He paused, trying to take in what he had just heard. Then he continued, "I am very interested in your investigations, Sergeant. Very interested. You will keep me informed, won't you?"

Windflower acknowledged the last remark and led Michael Howse to his office where he left him with the lawyer.

Windflower had a lot more to process, including another call to the Crown to see if Michael Howse could be released on his own recognizance with his lawyer as surety. Luckily, this could be done without a hearing, and Lauren Bartlett was her usual helpful self in managing the request. An hour later, Howse and his lawyer were walking out of the RCMP offices.

The media, on the other hand, were not very helpful at all. They were pushy and insistent and camped out just outside the front door until Windflower gave them a short statement. They also were causing all kinds of problems out at the scene, and Jones reported having to chase more than one of them off the property as they tried to get shots of the inside.

"It's crazy," said Betsy, when she came to drop off another stack of messages, all of them requests for interviews. "I guess we should expect it when a famous person, at least for Grand Bank, dies suddenly."

"I guess so," said Windflower. "Especially when it involves an explosion and a rich person that most people don't really like."

Betsy sighed at that last remark. "So true, but still sad," she said.

"What's true?" asked Evanchuk as she came in while Wind-flower and Betsy were talking.

"The demise of Cecil Howse," said Windflower. "How did you make out at the clinic?"

"They sedated the woman shortly after we got there. But before that she started to talk about being really scared, that maybe whoever did this to Cec Howse would do the same to her."

"Was she his girlfriend?"

"One of many was how Ms. Noseworthy described it. But she'd been at the house many times before and said it wasn't unusual to have people coming all hours of the day and night. Sometimes they dropped things off, sometimes they picked up. I'll go back over in the morning and see what else I can get from her."

"Okay. I'm going over to see Jones, and then I'm going home if anyone needs me."

Windflower drove over to the crime scene where Jones was explaining to another TV crew that they couldn't go onto the prop-erty. They moved away and went back to their truck when they saw Windflower approaching.

"Thanks, Boss. Come here anytime," said Jones.

"Everything okay?" he asked.

"Apart from those guys," she said, pointing to the two remain-ing TV trucks. "It's quieted down now. Most of them have gone to post their stories."

"Yeah, and by tomorrow this will be old news to them. Where's Smithson?"

"He's picking up his camera gear and then coming over. We're going to split the shift tonight, part here and part back at the station, if that's okay."

"Sure, it's okay. Forensics will be here in the morning. Call if you need me," Windflower said.

Jones went back to her cruiser, and Windflower took one last look at the house where Cec Howse had lived so well and died so horribly. A quote came to mind, which was interesting because they weren't coming as readily these days. "All that lives must die, pass-ing through nature to eternity." Very interesting indeed.

59

That evening Windflower was very happy to have some time with his family. It had been a long and somewhat brutal day. It let him realize that life wasn't about crime, criminals, death and horrific events. It was about smiles and giggles, cuddles and a friendly smile from a dog that adored him. Even a smirk from the cat who knew she was better than everyone else, but tolerated them anyway, felt not just normal, but absolutely glorious.

Supper was simple, consisting of warmed-up turkey soup from the freezer with a fresh baguette and green salad, and a fruit and cheese plate for dessert. Sheila looked after Amelia Louise's bath time while Windflower had a nice long walk with Lady. He was just coming back to his house when Eddie Tizzard pulled up beside him.

"Got a minute?" asked Tizzard.

"Sure," said Windflower. "Do you want to come in?"

"Nah, I don't want to bother you and Sheila."

"Let me put Lady inside, and I'll come back out." When he returned, he sat in the front seat of Tizzard's car.

"What's up?" asked Windflower.

"Majesky phoned me. I'm going to get a letter, but he wanted to talk to me first. They're going to suspend me for three months. I understand that. But they also want to bump me back to constable," said Tizzard.

"What else did Majesky say?" asked Windflower.

"He said that he thought I was a good police officer and that he hoped I would stay. I mean, that's nice and all, but they want to take my stripe."

"I know. It's tough. But it's more a message to everybody else not to engage in that type of behaviour than it is about you."

"It's me getting busted down," protested Tizzard.

"True. But remember when you were lying in bed in hospital out in Stephenville, not knowing whether you would live or die? I do. And I remember how hard you worked to stay alive and then how hard you worked in rehab because you wanted to be a Mountie."

Tizzard looked at him and stared hard. He exhaled a long breath. "I dunno," he said.

"What did you tell Majesky?"

"I said I'd think about it."

"Then do that. And talk to people, like Carrie and your dad. To the other people you trust. Whatever you decide, we'll support you."

"Thanks, Sarge."

"See ya, Eddie," said Windflower, and he got out of the car and walked inside.

"I saw you talking to Eddie," said Sheila. "What's going on?"

"I have no idea. Let's go to bed. I've had enough of today."

When Windflower woke in the morning, he could hear Sheila singing to Amelia Louise through the monitor. He had somewhat recovered from the events of the day before but could feel his body and his spirit dragging. He said a quick good morning to Sheila and kissed his daughter before putting on the coffee and grabbing Lady for a morning run. It was damp, dark and gloomy, but neither man nor dog minded the weather.

Windflower found the mist on his face refreshing, but not so much when he came around a corner and the fierce wind whipped it at him. But it did make him forget his problems and concerns, and that was exactly what he was going after. Even though e was hot and sweaty by the time he returned, he took his smudge bowl out to the back before having his first cup of coffee.

He needed to smudge this morning so he could be free to do what was needed today. It was his way of releasing the energy that had built up inside of him. It also connected him with his spirit and the spirit world, where true energy resides. He needed that today, too. As the smoke wafted around him, he let himself drift into that other world, the place where he could reconnect with Creator and his ancestors and allies. After smudging, he said his prayer of thanks, and at the end, he laid down some tobacco for the spirit of Cec Howse because that spirit, too, needed help on its journey.

Windflower went back in and ran upstairs to have a shower and get cleaned up for work. When he came down, Sheila had made oatmeal which Amelia Louise had started to eat, a little, and smear all over herself, a lot. He laughed and poured himself a coffee while Sheila served him a bowl of the hot cereal. He poured a spoonful of maple syrup on top and mixed it in.

"I love oatmeal," said Windflower.

"You love food," said Sheila.

"True." Windflower scooped another spoonful into his mouth.

"Too," said Amelia Louise. "Too, too, too."

"Don't you start," said Windflower. Sheila laughed and Amelia Louise followed suit. Then she dumped the remainder of her bowl over the side.

"I guess she's done," said Sheila, bending down to wipe it up. "Busy day today?" she asked as she put the mess into the garbage can.

"Is that your way of trying to talk about Cec Howse?"

"Oh, the smart detective. But yes, whatever you can tell me. The rumour mill can fill in the rest."

"You probably know more than I do."

"Well, I heard that there was an explosion and that there was a woman with him."

"That would be correct. Do you know who the woman was?"

"Mandy Noseworthy from Red Bay," said Sheila. "People are really trashing her."

"Like what?" asked Windflower.

"That she was a low woman and other words that I won't repeat. That she was getting paid for her services."

Windflower shrugged. "That doesn't really matter much, does it?"

"Not to me." Sheila waited patiently. "So, no scoops?" she asked.

"I really don't know much more."

"Or you can't say much more. I guess that's why you're the cop. You got all my info without giving up any of yours."

Windflower smiled and went to give her a kiss and a tight hug before he left. Amelia Louise demanded the same from her dada. He wiped her chin and kissed her on the forehead. "See you all tonight," he said as he walked out the door.

60

When Windflower arrived at the detachment, a sleepy Smithson was coming out of one of the cells.

"Morning, Boss," said Smithson.

"You sleep well?" asked Windflower.

"It's pretty comfortable," said Smithson, not picking up his sergeant's sarcasm. "I went out last night to set up the camera, and it's all good to go. But you know they have a perimeter security system."

"What does that mean?"

"It means they have cameras mounted on all edges of their property and have 360-degree camera views. So we don't really need our camera. We just need access to theirs."

"Can we do that, get access to the security camera footage? Like for the past 24 hours?"

"Sure. Do you want me to call the company?"

"Yes. Then I want you to go through the footage and make a record of everybody who came and went from the house during the last couple of days. In particular, we're interested in anybody who dropped off a package or anything else at the house."

"Got it. It's a local security company. I'll go see them when they open this morning. Right now, I'm going for breakfast. Do you wanna come?"

"No, but thank you," said Windflower. "I'm going to hang around until the forensics crew gets here. But Smithson, I want you to know that I'm glad you're here. It's good to have someone around who understands technology."

"Well thanks, Boss," said Smithson. "I'll let you know what I find out."

Windflower had a cup of coffee with Betsy when she came in, and soon after that they got a call from Jones that forensics had arrived. Windflower drove over to meet them. His old buddy Ted Brown wasn't with them. But he recognized Peters from the last time.

"Good morning, Sergeant," said Peters. "We're ready to go."

"Brownie's not with you?" asked Windflower.

"No, he's working with another crew on the Murray case in Clarenville," said Peters. "An explosion here?"

"Yeah, we think it might have been some form of package. There's quite a mess in there."

"Okay, we'll take it from here." Peters directed the rest of his crew to put on their hazmat suits and to start bringing in equipment.

Windflower spoke to Jones, who was sitting in her cruiser. "You look beat," he said.

"I'm tired," she said. "But I guess we need to keep a presence here 'cause once the media wake up and find out that forensics is here, they'll be back over in a flash."

"Yeah, we need someone. But why don't you go over and see if Richard Tizzard is around. If he'll do security, you're off the hook. I'll stay here until you get back."

He didn't need to tell Jones twice. She sped off to look for the elder Tizzard. If he could come, she could go home. That was a big incentive.

Windflower hung around outside. He had no reason to go back in the house. Forensics would look after the collecting and cleaning up that needed to happen. Evanchuk came by to let him know she was heading to the clinic to see their witness. She told him she would let him know how it went. As she was leaving, Jones was pulling up.

"He's on his way," said Jones. "Richard is more than happy to help out. I told him I'd stay for a few minutes with him, but I think he'll be fine."

Windflower left Jones and headed back to the detachment. He passed two TV trucks, likely on their way to film the forensics crew in action, he thought. Jones and Richard Tizzard would deal with that.

Once at the detachment he wanted to know what, if anything, Smithson had found. The constable was in the small boardroom that had somehow been transformed into a mini-studio. Smithson had hooked up a large screen TV and speakers and had two computers running alongside them. One computer had a live feed from the Howse property, and Windflower could see Jones directing one of the TV crews back from the house.

"That's amazing," said Windflower. "What's on the other computer?"

"That's the recording feed," said Smithson. "I'm going to put it up on the big TV. Here it comes now." The big screen had eight small sections. "Those are all the cameras," said Smithson. "I'm going to centre on the front door camera. Here it is now."

Windflower watched as the screen collapsed to a single large view of the front steps and the driveway. Then Smithson started moving the recording forward. "I'll do it fast until we see something," he said.

"There," said Windflower as shadows moved across the screen. Smithson slowed the feed down. "That's Cec Howse," said Windflower. "Clear as a bell."

Smithson sped the tape up again until they spotted something else. When it slowed down, a woman became visible standing on the front steps. "That's our witness, Amanda Noseworthy," said Windflower. They could see the door open and the woman walk inside.

They watched the feed for quite some time afterwards, and it felt to Windflower that they might be out of luck. But then he saw it. "Stop!" he shouted in excitement. "Move it back a little." When Smithson did, they could see the headlights of a car and then the car pull into the driveway. Then they saw a woman walk up to the front door and ring the doorbell. She had a package in her arms.

"Freeze that," yelled Windflower.

The two RCMP officers stared at the picture on the large screen. "Can you get a screenshot of that?" asked Windflower, surprising himself that he even knew the term for it.

"Sure," said Smithson. "I can blow it up, too."

He clicked, and the screen was then filled with the woman

holding a square package wrapped in brown paper in her arms.
"That looks like Daphne Burry," said Windflower. "But it can't be.
Can it?"

"I think it's her sister," said Betsy, who had walked into the
room. "Hannah Burry. I think she's back to using her maiden name."

"She has a twin?" asked Windflower.

"They're not twins. But everyone thinks so," said Betsy. "People
always mix them up. But there's some slight differences. That's
Hannah. She's two years older than Daphne. Her mouth curls up a
little on one side. If you look closely, you can see it."

Both men peered at the screen. "You're good, Betsy," said Windflower. "I would've sworn it was Daphne Burry."

"So would just about everybody else," said Betsy.

"Does she live around here?"

"She's got a house in Burin, from her previous marriage, but I
think she lives in St. John's now."

"Okay, thanks Betsy." Windflower then asked Smithson to run
the tape again, starting from when Hannah Burry arrived.

Smithson restarted the feed from the point where the woman
walks up and rings the doorbell. In the video, the door opens, and
she hands the package over. The door closes, and she walks back
down the driveway. "I'm assuming you can get a picture of the car
and whoever was driving," said Windflower.

"I'll get the driver and the plate number," said Smithson.

"After you do that, can you go to Burin and see if Hannah Burry
is still around? Although, I doubt she is. When you get the vehicle
info, give that to Betsy."

"What do you want me to do?" asked Betsy.

"Put her picture up as fast as you can," said Windflower. "Send
it everywhere, especially the airports. Then call the airport in St.
John's and find out if she's already taken a flight. In the meantime,
I need to call the superintendent."

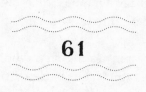

61

Windflower got through to Majesky on his first try. "I don't know if you heard, but Cec Howse is dead. An explosion at his house. And the woman we talked to, Daphne Burry, and her sister might be involved."

"An explosion, some sort of bomb?" asked Majesky. "What the heck is going on down there?"

"Good question, Sir," said Windflower. "But I think that everything is connected somehow. I just don't know how the pieces match up. But Daphne Burry is clearly more important than we first thought."

"What about Howse's son? Is he still around?"

"He's here but not very cooperative so far. We'll have to see how his father's death affects things. I'm also calling to ask for your help. We've identified a woman, Daphne Burry's sister, Hannah, as a person who delivered a package to Cec Howse before he died. We're trying to locate her down here, but I have a feeling she's gone to the mainland."

"Send the info directly to me. I'll push it on our end."

"Thank you, Superintendent."

"No worries," said Majesky. "Have you seen Tizzard?"

"I talked to him last night."

"What's he going to do?"

"I don't know, Sir. He was pretty upset."

"I hope he decides to stay," said Majesky.

"Me too," said Windflower.

After he hung up, Betsy came to hand him a file. "Hannah Burry," she said.

He took a quick look through the documents. There were

multiple arrests but only one conviction on a possession charge and a conditional discharge with probation. But the arrests were all connected to violent events like fights, domestic disturbances, and one for alleged theft of construction materials including explosives. She was found not guilty of the serious offences, but that really just meant there hadn't been enough evidence to convict her, not that she was truly innocent, thought Windflower.

Constable Evanchuk was his next visitor.

"How's our witness?" he asked.

"She's pretty shook up," said Evanchuk. "But she did say that she would be able to recognize the woman who came to the door."

"Hannah Burry. Smithson found the CCTV feed from the house. We're looking for her now."

"That's interesting. Ms. Noseworthy also said that there were other regular visitors, including Daphne Burry and Billy Sparkes. He's the big guy, right?"

"Yes, brother of the deceased Paul Sparkes," said Windflower.

"Other than that, not much else. Ms. Noseworthy is able to go home now, but I told her to stick around in case we needed her."

"Okay, thanks."

"Got another minute?" asked Evanchuk.

"Sure," said Windflower.

"It's about Eddie. He asked me what he should do. I told him that it wasn't up to me. That he should do what he thinks is right for him."

"That sounds fair. He has to follow his heart on this one. If it were you, what would you do?"

Carrie Evanchuk thought for a moment. "I would suck up the demotion and work my tail off to get it back," she said. "But then again, I've never been shot."

"Or attacked a superior officer," said Windflower. "I think there's some pride involved, maybe a lot of male ego baloney, too. But I think he's trying to look at the long term. Not just today but years down the road."

"What did you tell him? I know he came to see you."

"I told him that I wanted him to stay but that I would support him no matter what he chose."

"That's where I am, too," said Evanchuk. "Thanks, that helps."

It helped him, too, thought Windflower after Evanchuk had left. He thought about Tizzard and the difficult decision he had to make, but that was only for a few minutes because he had another visitor.

Betsy called him on the intercom. "Michael Howse is here to see you," she said.

"Send him in," said Windflower.

62

Michael Howse looked shaken as he walked into Windflower's office. The confident young man who had sat in front of him just a short time ago was gone. He looked like a frightened rabbit, thought Windflower.

"I need help," he said. "They killed my dad and I'll be next."

"What do you want us to do?" asked Windflower.

"Lock me up, protect me."

"You're asking me to put you back in jail? We just let you out. Have you talked with your lawyer about this?"

"Williams is gone," said Howse. "He was my father's lawyer anyway. If I need a lawyer, I'll just use Freddy."

"Why should we cooperate with you?" asked Windflower. "It seems a bit strange."

"I know stuff about my dad, about this operation, about Daphne Burry."

"Okay, I'm revoking your release and putting you back in jail. Are you ready to talk now or should we call Freddy first?"

"Let's get Freddy and then I'll talk," said Howse.

Windflower led Michael Howse to the back and opened a cell door. "Thanks," mumbled Howse as Windflower locked him in.

"You're welcome," said Windflower. "That's the first time anybody has ever thanked me for locking them up."

He was still smiling when he went to the front to tell Betsy about their returning guest.

"Can you call Fred Hawkins and ask him to come over?" he asked Betsy.

"Sure," she said, adding, "It looks like Hannah Burry has left the province. Air Canada to Toronto first thing this morning."

"Can you call Superintendent Majesky and give him that update? He's going to follow up on his end."

"Yes, Sir. Constable Smithson called. Obviously, he didn't have any luck in Burin. Even worse, his car broke down. He's waiting for a tow."

"Call him and tell him I'll come pick him up," said Windflower. "Where is he?"

"He's near the Frenchman's Cove exit," said Betsy.

Windflower needed to get out and clear his head. It felt like it was going to explode. Another thing that wasn't clear was the highway. There was a heavy-duty fog and periods of driving rain that made it slippery and even a little dangerous. Windflower adjusted his speed accordingly. He was slowly poking through the fog when he saw flashing lights in the distance.

That was good, he thought. Smithson put on his four-way flashers so he'd be seen in the awful fog. But as Windflower got closer, he could see it wasn't Smithson's vehicle. It was a semi-trailer, and the driver was on the side of the road waving frantically. Windflower sped up to him. Then he took in the whole scene.

Smithson's vehicle was lying upside down in the ditch. Smoke was billowing out. The driver was screaming something that Windflower ignored. He ran towards the overturned cruiser and could see Smithson's motionless body inside. He ran back to his Jeep and grabbed the industrial flashlight from the trunk. Racing back again to Smithson, he smashed the window, unhooked his seatbelt and pushed the opened airbag away from him.

Windflower managed to pull Smithson out of the vehicle as the smoke intensified. He pulled him alone for several yards until the semi-trailer driver finally came to help him. They managed to get back near Windflower's Jeep when they heard the explosion. It shook the ground around them and pushed flames 20 feet into the air. They could feel the heat and ducked as pieces of debris started to fly around them. Once they had recovered from the explosion, Windflower checked Smithson. He had a shallow breath, but at least he had one. He laid him on the ground and covered him with a blanket.

"You saved his life," said the driver. "That was crazy."

Windflower didn't respond. He watched the flames soar and realized that he acted on instinct and adrenalin. He didn't think, he just moved. If he had thought about it, there's no way he would have done that. He breathed out loudly, as if to release the tension inside him. He looked down as Smithson opened his eyes. "It'll be okay. Help is on the way," he said. Smithson closed his eyes again.

"So, what happened?" Windflower asked the semi-trailer driver as they heard sirens in the distance.

"I was coming down the hill, and it was too late by the time I saw him," said the driver. "I caught sight of his lights in the fog and just slid into him. I couldn't stop. Will he be okay?"

"I don't know," said Windflower. The first set of lights came over the hilltop. It was Evanchuk. The second was the paramedics. Evanchuk ran to Windflower. "Is he okay?" she asked. "What happened?"

The paramedics were close behind, and they took over looking after Smithson and soon had him up and into the ambulance. "We'll take him directly to Burin," said the head paramedic.

Windflower and Evanchuk watched the ambulance as it went down the highway. The driver stared at Windflower.

"He's a hero," said the driver to Evanchuk. "He just saved that man's life."

Windflower shrugged. "Take this man's information and get a statement," he told Evanchuk. "You can also get some photos while you're out here. I'll call it in and get highways out to clean up."

The fire had nearly burned out by the time Windflower got back in his car for the short trip back to Grand Bank. He drove slowly, partly because of the weather, which was still poor, but also to try to rebalance himself. He said a quiet prayer for Smithson along the way. The smouldering wreck would eventually be hauled away, and the driver of the semi-trailer would likely be exonerated after Evanchuk confirmed details with him. But Smithson's fate was uncertain. Windflower wouldn't know for sure about Smithson until the doctors in Burin had a chance to look at him. Windflower was no medical professional, but he thought that Smithson might be okay. At least he hoped so.

When Windflower arrived at the detachment, Freddy Hawkins

was sitting next to Betsy near the front door.

"Good day, Sergeant. I hear you are a hero," said Hawkins. "Congratulations."

Betsy lit up as she looked at her boss. She started to make a move towards him to give him a hug, but he moved quickly to guide the lawyer with him into his office.

"Did you talk to Michael Howse?" asked Windflower.

"My new client? Yes," said the lawyer.

"What does he want?" asked Windflower.

"He wants to do his civic duty and provide testimony to the police."

"What else does he want?"

"He wants love, life and liberty, like all of us," said the lawyer. "But mostly he wants protection. He thinks his life is in danger. He is prepared to give you the full details on the possible drug operation and some even more interesting information. People, places, names. He's got the whole package, so he says."

"Aren't you going to have a conflict representing him and Billy Sparkes?" asked Windflower. "Not that it matters to me."

"Billy Sparkes was a short-term client," said Hawkins. "He has released me. I am a free agent serving the Canadian justice system."

Windflower rolled his eyes. "Okay, let's see what he has to say."

63

Windflower brought Michael Howse into the boardroom and turned on the tape recorder.

"Winston Windflower, Grand Bank RCMP. Michael Howse, do you wish to make a statement of your own free will?"

"I do," said Howse.

"Proceed," said Windflower.

"I am seeking protection because I feel my life is in danger. My father is dead and so are two other men. They are all connected. I am a drug addict. I have been trying to deal with this for almost 10 years. I can't seem to get clean. I keep getting pulled back in. I want to go straight and live a good life. I don't want to die."

Michael Howse looked like he was going to cry but held it back and continued.

"My dad's death was the final straw for me. We didn't really get along, but I loved him. I wanted his approval. I would do anything for him. That's how I got into this mess. He was in trouble, big financial trouble. He had the house and the cars and the business, but that was all a fake. The banks owned all of that and more. They just let him stay in the house because they were trying to sell it, and it's easier when it's lived in."

He paused and opened a bottle of water that was on the table. He took a long drink to collect himself.

"He'd been bleeding the company dry for years, gambling. He loved to gamble. He just wasn't very good at it. That was closing in on him, too. He came to me with a plan. He wanted me to be the front for an opioid operation. I had some connections with the bikers in Ontario and could get the supply. Somehow, he got the pill presses and recruited Billy Sparkes and his brother to run it.

They made a lot of pills, and my dad would run them or ship them back and forth to Ontario. Sometimes, I did it too. But mostly he used Daphne Burry and her sister."

"Hannah Burry?" asked Windflower.

"Yes," said Howse. "That was his first mistake. Those women were mean. She killed Paul Sparkes at the trailer that night. Stuck him with insulin."

"Daphne Burry did that, correct?" asked Windflower.

"Correct," said Howse. "The second mistake was that Paul Sparkes, and probably his brother, too, started cutting the product with carfentanil and pocketing the extra profit."

"That's the purple heroin stuff?"

"Yeah. Some of that made it back on the street in Ontario, and my friends up there were not happy. Brought too much heat on their operations. That's who McMaster and Perreault were working for. I just took off and went back to rehab until things cooled down. But it looks like they were just heating up."

Michael Howse stopped talking and took another long swig of water from the bottle. He looked at Windflower.

"But they didn't kill my dad," he said when he spoke again. "That was Daphne. She's the one who made sure it happened. My dad had pulled her out of the operation, and she wasn't happy. She said he owed her money, which was probably true. But he had no intention of paying her and told her that. She had her own connections on the mainland and offered to bring him in as a way to recoup her money. I know he was planning on taking that and had no plans to give her anything. He was going to double-cross her. He told me."

"What else do you know?" asked Windflower when Howse stopped talking again.

"Daphne knew what he was planning, and told me she would get even," said Howse. "And I'd say she kept her promise. That's all I have to say until I know what happens next."

Windflower turned off the machine. "I have to talk to somebody."

He left the two men in the boardroom and called Ron Quigley.

"Hey, the hero of the day," said Quigley.

Windflower ignored that comment. "Michael Howse just gave

me a statement. He laid out the whole opioid operation. He's got connections back to Ontario. You should talk to him. He's pretty vulnerable now because of his dad's death."

"What did he ask for?" asked Quigley.

"Just protection because he thinks that one or more of them might want to kill him. But he didn't ask for a deal. That's a first."

"He will, don't worry about that. Why don't you ship Howse over to me? I'll interview him and see where it goes. I'm sure our Ontario contacts would like to talk to him, too."

"Sure," said Windflower. "I'll see who's around. By the way we're going to be down a person."

"Yeah, any word on Smithson, and are you okay?"

"I'm fine," said Windflower. "Nothing on Smithson yet. He's banged up, but I have a feeling he'll be okay."

"I hope so. I'll see what I can do about a replacement, maybe someone on a short-term basis."

"Thanks Ron," said Windflower. He had barely hung up the phone when his cellphone rang.

"Winston, are you okay? I heard about the accident," said Sheila.

"I'm fine," said Windflower. "Tired and a little bit shaken up, but I'm okay."

"Come home. I'll heat up some soup and you can relax."

Windflower started to protest, but Sheila would have none of it.

"I'll be home in an hour," said Windflower. "Promise."

"Okay, we'll see you soon."

Windflower couldn't leave right away because he saw the forensics truck pull up outside the building. Peters and another officer came into the building and were directed to his office.

"We're done for the day," said Peters. "We've taken samples and dusted for prints and have tons of pictures. We'll finish off in the morning. Then you'll need to get a forensic cleaning firm in there. There's a lot of blood spatters. And a representative from the bank came by. They said they owned the property. We suggested they talk to the Crown Attorney."

"That was good," said Windflower. "We're not getting in the middle of that. Did you do a general search?"

"We did the general area of the explosion and took a look around outside but nothing more than that. We don't normally do an extensive search unless we're asked," said Peters.

"Let me talk to the Crown," said Windflower. "Hang on." He called Lauren Bartlett and explained the situation. She said she would get a warrant and green light the search.

"We're good to go," said Windflower. "Do a full search. We're particularly looking for cash, drugs, and drug equipment and paraphernalia"

"More opioids?"

"See what you can find. I'll walk you out."

"Time for a drink?"

"Not tonight, sorry," said Windflower.

Peters and the other forensics officer left, and Windflower spent a few minutes with Betsy before finally getting out the door. He stepped outside and took a long, deep breath. He needed a break.

64

Getting a break was easy for Windflower once he got home. Amelia Louise didn't care about anything but getting a hug from her daddy. When he hugged her back, he didn't care about much else either. He bundled her up and took her and Lady for a trip down near the waterfront. It was cool and quiet along the way, and all three of them seemed a bit lost in just being together. The waterfront was one of Windflower's favourite places to get lost in.

When they came back, Sheila served up pea soup with chunks of crusty bread and a cheese platter that Windflower readily availed himself of. They made small talk during dinner, and Windflower reminded Sheila that he would have to start the weekend by working but would try to wrap things up early. He then had tons of fun with Amelia Louise as she played through her bath time. He changed her, read her a story and tucked her in with a kiss.

Downstairs Sheila had made them tea and laid out a cookie tray. "Carrie came by today," she said. "It sounds like Eddie hasn't made his mind up yet."

"Doesn't sound like it," said Windflower, grabbing a date square.

"I invited them over for supper tomorrow night. If you'll barbeque, I'll order some steaks from Warrens."

"That'll be perfect."

"Okay, now tell me what happened today, the accident."

Windflower didn't want to. He hated even the thought of going through it again and the way it would make him feel. But he also knew that he had to, and he was grateful that Sheila was such a good listener.

He talked non-stop for about 20 minutes, stopping only to fill his cup with tea. He talked about being afraid, first for himself and then for Smithson. Then he talked about running away from the car and the sensations of feeling it explode right next to him. And he cried when he remembered the sense of calm at the end.

Sheila came to him and held him tightly until the tears subsided.

"Hope you're happy now, making a grown man cry," said Windflower.

"I'm happy and proud to have a man who is brave enough to do that," said Sheila. "Go have a shower, and I'll pop Lady in the back. I'll meet you upstairs."

Windflower kissed her and went upstairs. After 10 minutes of hot water beating on his back and shoulders, he felt human again. Sheila was in bed when he got there, and she turned out the light. "Come hold me," was all he remembered.

When he woke in the morning, he got Amelia Louise from her crib and brought her to her mother. He dressed quickly and had a short jaunt with Lady. Back home, he made coffee for himself and Sheila. She offered breakfast, but he wanted to get to the office early. Minutes later, he was pulling into the detachment.

Jones came to see him as soon as she heard he was there.

"Smithson is fine," she said. "He's still in recovery, but apart from a couple of broken ribs and a smashed-up face, he's good."

"Wow," said Windflower. "That is great news. I guess the air bag must have saved him."

"Yeah, and he told me one time that he tightens his seat belt an extra notch. Said he saw a study about it on YouTube. I'm so glad he's such a nerd. How are you?"

"I'm okay. I have a life outside of here to keep me sane and grounded."

He walked to the back and got a cup of coffee and found a banana and a yogurt cup for breakfast. He ate the banana while his computer powered up and was opening his yogurt when his phone rang.

"Good, I was hoping you'd be there," said Majesky. "I have good news and not-so-good news. The not-so-good news is that we're still looking for Hannah Burry. But we've got a few leads to track down in Toronto. The good news is that the Crown has agreed to move ahead on murder charges against Daphne Burry."

"That is good news," said Windflower. "We have two witnesses now who claim that she injected Paul Sparkes with insulin, and we have the tox reports. It would be nice to tie her into the Cec Howse murder, too, and that may still happen."

"Exactly. What's going on with the son?"

"Michael Howse is over in Marystown with Inspector Quigley. They're going to see if they can link him up with the Ontario investigations."

"That would be good. It looks like you've managed to clear things off your desk."

"Mostly," said Windflower. "Forensics is doing a full search today at the Howse place, and Clarenville will look after McMaster and Perreault. Even Billy Sparkes isn't here anymore. He wanted to be transferred over to Marystown, too."

"Good," said Majesky. "It's not my place to do it, but I want to thank you for your act of bravery yesterday. Someone will be in contact with you about that."

"I was just doing my job, Sir," said Windflower.

"I wanted to check one more thing with you. You know Bill Ford, right?"

"Yes, I know him."

"I have a transfer request in on him. He had some trouble down there a few years ago. On a confidential basis, would you have any hesitation in recommending him or working with him?"

"None. Also, on a confidential basis, Bill Ford is one of the most competent and professional officers I know." Windflower paused and then added, "As long as he isn't drinking, Sir."

"Good, thank you for your thoughts and candour, Sergeant," said Majesky.

Windflower decided to finish his yogurt and go see the forensics crew before anyone else called. He scooped up the last spoonful and drove to the new crime scene. Richard Tizzard was out front and hailed him as he approached.

"Good morning, Sergeant. How are you doin' b'y?"

"Best kind," said Windflower. "I hear you're coming for supper. Sheila's going to try to get some steaks from Warrens."

"That will be wonderful," said Tizzard. "Not much goin' on here. The media have had their fun and are now onto the next tragedy. I wish they'd focus more on the good things that are happening, like you saving that young constable's life."

"Thank you kindly. But it was only my job."

"In any case, remember this," said Richard Tizzard. "'Receive what cheer you may. The night is long that never finds the day.'"

"Very true," said Windflower. "I'm going to see the guys inside."

He walked in the front door and could see the progress the forensics people had made. There were still blood stains everywhere, but a lot of the other stuff had been removed. The damage to the walls and surrounding areas was tremendous, but it was impossible to have a small bomb explode in such a contained area and not have that happen.

He found Peters coming down the stairs.

"We're clear on this floor, and the guys are finishing upstairs. Then we have the basement," said Peters.

"Find anything?"

"Some cash, not very much, maybe two grand. A couple of bags of weed and a smaller amount of cocaine. Plus, a large supply of amyl nitrite and a variety of sex toys and pornography."

"Poppers?" asked Windflower.

"They're illegal to sell," said Peters, "but anybody can get a prescription. Anyway, unless there's something shocking in the basement, we're out of here by noon."

"Okay, let me know if anything else turns up," said Windflower.

He left Peters and waved goodbye to Richard Tizzard. He knew he should go back to the office, but he needed a bit more outside time today, no matter the weather, which wasn't good at all when he got to the beach and started to walk up the hill towards the Grand Bank Cape. It was cool, wet and windy. But somehow, he didn't mind any of that. He trooped to the top of the first level and sat on a large rock to survey the town below him.

It felt like things were quieting down. That's what he thought as he watched the few cars and even fewer people moving around town. It looked calm and peaceful. Maybe it was worth a bit of fog and wind and rain to live in a place where very little bad happened. And when it did, the culprits got caught, and people could go on with their lives. With that pleasant last thought, Windflower strolled down the hill and drove back to work.

65

When Windflower got back to his office, he noticed the blinking on his telephone telling him he had voicemail. There were three messages. Two could wait until Monday, but one he wanted to return as soon as possible.

"Good day, Inspector," said Windflower when Ron Quigley picked up the telephone.

"Good day, Sergeant. I've got some news. We've made contact with the OPP, and they're coming down to talk to Michael Howse. I talked to him a little about what was going on in Ontario, and he seems to know what he's talking about."

"Good. What are you doing with Billy Sparkes?" asked Windflower.

"His new lawyer was banging on my door this morning telling us to let him go. I think we'll spring him for now but hold him in the area on conditions. Once the Michael Howse situation gets figured out, we'll probably charge Billy Sparkes with possession of the pill press and see if we can't have him plead to a fine."

"That would be good. Get some money back anyway."

"I'm also making some personnel changes." That got Windflower's attention. Quigley paused for effect or maybe just to tease Windflower.

"Okay, I give in. Please tell me, Inspector," said Windflower.

Quigley laughed. "However it works out with Tizzard, I'm losing my assistant," he said. "So I've decided to be proactive on that front. Bill Ford is transferring in as my new assistant."

"That is great news."

"Ah, but I have even better news for you. I've talked to HQ, and they've agreed to let Evanchuk stay in Grand Bank for another year."

"Excellent. Is there a catch, something you're not telling me?"

"O ye of little faith. 'Our doubts are traitors and make us lose the good we oft might win by fearing to attempt.'"

"In that case, thank you so much, Inspector, and have a wonderful day," said Windflower. "Oh, have you told Evanchuk yet?"

"I thought you might like to do that," said Quigley. "I'm sure she'll be pleased."

The rest of the morning blew by in a flurry of phone calls and media interviews. The local newspaper guy even came over to get a picture of Windflower for a story on the accident. That would show up later in the Southern Gazette as Mountie Risks Life to Save Colleague. At the café when he went for a late lunch, people came up to him to congratulate him. He was more than a little embarrassed, but he took the opportunity to talk and find out what was new in people's lives.

The second-best moment of the day came when he was walking back to the office and could feel the wind die down and the fog start to lift. By the time he got to the office, the sun was beginning to shine. The best was when he turned his office lights out and closed the door to head for home.

All the way home he passed people outside, walking and talking and trying to enjoy some of the first tastes of the warming sun that they'd had in a long time. When he pulled up the driveway, Sheila, the baby and Molly and Lady were all out in the backyard. Sheila had spread a tarp and blanket on the ground, and despite her best efforts Amelia Louise managed to crawl off it every five seconds. She crawled for him as Molly and Lady raced ahead to beat her.

He picked up his daughter and held her up to the sun while Molly mewed and Lady barked. Lady also decided to run full laps around the yard to show her joy at Windflower's return. He went to Sheila and handed the wriggling baby back.

"The steaks are in the fridge," said Sheila. "I put that dry rub on them that you like."

"Excellent," said Windflower. "I'll get changed and then start everything up."

He went inside and inspected the steaks. They were medium-sized T-bones, perfect for the grill. He laid them on the counter. Sheila had also cleaned a half dozen large baking potatoes, which

Windflower put in the oven to bake. Then he went upstairs and changed into his jeans and RCMP sweatshirt. When he came down, he could smell the spices and the meat combining. To him it smelled like heaven.

He'd found his perfect dry rub a few years ago: a little salt and pepper, garlic powder, paprika, onion powder, coriander and turmeric. It brought out the flavours of the meat without overpowering it. He enjoyed the aroma while he peeled and sliced carrots and put them in a tinfoil packet with butter and a spoonful of maple syrup. Then he sliced a couple of onions and mixed them with a can of button mushrooms and butter in another packet. He laid the packets in the fridge alongside the big green salad that Sheila had already made. There was a white box in the refrigerator, too, that he hoped was dessert.

All his preparations done, he went back outside and sat on the blanket with the baby and Sheila. "All set?" she asked.

"Ready to go," said Windflower as Amelia Louise crawled over him and tried to make her escape. He grabbed her shirt and pulled her back. "Bill Ford is getting transferred to Marystown. Ron Quigley told me today."

"That is good news. I like Bill. He's a great guy," said Sheila.

"Who's a great guy?" asked Evanchuk, who had come into the backyard while they were speaking.

"Great, you're here," said Windflower. "You can help me bring things out."

Evanchuk looked at Sheila, but she just shook her head as if to say, I have no idea what he's doing. Windflower opened the door, and Evanchuk followed him in.

"The great guy we were talking about is Bill Ford," said Windflower. "He's being transferred to Marystown to work with Quigley."

"What about me?" asked Evanchuk.

"That's what I wanted to talk to you about. You are being transferred back here for the next year."

"That's great news!" Evanchuk tried to give Windflower a hug, but he had anticipated that and so passed her the carrots instead. "I am so happy, and it will work out well for me and Eddie, too," she said.

"What do you mean?" asked Windflower.

"I'll let Eddie tell you his decision himself. Now, do you want some help?"

Windflower got her to take out the vegetables while he carried out the tray of steaks. He fired up the grill and put the vegetables on. He could hear Eddie Tizzard and his dad laughing as they came into the yard.

Amelia Louise started her "unca, unca" chant at first sight of the younger Tizzard, and soon he and the baby were rolling around on the blanket and then the ground. The ground was cold and damp, but no one really cared about that. Sheila got everybody drinks while Windflower put the steaks on. After taking all their orders from well done for Richard to blue for Evanchuk, he got to work on the barbeque. First, he seared the meat, sealing in the juices. Then he moved the steaks around to get the desired preferences. Finally pronouncing his work done, he turned off the grill and let the steaks stand for a few minutes before declaring that dinner was ready and corralling everyone inside.

"Oh my God," said Eddie Tizzard as he took his first mouthful of steak. "Kill me now. My life can never get better than this."

Everyone laughed, and everyone enjoyed their meal, especially Lady and Molly who both got a few scraps at the end. After the meal Windflower went outside to clean the grill, and the younger Tizzard followed him.

"Carrie told me she's getting transferred back. That's really good," said Tizzard.

"What about you?" asked Windflower.

"I've made my decision," said Tizzard. "I'm leaving the Force. It's not the demotion, although I have to say that hurts. It's more that I want something different. I want to work on the other side of justice. I'm going back to school, and if everything works out, I'll go to law school next year."

"But for now, you're sticking around here?"

"Absolutely. I don't know how many more years I'll get with my dad, and now that Carrie is going to be here, it'll be perfect. I was also thinking about setting up my own little security and investigation business."

"I think you'd be good at that. Eddie Tizzard, private eye," said Windflower. "Let's go tell Sheila the news."

Sheila was pleased to hear about Carrie's and Eddie's news, and she brought out the white box to help them celebrate. Inside was Richard Tizzard's favourite dessert, lemon meringue pie. "Fresh from Beulah, just for this occasion," said Sheila.

After everybody left, Sheila gave Amelia Louise her bath, and the baby fell asleep in Windflower's arms even before he could finish reading Goodnight Moon. He put her in bed and enjoyed a few quiet moments with Sheila before taking Lady on a long moonlit walk all over Grand Bank.

Windflower fell asleep as fast as the baby that night. When he woke, it was in his dream. The first thing he noticed was that there was no longer a fire. But the damage had been done. The house that once stood in the meadow was no longer there. Instead, there was a charred mass of smouldering ruins. It looked devastating, and he felt awful. Then he heard someone laughing. It seemed to be coming from a moose who was standing near the forest.

"What's so funny?" asked Windflower. "Look at what happened to the house, and where's the boy and my allies?"

This time the moose snorted. "Sometimes it looks like it's the worst. But it's simply the end of one thing and the beginning of another. We think that where we are is the best place ever. But what about if there was something better right in front of you?"

Windflower had many more questions, but the moose turned and pushed its way through the forest. Windflower ran after it. It was tough going for a few minutes until he thought he heard water. When he broke through the brambles, he could see the river. It was large and wide and flowing freely.

There, sitting beside the river was a young man, smiling and happy. There was a fire burning, and with him were all of Windflower's other allies. There was a pot with something that smelled delicious cooking on the fire. The hawk hovered above the fire and called to him. "Come have some stew. We're celebrating."

Windflower smiled and walked closer. Then he woke up, still thinking about that stew in the pot and the beautiful scene he had witnessed. It's all going to be okay, he thought. In fact, it already was.

THE END

ACKNOWLEDGEMENTS

I would like to thank a number of people for their help in getting this book out of my head and onto these pages. That includes beta readers and advisers Mike MacDonald, Andy Redmond, Barb Stewart, Robert Way, Lynne Tyler, Denise Zendel and Karen Nortman, and Bernadette Cox for her excellent support and copy editing.

ABOUT THE AUTHOR

Mike Martin was born in Newfoundland on the East Coast of Canada and now lives and works in Ottawa, Ontario. He is a long-time freelance writer and his articles and essays have appeared in newspapers, magazines and online across Canada as well as in the United States and New Zealand. He is the author of *Change the Things You Can: Dealing with Difficult People* and has written a number of short stories that have been published in various publications including *Canadian Stories* and *Downhome* magazine.

The Walker on the Cape was his first full fiction book and the premiere of the Sgt. Windflower Mystery Series. Other books in the series include *The Body on the T, Beneath the Surface, A Twist of Fortune,* and *A Long Ways from Home,* followed by *A Tangled Web,* which was shortlisted for the 2017 Bony Blithe Light Mystery Award as the best light mystery of the year, and *Darkest Before the Dawn,* which won the 2018 Bony Blithe Light Mystery Award. *Fire, Fog and Water* is the eighth in the series.

Mike has recently published *Christmas in Newfoundland: Memories and Mysteries,* a Sgt. Windflower Book of Christmas past and present.

He is currently Chair of the Board of Crime Writers of Canada, a national organization promoting Canadian crime and mystery writers.

You can follow the Sgt. Windflower Mysteries on Facebook at https://www.facebook.com/TheWalkerOnTheCapeReviewsAnd-More/